The Little Valley of God

by
CARLO COCCIOLI

Translated by Campbell Nairne

SIMON AND SCHUSTER — NEW YORK — 1957

LIBRARY OF CONGRESS CATALOG CARD NUMBER: 57-5672

MANUFACTURED IN THE UNITED STATES OF AMERICA
BY KINGSPORT PRESS, INC., KINGSPORT, TENN.

CONTENTS

(v)

The Little Valley
of God

The Priest Swollen with Pride

THE church of San Sebastiano stood somewhat below the level of the road. You went down a steep path that had been made more by use than by labor, and in a few minutes you reached the parvis of the little church, which served also as a fair ground. Going down another sixty yards or so among the white polished stones, you reached the edge of the river. That was what the people called it, but in reality it was only a wretched mountain stream that was almost always dry. The church was thus halfway between the dusty road and the dried-up bed of the torrent. The road ran along the Little Valley of God from one end to the other.

It was evening, and Don Marcello was making his way along the parched road toward the church and the priest's house. Hens were flapping their wings beside the mulberry bushes, briskly pecking away at the soil they had turned up so many times, fighting with each other over the tiniest grub, the smallest worm. The sun's rays were gilding slopes covered with vines, olive trees, and yellow sheaves of corn. Swallows flew low, twittering and almost touching the ground with their white throats; then they took to the upper air and darted like arrows into the setting sun. The shrill cries of children rose all around; a man was singing at the top of his voice. All this was going on at the exact spot where the path leading to the church of San Sebastiano leaves the highroad and goes down among the pebbles. Here there was a cluster of houses and a general store, kept by a woman, which sold wine and spirits. The people used to come here, buy some wine, and drink it leaning up against a rustic counter that showed the wear and tear of the years. Outside there was a summerhouse that backed onto a squat old oak. This store was, in short, a sort of tavern; but, in the Little Valley of God, one preferred to call it the Shop.

Don Marcello heard neither the singing nor the cries of the children. He did not see the hens flapping their wings or the swallows skimming the ground. He was walking with his head down, looking at the powdery, burnt-up earth, and there was a white circle of dust on his cassock. He was old and bent, with a long thin face, and deep-set, almost mysterious eyes; at times a flash of light would travel across them, a sudden but rare illumination. Just now he saw neither the sunset, nor the red sky, nor the dusty road; he was holding his satchel against his heart, and he was happy.

A man came out of the shop: a youth with a curly head, short trousers, and an open shirt which revealed a chest covered with black glistening hair. He stopped on the threshold, looked at the priest and, with a peculiar sort of determination, began to blaspheme.

"Marco," said Don Marcello, and stopped.

The youth went on looking at him without any expression of hatred. Now the priest was in front of him, his head a little on one side, one hand clasping his satchel at the level of his heart. They gazed at each other for a moment; then the young man raised his head with a defiant air, leaned against the wall, and once again blasphemed in a loud voice. This time he began on the Virgin Mary.

"Marco," the priest repeated gently. The unknown man who had been singing a moment ago had fallen silent.

The youth smiled.

"I want to blaspheme," he said quietly. "I've been working like a black all day; now I want to take it easy and blaspheme." He drew himself up arrogantly; nevertheless there was a slight trembling in his legs. "I'm a free man! I want to blaspheme and no one's going to stop me."

(4)

"You're being rather rash," said Don Marcello with the same gentleness.

The youth looked him up and down, a little surprised. "I'm a free man," he repeated.

"A rash one."

"A free man . . ."

"I didn't say you're not a free man. I said you're being rather rash, Marco. Besides, you've been drinking."

The young man protested.

"You mean I'm drunk? Well, you just shut up. I'm not drunk, I tell you. I . . ."

The priest interrupted him.

"You've been drinking. I'm not saying you're drunk. I'm saying you've had a drink."

"That's enough!" shouted the lad. Then he seemed vexed and, as if stating a self-evident truth, he remarked, "I could beat you up, you know."

The priest shook his head.

"No, no."

"What d'you mean, no? I tell you I could. Look at the strength of my muscles. If I wanted to, I could beat you up. I've only to feel like doing it and that would be enough. I could even crack your head open if I wanted to, or throw you in the river. You don't know all I could do to you if I felt like it. Am I stronger than you—yes or no?"

The priest continued to look at him.

"You won't do it," he said.

"Oh, won't I? I'm a freethinker, I am. I don't like priests."

Don Marcello said in an even voice, "You would be cursed, Marco."

The lad gazed at him with an air of astonishment.

"You'd curse me?"

An uneasy light could be seen in his eyes and a hint of fear showed in his voice.

"I might," the priest said after a moment's reflection. Then he fell silent again and waited.

The lad looked at his hands. In the silence he asked, "And I would die?"

(5)

"Perhaps not," said the priest. "But you would live in hell. The Demon would be in you."

It was a solemn statement; nevertheless the youth still had a smile on his face.

"I know six or seven peasants who can drive out devils," he said with an air of defiance.

"That's true," said the priest.

"They write a few words on a scrap of paper; there isn't a devil that can stand up to that."

"I know, I know," the priest repeated.

"Not even the most powerful. Not even Satan, not even Lucifer. Have you ever seen a car that won't go? All you have to do is to put a bit of paper into the engine, a paper one of these peasants has written on, and you can be sure that if there's a devil inside he'll come out."

"I know."

"Even if he's very powerful, even if he's Satan himself."

At this point the lad was silent for a moment; then he burst out laughing.

"What do your devils matter to me? Let them loose if you want to. I'll go to people who know about devils. Leopoldo Trivelli, Simone Lamorte, Angelo Furiano, Renato Dolce-cuore . . ."

"Desiderato Atté, Benevenuto Nicola. Is that right?"

"Yes, those are the people I mean. What then?"

"They wouldn't drive out my devils," said Don Marcello.

"Not even Renato Dolcecuore?"

"Not even Renato Dolcecuore."

"Not even Desiderato Atté?"

"Not even Desiderato Atté."

"But why? They're very powerful, aren't they?" Once again there was a quiver in the lad's voice and a dim, hidden watering in his eyes. Don Marcello raised his head.

"My curse would make the devils even stronger. For such is our power. . . ."

Marco lowered his eyes.

"With words?" he said.

(6)

"What's that?"

"I'm asking if you'd use words."

"Certainly," said the priest. "And they are terrible words: May a devil light upon him and may the Enemy hold fast to his right hand. When he passes before the Judgment Seat, let him come forth damned."

"That's enough!" cried Marco. "That's enough! Don't curse me, Father!"

The water rising in his eyes was now brimming over.

"I could do it if I wanted to," said the priest.

Marco was on the point of weeping; his face was pale.

"Ah, what a sinner I am," he groaned. "Don't curse me, Don Marcello. I did wrong to blaspheme, I'll go and confess tomorrow morning. Ah, don't curse me!"

"You're afraid?" asked the priest. It seemed that he was rejoicing over the boy's fear, taking a subtle pleasure in it.

"Yes," the lad said. "I'm afraid, Father."

The priest smiled and began to look at the ground. Then he lifted his head and gazed at the young man, who was leaning back against the wall, and trembling. The movement of his great body, his strong hairy legs, his black chest, and his flashing teeth gave visible proof of the overmastering terror that had seized him.

"Don't curse, me, Father," he pleaded. "Don't curse me, I repent!" The misty water in his eyes had become a flood that was overflowing its banks.

Behold the flesh crushed by the spirit, subdued by the spirit, thought the priest. The Spirit I serve . . . And he smiled in his heart, proud of such strength and of his Lord from whom he received it. "The nations are sore afraid and the kings are upon their knees," he recited under his breath. Then he turned again to the lad.

"Fear nothing. I won't curse you, Marco."

He looked at the horizon, then at the sky.

"This country is a good country," he said. "Our fathers called it the Little Valley of God, and surely not without reason. I believe God loves this country and the men who live in it. I would

(7)

like to think that almost everywhere in our valley He has His dwelling. Yes," he went on, "it must give Him pleasure to walk about in a country that bears His name; to trace His sign on every clod of earth, on every pebble, on every drop of water, inside every grain of wheat, in the heart of every animal, in the insects. You understand that, Marco? But away with you, get out, go, go!"

He was almost shouting now. Marco started; a kind of sob burst from him and he ran back into the nearest house.

Don Marcello made his way toward the path. The sunset was golden upon the hills, the sky was red and deep blue, a soft breeze was caressing the earth, herald of the approaching night. The swallows went on twittering. There was a smell of the stable and of bread, the tender fragrance of evening. A man was urging on his beasts with dull cries, a low bellowing answered him. Thus it was with all things; they were familiar and yet at the same time profoundly mysterious.

Don Marcello went up to his house, beside the church, and raised his head to look at it. The façade was rude and bare; hard herringbone stonework that the masons of long ago had never carved; but it was beautiful in the old man's eyes. My Roman church, he thought with emotion. And within him he felt a swelling of happiness.

In a moment he would go inside his house, he would wash his hands and face, refresh himself with a glass of wine, and then sit down to supper. Giuditta would serve him with her soft dark hands, the daylight would gradually fade, and with the coming of night a profound peace would descend from the sky. How beautiful it was to stand at the window and, in the darkness, gaze at the stars! Then Giuditta would light the lamp and he would reread his work: *Essay on the Roman Origins of the Church of San Sebastiano*—the pamphlet he was carrying in his leather satchel, the first edition still damp from the press. I mustn't puff myself up, Don Marcello murmured gently to himself; but, at the same moment, he knew in his heart that the Lord would forgive him even his pride, such as it was. After all, he thought, it's a way of praising His holy name. He raised his head and called out, "Giuditta!"

(8)

The old servant came to the window and asked, "Have you brought it, Don Marcello?"

"Yes," he replied, and he showed her his satchel. "It's inside."

Giuditta disappeared like a flash, and the priest heard her murmur, *"Madonna mia!"*

"Lord, make me not overproud," he prayed again.

(2)

In Which We Hear of a Young Man in Love and One of the Countries of the Wide World

In this story of the Little Valley of God there is a mortal character who is more important than the others—at least so I thought until lately; his name is Silvano. I am very much attached to him and it's difficult for me to begin speaking about him, for he means a great deal to me.

On a morning in August Silvano was making his way toward the house in the Little Valley of God that was to give him bed and board. It was nearly midday and it was hot. For three hours he had been walking in the sun, in clouds of white dust, and he was dragging with him a heavy suitcase which he kept changing from hand to hand. This was because there was no post-bus that day; the men were in fact on strike—just what would happen. Silvano was exactly twenty-six years old, but even at that age a man can feel weary, he can even be overcome by the heat and dust of the road; and after walking for three hours in a stifling atmosphere Silvano had begun to think that his luggage must be filled with stones. The cicadas were shrilling away beneath the chestnut trees on the slope, a piercing and unceasing chorus that made this trudge under the burning sky still more fatiguing. Yet in spite of the heat and his weariness, Silvano was extremely happy.

(10)

For I'm in love! he was saying to himself. That's why I have this feeling of happiness inside me, everywhere and always; it's because I'm in love. He stopped for a moment to wipe away the sweat that was running down his face; his thoughts were throwing him into a state of agitation, and when a man gets upset his emotion naturally intensifies the heat of the air around him even in the most torrid of summers. Silvano put his suitcase on the ground, pulled a handkerchief from his pocket, and mopped his face with it. Looking about him he noticed that tufts of yellowish flowers were growing at the edge of the road. He plucked two or three and thrust them into his cuff, under his wrist watch, between the leather strap and his skin. Perhaps these flowers will bring me luck, he thought. It was in such ways that he justified—to his own satisfaction—the inordinate love he had for the slender flowers of the field.

Then he scanned the countryside, and in the distance, perched at the summit of a pass, he discovered the manor of Ca' d'Orso, a cluster of roofs and turrets partly lost in the sky. He began to study them carefully and meanwhile he felt his heart swelling more and more with love. When a man loves a woman he loves also her clothes, her brother, her slippers, her grandmother, her dog—or the house she lives in. Ca' d'Orso was in fact the home of the girl Silvano loved, and that was why he had just looked at it with such deep tenderness.

He stood silent for a moment, affectionately contemplating the scene, and slowly passing his handkerchief over his streaming face. Suddenly a thought struck him. These fields must also belong to Barbara, he said to himself. They were fields of harvested wheat, interspersed with vines and olive trees and edged with scarlet poppies. And Barbara was the name of the girl he loved, the girl for whose sake he had come to this country. He thought a little, then decided that these fields must indeed belong to Barbara. And suddenly he found them marvelous and fell head over heels in love with them. How well kept they were, how carefully the vines had been pruned! And weren't those long rows of corn, so well arranged, like the battalions of a marching army?

With very little prompting Silvano would have knelt down

(11)

and kissed this sacred earth, embraced the twisted olive trees, and prostrated himself before the lonely golden majesty of the harvest fields.

Silvano was in love, and when a young man is in love one must not be surprised if these things happen to him.

A wandering singer once chanced to pass through the Little Valley of God; it was evening and a fair had been going on all day in front of the Shop. The people were a little weary, there had been drinking and bargaining, and the earth was churned up by the trampling of men and beasts. The singer was a middle-aged man with a long withered face. He climbed onto a chair and began to sing. He was wearing a fur cap and from time to time he took it off as he sang, then clapped it back on his head. The people felt a stirring of emotion, they came out of the Shop and surrounded this singer perched on a chair. Suddenly he fell silent. Then he said, "And now I challenge you to describe your country."

The men looked at each other. The singer plucked his cap from his head and put it back again. "I challenge you!" he cried. And again he was silent. The men remained dumb, until at last a graybeard spat into his hands and said, "Aye!" The singer became very friendly, leaned toward him, gave him a broad smile, and asked, "You'd like to say something?"

"Yes," said the old man. "What d'you mean exactly?"

The singer took off his cap and put it on again; he did this automatically, apparently unconscious of what he was doing. The peasants looked at him with a slightly intimidated air and they all seemed curious to hear him speak. To describe your own country seems quite easy; but, when you come to consider, how do you do it and what do you say? So they all kept quiet and, in the stillness, the singer began.

"I'm a newcomer to this country," he said proudly. "This is the first time I've set eyes on it. Yesterday I didn't know it existed and even now I've no idea what's it called. Hi, you, boy, what's the name of this country?"

The boy glanced all round before he replied, "The Little Valley of God." The men were still silent.

"The Little Valley of God!" echoed the stranger, erect on his chair. "A pretty name; accept my compliments. Well, as I was saying, this is the first time I've come here. And yet I'm able to describe it for you as it is. I'll wager there's no one here who can describe it as I can—I, a stranger. Do you believe that or don't you?"

One of the men said, "Go on, we're listening."

The singer took off his cap and put it back again. "The Little Valley of God!" he announced. Then in a singsong, chanting voice he began: "It's made of sky, earth, and vegetation, of people who live and breathe. The sky is ours; there's the moon by night and the sun by day. The sky sends us rain, snow, hail, tempest and fine weather. The earth comes to us out of the depths of the past. Our fathers lived here before us; when a man dies he is put into the ground—dust thou art, O man, and unto dust returnest. The earth furrows itself, seeds itself, and in due season brings forth corn and all that is useful to man. Men and beasts are the creatures that inhabit it. Men live in houses, cattle in stables, fowls in yards, fish in the water, birds in the air. Men are born, they grow up, they marry and bring other children into the world. Then they die and return to earth. Their sons take wives and beget children; these children grow up and marry. And so on from age unto age, amen. It's the same in the animal kingdom. It's the same in the vegetable kingdom. There are all sorts and conditions of men: landowners, peasants, tailors, barbers, innkeepers, undertakers. In the animal kingdom there are kine and goats, horses and donkeys, hares, fish, woodcock, flies, vipers. And dogs, ah yes! I must not forget dogs. In the vegetable kingdom there are chestnuts, poplars, junipers, vines, fruit trees, corn. Men have their mayors, priests, police sergeants, public women; they have churches, town councils, inns, graveyards, brothels. Tell me, sirs, isn't that how it is in your country?"

The singer took off his fur cap and put it back. He had got a little heated. "Who will give me a glass of wine?" he asked, looking round the company.

An old man told an urchin to take him a glass of wine.

The singer drank and said, "That isn't the end of my story."

(13)

The men were silent, spellbound by what they had heard. Things were like that, that was how it was. In a few words he had described the whole of the Little Valley of God and the whole of their lives. At last one of them spoke up. "That's just how it is. You'd think it would be difficult to explain, but it's really quite simple. We're like that and our country's like that. Go on, get down from your chair and come and have something to eat."

The singer made no movement. He was looking curiously round the company and he seemed to be getting ready for another declamation that would be finer still. "How is it that no one's laughing?" he asked suddenly, with an air of surprise.

The man who had invited him to supper turned round. "You're right," he said, and he too seemed surprised. "You're right. No one's laughing."

"What I've told you ought to make you laugh," said the singer.

"That's true," the man agreed, speaking for them all. "It was so odd. . . ."

"And there's no one laughing?" the singer persisted. He continued to look round him. Someone, meeting his gaze, tried to smile, but could not.

"Now I'll tell you why," said the singer. And he announced: "Why you don't laugh." Then he began again in his singsong chant.

"I described your country. I described you who live in it. Then I said: That isn't the end of my story. Because, you see, there's still something to add. Can you guess what it is? I'll tell you. Men can never be happy. None of you can be happy. None of you has ever said: Look, at this moment I'm happy—not even the oldest among you, those who are fourscore, those who have lived to be nearly a hundred. Each one of you gets up in the morning and says: Today I mean to do this and that; and you think: if I succeed in doing this or that I shall be happy. But afterwards, in the course of the day, when you have done the things on which your happiness ought to depend, you realize that you are not yet happy. One never is. No one is ever happy in the present. That's how it is in the Little Valley of God, in

London, Pekin, Paris, Australia. And do you know why? Because it's too easy to be happy. Man imagines heaven knows what, and yet there's nothing easier than to be happy. It's enough to say: I am happy. All you need say is: There's happiness within me. It's enough to say: Happiness isn't going to come tomorrow, or in a couple of hours, or when I get married, or when I have done this or that; it's within me here and now, at this very moment. And now I've really finished. Which of you was it that invited me to supper?"

The men stood silently around the singer. He got off the chair and said, "Lord, how hungry I am!"

(3)

Concerning the Death of a Dog Called Fiorella

IN the Little Valley of God, when an animal, dog or cat, began to give trouble, the custom was to kill it. That happened, for instance, when a cat got mange or stole the joint of meat that had been left on the table; or when a dog that had been taken out hunting did not seem to enter into its master's plans. In these cases and in others of the same kind the animals were strangled with a steel wire or flung into a well where no one had drawn water for a long time, or else they were knocked over the head with a heavy stick. There was talk of a man who had put a cat in a stewing pot, closed the lid tightly, and put the pot on the fire. But this procedure had seemed a little extraordinary and even the people of the Little Valley of God had thought it rather cruel to the cat. Besides, the man who had resorted to such an expedient had been seen lying in the grass in broad daylight with little boys; the blind alleys of Nature are as inscrutable as the highroads of the Lord. In short, most people preferred to use the stick for cats and the steel wire for dogs.

Young Toni had a setter bitch which he would have to kill. It was a little pearl-gray animal with white soulful eyes and its name was Fiorella. It had been attacked by a lean hairy dog and was savagely bitten. The dog had been put away a few days later and the vet said it had been a case of rabies. So Toni now had to think seriously of killing Fiorella.

He was a boy of almost sixteen, but he did not know what to do; or rather he knew very well but was absolutely certain that he could never bring himself to do it. First of all he went and talked to his father, who replied, "Get a peasant to knock her over the head." It was evident, however, that his father's thoughts were elsewhere; when Toni came into the room he had in fact been debating with himself what action he should take to spread confusion among his tenants, who were claiming sixty per cent on the crops. For at this time socialistic propaganda was making great progress in the Little Valley of God. That was the reason why Toni's father went on to add, "One of those damn clodhoppers!" He was a stout plethoric man with curly platinum-gray hair.

Toni detested the peasants for the same reasons as his father and he would never have dreamed of entrusting Fiorella to these people. The very idea of putting his bitch into their cruel hands caused him intense misery; he knew, however, that there was no time to lose and that the vet was keeping an eye on him. He thought about it a whole night. Then, at dawn, he got up, jumped on his bicycle, and went off to find Don Marcello.

The priest had just celebrated mass and was eating his breakfast in the kitchen, while Giuditta waited on him. He told her to bring the boy a glass of sweet wine and a biscuit. It was well worth while to make a certain fuss over Toni, for later on he would be one of the biggest landowners in the valley. Don Marcello finished his meal and it was only when he had risen from the table that he asked benevolently, "Well Toni, what is it?" This quiet, gentle lad had always pleased him.

But at that moment Toni seemed very upset. He had not been able to get a wink of sleep and he felt as if there was a heavy weight on his stomach. "I must kill Fiorella," he stammered.

"And who is Fiorella?" asked the priest, looking at him over his glasses.

"My bitch," Toni replied.

Don Marcello continued to gaze at him.

"And why must she be killed?"

"She's been infected by a mad dog. It bit her."

"Pity," said the priest. "She's a very pretty animal, I believe,

(17)

and a good hunter." He said no more for he did not know what turn the conversation was going to take and he was unwilling to commit himself.

Toni sat for a moment in silence, bolt upright on his chair. Don Marcello also kept silent; he wondered whether this might not be an opportune moment to show the boy his *Essay on the Roman Origins of the Church of San Sebastiano.* Then he decided that it was not, and asked, "Well, my son?"

Toni fidgeted on his chair. He continued to see Fiorella's white eyes in front of him, and her tender soulful gaze.

"Have they souls?" he asked sharply.

"Who?" said the priest, starting up. "Who—o?" And his voice tailed off into a sound like an owl's hoot.

"Dogs."

"No!" cried the priest angrily, amost shouting. "No, no, no!"

Toni got up. He was very pale and he was still seeing Fiorella's white eyes in front of him. He said stiffly, "Good-by, sir." And he went away.

He returned home, took his shotgun, and whistled to Fiorella. The bitch came joyously to heel. They took a path across the fields, leaving the highroad behind them.

The sun was high in the heavens, larks were trilling as they soared into the blue sky. Numb with misery, the boy walked for a long time with his eyes on the ground. The bitch followed him with a timidity that was most unusual; she was no longer frisking about and she too seemed depressed. At last they reached the edge of a stream flowing between two rows of silvery willows; blue dragonflies were darting above the water, a bird sang in a nearby bush. There was a great white boulder in the shade of an oak. Toni sat upon it and laid his gun at his feet. Then he called Fiorella beside him; the bitch lay between his legs. He took her head in his hands and stroked it gently, with tears flowing from his eyes. "Fiorella, Fiorella . . ." he said.

At last he got up, took the gun, and put the barrel against the dog's head. She raised her soft eyes and as she looked at him she began to tremble. Toni closed his eyelids; then violently he pulled the trigger.

(18)

Silvano was busy on a short story that a review had been expecting for a month when the maid came in and announced that young Signor Toni was outside. He put down his pen. "Please show him in." He felt a little dazed as he always was when he had been writing something that disturbed him emotionally. In fact he had just been dealing with a burning subject—unrequited love; and it made him think of Barbara, Barbara. . . .

The boy came in.

"What's the matter, Toni?" Silvano asked.

Receiving no reply, he said, "Sit down, Toni." He could not drag himself away from his story or get the name Barbara out of his mind. Consequently he felt very agitated.

Toni sat down and said, "Silvano, I've killed Fiorella."

At this point Silvano noticed the boy's pallor and the beads of sweat on his brow.

"Let's go out for a little," he suggested. He arranged his papers as best he could and left the room. The boy followed him without a word. They left the house and took the road leading to the wood, Silvano a little in front, both with their heads bent. They walked in silence for a moment and then Silvano turned round.

"Let's sit down, Toni."

There were two large boulders at hand; they sat down on one of them.

"So you've killed Fiorella," Silvano said in a low voice, as if speaking to himself."

"Yes," said Toni.

Absently Silvano began to trace marks in the loose earth with his forefinger. "Poor Fiorella. Poor old Fiorella."

Toni said calmly, "I'm losing my reason, Silvano. Help me. For two nights I haven't slept. Everywhere I see nothing but her white eyes. I'm going out of my mind. Help me, Silvano."

"Yes," said Silvano.

"Her white eyes," Toni repeated. There was pain and despair and helplessness in his voice. He seemed to be saying: Oh, I wish I had never been born.

"How did you kill her?"

(19)

"With my shotgun."

"She died instantaneously?"

"Yes."

"Perhaps she didn't suffer."

"Perhaps not."

They were silent for a moment. In the shadow and stillness even the song of the cicadas could no longer be heard. Silvano said, "Who knows where she is now?"

It was some time before Toni could bring himself to answer. Then he replied very softly, as with a foreboding of what Silvano was going to say, "Fiorella, you mean?"

"Yes."

"I don't know." Then Toni asked, "Do you believe that dogs have souls?"

Silvano replied quietly, "Of course they have. All living creatures have souls."

"Don Marcello said no," the boy murmured. "Did he deceive me?"

Silvano said, "Don Marcello didn't deceive you. Probably he doesn't know these things, and even if he did know them perhaps he couldn't say them."

"Are they so difficult then?"

"On the contrary, they're very simple," Silvano replied. "But just because they're so simple . . ."

Toni kept his eyes on the ground. "Where is she now?"

Silvano was asking himself that very question. "Who knows? Perhaps in a paradise. Perhaps at this moment Fiorella is chasing golden partridges. . . ."

"Golden partridges?"

"I think so. Dogs must love golden partridges. Don't you know they love the things that most deserve to be loved? There are dogs that love roses. Others love butterflies; others again love their masters' hands. Every time I look at a dog I see what he's fond of. I see his soul. You won't think I'm mad?"

There was a great silence. "No," Toni said at last. "I know that's how it is."

It was like a declaration of faith.

(20)

I dedicate this chapter to the memory of my dog Jack, need-lessly put to death by those who loved him, at the end of the summer of 1947. And if such a dedication makes people talk, let them talk; I care very little what they say about me.

Jack, do you remember when the two of us gossiped together? Let this story of the bitch Fiorella be a tribute to your memory, Jack, you who are a symbol of the living creatures we deliver up to the power of Satan, creatures we neglect, despise, and slaughter without knowing why, without recognizing the spirit that ani-mates them. The storyteller will have a lonely part to play in this tale of the Little Valley of God: he must stand in the wings, setting down what he sees and hears, and he will not be able to escape from the logic that governs the scheme of things on this earth. He will see death coming silently upon his characters and he will be unable to shed tears for them; he will witness the miracle of life resurrecting itself from forgotten graves, and he will be unable to rejoice; he will hear the soft tread of Love, and he will be unable to love him. The storyteller must trample on his heart; he must stifle his cries, tears, and laughter; he must hold aloof from this life he is creating. If it were not so, I would raise a song to you, Jack, in all the languages of the earth; yes, I would not stop short of humbling the great and powerful, and those who are beautiful in face and body, in exaltation of you, Jack; you are symbolic of faithful friendship and a pledge of innocence and imperishable love. And I should tell what came to pass that morning, through Toni's declaration of faith.

I should say that a breath of wind passed suddenly through the wood, that the plants rustled and the insects droned, and that upon grass and water ran a light trembling. I should say that everything was bathed in a new dawn and that Silvano and Toni lifted their eyes and then flung themselves on the ground and buried their faces in their hands.

And I should say that afterwards they saw in front of them a luminous globe, a light suspended in the air by its own mo-mentum, a burning heart plucked from a sacred image. And that in this globe trembled the reflection of all the dead in the world: men and dogs and insects and flowers of the field; all the

(21)

creatures that have been born into this world, lived there in simplicity and innocence, and left it—like you, Jack, put to death by those you loved. And that a song rose from this glorious company of simple spirits, the very song of the universe, the song that rises from atoms and planets, to the eternal glory of the Creator, in token of His power and beauty.

And that at last this vision faded, and that it left behind a sense of mystery, like the perfume of roses in the morning when there has been rain in the night and their petals shine with the risen sun.

(4)

The Appalling Story of Simonetta Grei

APART from the chronic wranglings between landlords and tenants, the alternation of rain and fine weather, and the dubious escapades of youths with girls, there were many other happenings in the Little Valley of God that were capable of stirring the curiosity of its inhabitants. There was, for instance, the frightful story of Simonetta Grei.

It was one of those stories that the men were in the habit of relating at the Shop, on Sunday afternoons when they were tired of playing bowls and cursing the weather. Someone would launch forth and the others would listen to him in silence. Hearken, good people, to the story of Simonetta Grei. It was a wartime adventure and that was why it could still raise a shudder of fear in the Little Valley of God, whereas everywhere else it would only have succeeded in provoking a smile. The passage of the armies was still too recent a memory for anyone to have forgotten it.

The Little Valley of God has more or less the shape of a funnel opening on the plain. In the middle of the plain rises a modest agglomeration of civic buildings that goes by the name of the Town. It was there, in this torrid summer during the war, that Simonetta Grei was living with her old father. She was plump and short and wore spectacles with very thick lenses. I am naturally too discreet to say how old she was, but the calculation would be a simple piece of arithmetic, seeing that her father, who was then over eighty, had been forty when she was born. He was a little man dressed in black, of frail and delicate appearance, who wore a white goatee beard. He was usually known as the Chevalier Catone.

In this month of August all the townsfolk had fled, dragging behind them their children and the barest necessities of life, which they had loaded onto creaking carts. Heat and terror had taken possession of the plain. The front was coming nearer, guns were peppering the sky with yellow powder, and heavy rumblings shook the ground. German soldiers were entering houses and doing violence to men and women. So the whole population had fled into the mountains, except for the Bishop, the hospital doctors, and the Chevalier Catone. As for Simonetta, she had offered herself as a nurse, in accordance with the motto of her father's family: "In the face of pain the Grei remain."

The Chevalier Catone had stayed behind by himself in the old house that even his most venerable and trusted domestics had abandoned. He spent his days playing the arias of Bach on the piano, especially the chorale: "O man, weep thy great transgression." He considered that this war was a divine judgment upon sinful men and for that reason he accepted it with a good grace, I will even say with a certain satisfaction. He only got really annoyed when the noise of the guns prevented him from hearing the sound of his own instrument; for, being so advanced in years, he was a trifle deaf. Meanwhile Simonetta Grei was dragging her massive body along the half-destroyed corridors of the hospital. That summer she felt that a new strength had come to her and it was as if she had acquired a new awareness of life.

One day, using a pale little priest as his envoy, the Bishop asked her to come to his house. The Bishop was tall and incredibly thin, incredibly old and withered. But his eyes shone with an inner glow and with love. He motioned to her.

"Sit down, Signorina Grei."

Simonetta sat down with a certain caution. On her way to the Bishop's house a shell had fallen not far from her and a splinter had ripped the hem of her dress. So now she was careful to put her hand over the rent. She would have been displeased if the Bishop were to see it.

(24)

"I await your commands, Monsignor," she murmured.

It was almost midday, and the heat was intense. The Bishop passed his hand over his transparent face; in his black and purple robes he had a noble presence. A great chain with a cross glittered on his breast. He pressed a bell and a little abbé ran up. The prelate ordered, "Refreshments for Signorina Grei."

Then he courteously asked after her health and her father's, speaking of this and that until his guest had refreshed herself. He interrupted himself only when a shell fell a little too close; then it could be seen that his thin white lips were soundlessly trembling. He came at last to the reason for his summons.

"I have received word," he said, "that the old Marchesa Mariana is all alone at Ca' di Leone; her servants have deserted her. She is a paralytic, as you know, and I believe she is nearly seventy. We grew up together; I remember her as a little girl with braids down her back. She had a personality of her own, I would even call it a little autocratic. But all this belongs to another age."

Simonetta Grei bowed her head.

"Yes?" she said, and now there was a kind of resignation within her.

The Bishop also bowed his head.

"I know," he said, "I know."

She was silent.

"Ca' di Leone is a long way off," said the Bishop. "Several hours' journey by road. It's hot and the guns are active."

Simonetta raised her head. "The Marchesa Mariana is alone?"

"So they tell me, yes," replied the Bishop.

"We must go and fetch her," cried Simonetta in a very loud voice, and she got up with an air of decision. "But who will come with me and where shall we find a stretcher? Every second if precious, we must set out immediately, Monsignor, immediately!"

The Bishop also rose to his feet.

"Yes, Signorina," he said, and rang a bell.

When they began their journey it was almost two o'clock. The sun was beating down and a great silence enfolded the streets of the town. Leaving the skeletons of the shattered houses behind them they began to follow the bank of the torrent. First of all came Simonetta, flourishing in her right hand a great white flag with a red cross at its center; then four young priests, who supported the stretcher. It was a large chair of red damask slung on two stout wooden handles; it was extremely heavy and so in next to no time the four bearers were gasping for breath and their faces were running with sweat. Clad in black from head to foot, dark spots under the blazing sun, they seemed to be taking their duties with the utmost seriousness. The torrent had completely dried up and the air was like a blazing furnace. Simonetta went forward as rapidly as her corpulence allowed. Sweat was running into her eyes, and her right leg was causing her acute pain, which she had not noticed until she was on the road. My talisman, she thought, my talisman. She felt as if she were swathed in heat, plunged into a bath of fire. She could only murmur in a half whisper: "Oh, my talisman." In her left hand, within a little gold reliquary, she clutched the revered relic of St. Simon, her patron saint. She had barely had time to snatch it up before leaving. It was an heirloom. It will surely protect me, she thought. Who knows how many people it has protected in days gone by? Heat, cicadas, lamentation—could any heat be worse than this? St. Simon, oh, St. Simon!

They walked for more than an hour without meeting a soul; the country was deserted. From time to time as they followed the torrent they passed a few houses, but these too seemed empty. The peasants had deserted the plain; only the mountain could offer them shelter. In the fields the unharvested grain was drying up; the doors of the houses stood wide open and defenseless; a few terrified dogs roamed about in the stillness. An immense grief, a pitiless solitude reigned in this deserted countryside. Even the song of the birds was a dirge. The gunfire was now dying down; after the uproar of the morning the gunners were no doubt stretched out beside their guns (perhaps they were asleep, perhaps they were dead; who could tell?); but there were traces of the firing in the reddish dust that still hung in mid-air and intensified the savage heat of the sun. There were other signs; olive trees were lying on the yellowish earth, eloquent of helplessness and solitude.

(26)

The procession went on. The priests were silent; tall and black, they reflected the glare. Simonetta continued to squeeze the relic in her left hand; from now on the red and white flag began to weigh heavily on her right arm. My talisman, my talisman—oh, St. Simon! The pain was becoming almost unbearable. I shall fall down, Simonetta said to herself, I shall fall down unless the Bishop prays for me. I shall fall, and I shall be dust in the dust. The white banner was a flaming light. St. Simon, I'm going to fall down. How the reliquary burned in her small, plump, moist hand! . . . Unless the Bishop prays for me. Bishop, pray for me. . . .

Presently one of the priests said, "Let's stop a minute, for God's sake!" He spoke in a soundless voice, but the others understood and without a word they deposited the chair on the dried-up grass. The sun was making the red damask shine and the metal plates gleamed like beacons. For a moment all were silent; they could be heard gasping for breath. Then one of them said, "Sit down, Signorina." Simonetta sat down on the chair, still clutching the reliquary in her hand. She sat as if dazed, lost in a dizzy whirl of pain.

No one dared to look in the other's eyes. All was still; even the never-ending chorus of the cicadas.

Simonetta remained seated for an indefinite length of time, stiff and numb, with the banner at her side and the four silent priests surrounding her. At last she got up and said, "We must go. It's a long way to Ca' di Leone."

Without a word the four priests took up the litter and Simonetta raised her flag.

When they arrived at Ca' di Leone and climbed the great stone staircase it was clear that the Marchesa Mariana had been warned of their coming. In the half-darkness of her drawing room she was sitting bolt upright in her armchair; everything about her shone with intense life—her white ringlets, her lace collar, her eyes. She caught sight of them and exclaimed with a kind of scorn, "It's after three o'clock, gentlemen."

They were dead tired, a heavy weight was robbing them of the power to move, they could feel the blood pounding in their temples. As if struck by a thunderbolt, they stood for a moment in silence, incapable of action, trying to accustom their eyes to the gloom. Then Simonetta said, "We have come to fetch you, madame."

"I'm well aware that you haven't come to play bridge," retorted the old woman. "But how d'you think you're going to carry me? Have I got to make a public declaration of the state I'm in? Don't you know that I'm paralyzed?"

Simonetta reddened.

"We have a sort of litter; the abbés will carry it."

"Who are these abbés?" In the old woman's voice there was a note of suspicion, perhaps a trace of scorn.

One after the other the four priests bowed low and said, "Don Gustavo, Don Aldo, Don Ferrante, Don Leo." Sweat was still pouring off them; they were bathed in a dim sea of heat.

"I am highly honored," said the old lady. "You seem all alike to me, but no doubt that's because it's dark in here. It was the Bishop who sent you, wasn't it? I knew he wouldn't have forgotten me. The little pet! Would you believe it, he was once in love with me; we went to school together; he was a tall boy as shy as a girl, and the least little thing used to make him blush. One day he kissed me on the mouth in front of everyone. He turned as white as a sheet, then as red as a turkey cock." The Marchesa pointed to Don Ferrante. "As red as you are at this moment, sir priest. What did you say your name was?"

"Don Ferrante, madame."

"Well, what's the matter with you? I haven't kissed you, Don Ferrante." She laughed. "I don't kiss anyone nowadays, my son. But what are we doing here? Haven't you come to fetch me? Why don't we set off?"

"Straight away, madame," said Simonetta, and her voice was a mere thread.

The Marchesa seemed very agitated. "Let's go then, let's go. I'm putting my old bones in your care, and they're more precious to me than anything in the world. Off we go!" One would have thought she was about to get up and run.

The four priests brought in the litter and helped the old lady to get in. They were extremely embarrassed and set about it very clumsily; the Marchesa made a fuss and complained that this wasn't helping matters. She declared suddenly that a chair of red damask was hardly the right sort of conveyance for a country excursion of this kind and that she thought they would at any rate have brought something more comfortable for her to sit in, a real sedan chair and not a rickshaw like this. In the end she seemed to grow calmer. Holding out her hands, which were extraordinarily small and knotted, she commanded Simonetta to give her her handbag. "My reticule, give me my reticule, please." It was a satin purse which lay on a lacquer table beside her armchair.

Simonetta handed it to her and the procession made its way toward the door. Before she crossed the threshold the Marchesa looked round the drawing room with a searching gaze that seemed to take it all in. Then she said in quite a different tone, "These gentlemen must forgive me for not having done them the honors of the house. My rascally servants have deserted me."

She ended in a firm voice, "Off we go, then, in the name of your Lord."

They had scarcely emerged from the house when the first shell screamed overhead and exploded in the distance with a frightful uproar. It was a terrifying noise and Simonetta frenziedly clutched the relic in her hand. The Marchesa declared with an air of indifference, "It's starting again. The thing's in very poor taste." She seemed in no way frightened.

Painfully continuing their journey, while shells screamed across the sky, they came to the narrow uneven track that ran along the edge of the torrent. When the shells fell too close the four abbés could be heard murmuring in chorus, "Jesus Mary Joseph." Finally this got on the old lady's nerves and she burst out suddenly, "What rubbish! Can't you go a little quicker?" Without replying the four priests tried to quicken their pace.

Then three or four shots split the air as they whizzed past. This was not the rumbling of gunfire but something sharper and closer. And someone shouted, "Halt! halt!" with a voice that resounded in the stillness. Three men appeared, waving weapons in their hands. They were young, very fair-skinned, and they had not a stitch of clothing between them, except for their caps and the leather belts they wore round their waists.

The priests stopped without putting down the litter. The old Marchesa did not speak. With one hand Simonetta Grei brandished the staff of her flag in desperation while with the other she gripped the holy relic so tightly that it hurt. She felt its ridged surface clamped against her sweating flesh.

The naked youths drew near. Their hair was so blond that it seemed white, and their hòrrible porcelain-blue eyes glittered in their pink and white flesh. So clear were they that they resembled luminous pits dug deep in their faces. When the youths reached the path they halted, and one of them, taking aim, called out, "You, Italians, where are you going?"

With a sigh the priests put the litter on the ground, as if they had understood that there was nothing else they could do; but not one of them opened his mouth.

Simonetta came forward and said, "We're taking this patient to hospital, to hospital. Understand, hospital? Lazarett, lazarett. This lady sick, I'm Red Cross nurse. Understand, Red Cross? Is it dangerous here?" As she spoke she tried not to look at the naked men.

One of them flung out his arms and began to laugh. His lips were lighter in color than his gums and he had strong teeth set widely apart.

"You fat old cow!" he exclaimed, and with his hand he struck Simonetta Grei a heavy blow on her broad bosom. Brutally he ordered, "You, Italians, come with us." He seized one of the poles of the litter and his two companions followed suit; without a word Don Ferrante took up the fourth.

Leaving the path that ran along the torrent they made their way across the ravaged fields until they reached a little concrete structure that seemed to have sprouted from the ground. They put down the old lady, who had preserved a stubborn silence, and shouted something in German. Other men came out of the concrete shelter, which was doubtless a pillbox, and approached the curious procession. It was at that moment that the Marchesa opened her mouth and called out, "These men have clothes on."

Memorable words which Simonetta Grei was not then in a

fit state to appreciate. And that was a great pity, for later, when she was recounting her adventure in detail (as she was often asked to do) her audience always demanded enlightenment on this particular point. It was a fact that the Marchesa had called out, "These men have clothes on," and then struck the nurse's shoulder with her bony fingers. "Courage, my girl. They're young too and perhaps a little less ugly than the others; but I don't suppose you've even noticed that, my dear."

Simonetta Grei said nothing. What could she have said? She waited, holding her flag in one hand and tightly clutching the holy relic with the other. Everything, even the pulsing of her blood, was now concentrated on what lay in the hollow of her hand. She could barely see, a black mist had blotted everything out; she was conscious of the drumming in her temples, a pounding and throbbing that never stopped, never stopped.

One of the men who had their uniforms on was plainly an officer. On his tunic he wore a black and red ribbon and epaulettes that glittered in the sun. He began to talk in voluble old-fashioned Italian.

"Why do you take the liberty of walking here? Don't you know that there's a curfew? What are those priests doing with the old lady? Ach, I kill you all. You have no more brains than a hen."

Neither the priests nor Simonetta said a word. If the officer's language was queer, it was abundantly evident that there was nothing to be said in reply. Rooted to the ground, not daring to move an eyelash, not daring to breathe, they waited for something they felt would come—must come. And while they waited a terrible stillness reigned over the sun-drenched countryside; a stillness that hooded the blinding light of the afternoon so that it lost some of its strength. Suddenly the stillness vibrated and the Marchesa was heard speaking to the officer. She spoke to him sharply as if she were dealing with an impertinent boy.

"Look here, young man, please pay attention to what I'm saying. I have nothing whatever to do with these four priests. Get that into your head, will you? Otherwise, as sure as there's a God in heaven, I'll box your ears for you."

"*Was?*" screamed the officer, standing back. His scream was so high-pitched and prolonged that for a long time the echo of it hung over the vast plain, a lofty spiral of sound.

The soldiers' blue eyes opened wide in astonishment but they gave no other sign that they had heard. No one dared to move or speak; and a still more profound silence seemed to engulf the four priests, standing there in their black robes, with white faces and hollow, brilliant eyes. It was in this unnatural silence that something came to life all of a sudden in the old lady's brain. She turned to Simonetta Grei, who was standing petrified beside her, and asked in a tone of entreaty, "Will you tell me what that man wants, for God's sake?" She drew out the last word so that it sounded almost like a moan.

The officer continued to glare at her ferociously. It was a fixed, savage look that he gave her. Above all it was the look of a man thirsting for a cruel and unaccustomed pleasure. It lasted two or three seconds, centuries in the stillness; then something struck Simonetta Grei like the crack of a whip. The man's hand was moving. It slid along his tunic, it rested on the butt of his revolver. A sudden confidence flooded into Simonetta's heart; she felt something descend upon her from on high, shake her, and banish the numbness from her burning limbs. She found that she could move forward.

Holding the relic as a last but sure weapon of defense, she called out to the officer in a very loud voice, "No, no, don't kill her!"

And waving the relic before his face she made the sign of the cross with it: "In the name of the Father, the Son, and the Holy Ghost, amen." She stood motionless, her arm stretched out, filled with a crazy terror.

Then took place the miracle that was latter called the Miracle of St. Simon. The Marchesa stirred, seized the satin bag that hung at her side, searched it rapidly, and produced something. Two fat cigars with gold bands, two rich and expensive cigars. She stuck one in her mouth and offered the officer the other.

"Take it, *mein Herr,* and let's be friends. Give me a light, please." And she waited, with her aristocratic wrinkled face held out.

Something snapped in the officer and his men, and their stout bodies were shaken with fits of laughter—hysterical, piercing, almost painful laughter. It lasted for what seemed a long time. They laughed so uproariously that one of the young men fell on the ground, where he hugged his belly with his hands, so convulsed with merriment that great tears rolled from his eyes.

At last the wild laughter died away and the officer was able to talk. He took the cigar that the old lady was still holding out and he put it in his mouth. Then he pulled a lighter from his pocket and offered the Marchesa a light.

"You can go, gentlemen," he said with a low bow.

The four priests took up the litter and Simonetta lifted her flag. She was no longer capable of mental effort; she thought only of her talisman, the reliquary that burned in her sweat-drenched hand.

(5)

In Which the Death-bell Tolls

A CHANGE usually comes over the countryside when the bell tolls to spread the news that someone has died. The quivering of the warm air is stilled, the sky clouds over, the flowers of the field droop their heads toward the ground, an icy shiver passes across every inanimate object. Dogs get to their feet with the hair bristling on their backs and set up a mournful howling; cattle low uneasily in their stalls. A human soul does not leave the earth without causing a disturbance in Nature.

Silvano always felt a painful sensation when he heard the death-bell tolling. It was not a sharp and unbearable grief that pierced his heart but rather a feeling of sadness, a feeling of melancholy resignation. He usually stopped whatever he was doing and plunged into thought; when he was alone it was also his habit to cross himself on his forehead, mouth, and heart. And that is what he did now.

The bell went on tolling its single peal—slow, measured, and leaden. There was not a flower of the field that had not drooped its head; even the sun, which had been shining gloriously a few minutes earlier, had vanished behind a screen of clouds. Who can be dead? Silvano asked himself, mildly curious. Whose soul is it that's mounting now into the blue of the heavens?

His hostess, Signorina Carmela, came into the room and announced, "Farmer Crispino is dead, Signor Silvano." She was the only person in the Little Valley of God to use this mode of address; everyone else called him "Professor."

He saw that she was very pale and asked, "Are you ill, Signorina?"

"No," she answered, "but it's a great loss. Crispino is a very wealthy man—or rather he was."

"Rich or poor," Silvano observed sadly, "death comes to us all."

"Yes, alas," agreed Signorina Carmela. She sighed; obviously she thought it was unfair.

She went out and Silvano returned to his work. For three days he had been toiling away at his story and it could not be said that he was making much headway. He had embarked on a very melancholy theme: that of a young man in love with a girl who does not love him. Now he was debating whether he ought to put his hero out of his agony by letting him die, or whether he ought to keep him alive. The first solution seemed to him rather grim, but in his sadness he thought that on the whole it was preferable to the second. When a young man's love is unrequited, Silvano said to himself, what can he do except die? The fact that as yet he had not once set eyes on Barbara added to his inner confusion. He had a naturally trustful disposition, but some doubts were beginning to enter his mind. He had been three times to Ca' d'Orso, and Barbara had never once showed herself. And why not? Silvano wondered. Why not? In his state of mental anguish it was very hard for him to concentrate on the subject of his story.

The following day Signorina Carmela asked him if he would like to go with her and visit the deceased. Silvano said he would, not that he had any particular wish to see the corpse but because the dead interested him. And indeed few things on earth are as interesting as the dead. It often happens that when a man dies he acquires a personality he never had in life. Besides, Silvano said to himself, there's a good chance of meeting Barbara; for in the Little Valley of God visiting the dead was considered an important social duty. On such occasions the girls put on their prettiest dresses and the young men wore their Sunday best. The result was that many a marriage had been brought about by a lifeless corpse and one could say without fear of contradiction: In this country even the dead are of some use.

When they got to Farmer Crispino's house Silvano and Carmela found quite a gathering of his friends and relations. None of them could have had any illusions about him; he had been tightfisted in spite of his wealth, a miser. A man can have only one real love in his life, and Crispino had made money his god. The dead man's sister, who had never married, was doing the honors. Signorina Carmela kissed her on both her faded cheeks and said, "You poor dear." She showed the newcomers into the little drawing room. "Sit down, Professor," she said—for in the Little Valley of God there was no one who did not consider Silvano a person of importance. Then she told the servant to bring them a drop of *vinsanto*.

When Silvano had slaked his thirst he asked, as politeness demanded, "May we see the dear departed?"

The old maid bowed her head and sighed, "Of course, I'll lead the way."

Farmer Crispino had been put into a handsome coffin. He was swathed in black and there was a wreath between his waxen hands. As he had been a very tall man there was scarcely room enough for him in the coffin and his knees were a little bent. They must have taken their measurements badly, Silvano thought. There was a sickly fragrance of flowers and candles in the air, and mingled with it an odor of putrefaction like the smell that hangs round butchers' shops in summer. The dead man's face was very white and he had a handkerchief bound round his head, no doubt to keep the jaw from falling back. Silvano imagined what would happen if the knot came undone unexpectedly and the mouth clicked open. The people would run away shrieking, women would faint, or . . . well, who could say? In the country there is often such callousness in the face of death.

Around the coffin candles were burning and people were kneeling in prayer. Carmela kissed the dead man's brow and said, with some emotion, "Poor man!"

All her affection for him was in those words. There wasn't much in his hostess's life that Silvano did not know about, and

(36)

he knew that long ago Carmela had been vainly in love with Crispino.

She went on, *"Requiem aeternam,* sleep well, my friend."

"Why are you keeping the window like that?" Silvano asked a servant. He had seen that the window was half open and what he meant was: Why don't you throw it wide open? The servant misunderstood him and explained, "It's open so that the soul can get out."

"The soul?"

"Yes, so that it can get out."

"Of course!" Silvano replied gravely.

All of a sudden there was a movement among the spectators; the women whispered together and distracted Silvano from his thoughts. He saw the dead man's sister lean toward Carmela and heard her talking excitedly.

"Look, there he is, that's him! What nerve!"

A young boy came in. He might have been fourteen or fifteen; he was tall for his age, fair, and remarkably good-looking. Pale-faced, he stopped on the threshold. The spectators stared at him curiously, the murmur of the prayers died away, and everyone waited to see what would happen.

As he watched, Silvano's heart went out to the boy. It was clear that he was feeling his position keenly and was aware that he had a cruelly difficult role to play. Nevertheless he played it with a natural dignity. Silvano turned again to the servant, who was still standing beside him, and asked, "Who is he?"

The servant whispered in his ear, "They say he's Signor Crispino's bastard. He's very like the master in appearance, isn't he? The very image of him!"

"Yes," Silvano agreed. "It's a frightening resemblance."

Meanwhile the boy continued to stand at the door, pale and rigid, looking now at the corpse and now at the dead man's sister. The servant murmured again, "If she kisses him that will mean that she accepts him as the heir. There's a matter of forty million lire involved."

Silently they all waited. At last the dead man's sister made a movement; she took two steps toward the boy, raised her right hand, and whispered, "Get out!"

(37)

The boy said nothing. With his blue eyes he gazed at the dead man; he was trembling slightly.

"Get out!" the woman repeated.

Then the boy said loudly, "All right, Aunt. But first I want to pay my respects to my father."

He drew near the bed, made the sign of the cross, and kissed the dead man on the brow. Then he moved to the door. Before he stepped over the threshold he said with gentle politeness, "Good night, Aunt."

This is about as much as I can stand! thought Silvano. The smell of flowers and wax, the vague whiff of the butcher's shop, the white cloth around the white face of the dead man, the hardness that glittered in the eyes of the old maid—O God, it's too much, I've had more than I can stand! What am I doing here? This dead man in his luxury coffin—what is he to me? What am I doing here in the midst of all these people? God, I've had enough!

And he went out quietly.

Outside the house he drew the fresh air deep into his lungs. He was still upset, but now he could examine his emotions. Why had he suddenly felt so agitated? He drew another deep breath; then he smiled. It was the hour of sunset and a light breeze was caressing the earth. On the horizon the mountains were dark blue, sharply outlined against the reddish sky; a few clouds embroidered the heavens. Distant voices could be heard, a goat bleated; and from very far off came the slow tinkling of a bell. And all these signs of human life were sinking into a chill and desolate hush, losing themselves in it, making it yet more profound. Silvano was still conscious of the restlessness that had suddenly come over him in the dead man's room, of the unendurable feeling of weariness that had driven him to ask: What am I doing here? But now the sky had cleared. He drew a deep breath and turned round. And at that moment he saw Barbara coming toward him.

She was wearing a pearl-gray dress; she was walking leisurely and in her hands she carried a black prayer book. Her step was light, she looked straight in front of her as she walked, she seemed the delicate creation of a dream. Silvano felt his heart beating, but he went bravely forward.

"Barbara," he said, and stopped.

The girl held out her hand and smiled faintly. Her face was lightly freckled, and she had fair hair and misty gray eyes; she gave the impression that within her was a muddied stream, flowing slowly between high banks, out of sight of the poplars that soared heavenward above it. Rather distantly, but still smiling, she asked, "How are you, Silvano?"

Ah, that smile! Silvano's mind went blank and he felt a wave of weakness sweep over him. Bereft of his strength, limp, unmanned, he recognized that he was a failure in life—no good for anything. He looked at his watch and muttered, "Good-by, Barbara, I must run, it's getting late; but we'll see each other again, won't we?"

"Good-by," Barbara said, and she was still smiling.

(6)

"And they shall call his name Emmanuel"

ONCE upon a time the threshing of the corn was a festive occasion in every household, for both masters and men. Under the fierce August sun the people carried sheaves to the great dusty threshing floors, sang ballads of long ago, and drank the best white wine. The hum of the threshing machine rose into the splendor of the summer sky, dogs scampered joyously among the workers, and hens fluttered about looking for fallen grain that had been left on the ground. Birds wheeled overhead, in the full blaze of the sun, and the heap of straw cast all round the threshing post was like a hymn to the glory of Almighty God, creator of all things. At this season any poor man who came to the doors of the farmsteads could be sure of receiving a loaf of bread, a piece of cheese, and a flagon of wine; and even the beggars whose lot was hardest forgot their hunger and misery and sang lightheartedly with those who were carefree and happy. In the evenings there was a great feasting and dancing on the threshing floor. Landlords and tenants ate together, proposed healths, drank to the harvest, to the fertility of the bountiful earth. Emboldened by wine, the youngest members of the company dragged girls into secret corners of the barn; and so it was that many infants saw the light for the first time in April, exactly nine months after the threshing season.

But in the burning summer of our story all this was but a memory of days long vanished. Joy, Concord, and Charity, whose presence had once inspired and gladdened the Little Valley of God, had now departed from it; and a poison had instilled itself into men's souls. The poison (according to the landowners) was the socialistic propaganda of the peasant unions. The poison (according to the tenants) was the avarice of the landowners— heartless brutes who turned a deaf ear to every appeal. But the landowners retorted: Here are people who can't tell a bull from a cow, or an elm from a chestnut, and yet they come here and make speeches, and incite you to break the old agreement between us, under which we go half shares in the fruits of the harvest. We pay the taxes, don't we? And haven't we the responsibility of finding a market for your produce? Wasn't that the way of it with our fathers and grandfathers and all bygone generations? They spoke these words with an assumed air of friendly reproach, and the peasants did not know what to reply. They stood before their masters, not daring to look them in the eyes, and twisted their much-worn caps in their blackened hands. Then the representatives of the unions intervened: men with red congested faces who kept their hats on their heads and talked of claims, the proletariat, and sacred rights (everything is sacred for those who want it to be sacred). Then, turning to the peasants, they alluded to certain happenings which often disturbed the serenity of the hours of darkness; for instance, those deplorable outbreaks of fire in the haylofts. It so happens that in our country the peasants are rather resistant to political propaganda; all the same they feel much more disposed to listen when someone comes and warns them: Close your ranks; otherwise your house, your barn. . . . And most men in our country attach great importance to their houses.

So it came about that in the Little Valley of God that summer the tenants hated their landlords, and the landlords hated their tenants. A frigid silence reigned in the farmsteads. Sadness, Discord, and Violence held dominion over men's hearts. The landowners went about with revolvers in their pockets, and by night the peasants greased the Tommy-guns they kept hidden in the haylofts. Oaths and blasphemies had taken the place of songs; for when men have brought misfortunes upon themselves they usually try to shift the responsibility to someone else's shoulders, and very often their scapegoat is He whose name is written with a capital letter, He who will come to judge the quick and the dead.

There was so much wheat in the peasant Leopoldo's barn that at ten o'clock in the morning barely a fifth of it had been threshed. Signorina Carmela was there, sitting apart, and every time she saw a sack carried up she cut a notch in a stout ash stick. She had been at it since sunrise, and with her gleaming knife she had already cut into more than nine long sticks. The wheat was a beautiful golden color and the grain was bursting from the ears.

"I wish I knew what these good-for-nothing rascals have to grumble about," Signorina Carmela said suddenly. "They're never pleased. No one has ever seen such a harvest as there is this year."

"By nature man is never content," sighed Silvano. He was sitting hunched on a big stone and trying to read a book. But between the pages he kept seeing Barbara's gray eyes and her tiny white hands.

"And why not?" Signorina Carmela burst out. She was a stout asthmatic woman with too much blood in her veins. It was said that she might die suddenly at any moment. She knew it and made her communion every morning so as not to die in a state of mortal sin. Silvano often wondered what this mortal sin she was always talking about could possibly be, but he was too discreet to ask.

He answered, "I don't know. Perhaps because the Lord wants it to be like that, perhaps it's His will." He knew that an argument of that kind would leave Signorina Carmela with nothing to say.

She was in fact reduced to silence; and at that moment a young man appeared on the threshing floor. He was of medium height, thin and pale, with light chestnut hair that fell curiously about his shoulders. He was wearing clothes that did not match, trousers of a nondescript color and an old tunic that appeared to be of military origin. Slung over his back was a haversack. "May I come and join you?" he asked, and his voice made the

(42)

men and women turn round, quieted a barking dog, drowned the rhythmic chuffing of the engine.

Leopoldo gazed at him for some time. Then he said slowly, "Yes." He spat on the ground and added as if in self-justification, "We can always do with extra help at threshing time. Even on a morning like this, when the devil himself seems to be lending us a hand. We're short of a man as it happens; Fioravante isn't here. You can take his place."

Silvano thought that even Leopoldo did not believe a word of what he had just said. It must have been for some quite different reason that he had allowed this stranger to stay and share in their labors.

The newcomer put down his knapsack at the foot of an olive tree, glanced round him, and ran his hand through his hair. Silvano noticed that his hands were white and delicate and this discovery surprised him considerably. The man moved toward the threshing machine. Silvano said to himself: I'm sure I've seen this man somewhere else, in different circumstances. Yet he did not succeed in remembering where or when, though he racked his brains. And the result was that he felt disturbed.

Meanwhile the youth had approached the machine. The driver asked him sharply, "What can you do?"

He smiled. "A little of everything. I'm a peasant too, you see."

The driver looked at him and smiled back. "Go and take over from that fellow who's loading the sheaves," he ordered.

The young man climbed onto the machine. In spite of his emaciation and his delicate appearance he showed by the way he jumped up that he was very agile in his movements. Nevertheless the youth who had been feeding the sheaves into the opening began to laugh. He was half-naked, with a hard dry body, corded muscles that stood out, and crimson scarf round his neck. He laughed and pointed to the newcomer's shoulders.

"So, you want to take over, eh?"

"Yes," said the other mildly.

At that moment everyone stopped talking and listened. No one could have said why it was, but there was really something quite extraordinary about these two young men standing up there on top of the threshing machine and shouting to each

(43)

other above the hum of the engine. One was dark-skinned, aggressive, and robust; the other was rather fair, with a serene expression, long hair that fell about his shoulders, and white sensitive hands. The stranger said again, "Yes . . . Elia."

It was at that moment that the engine suddenly stopped. There was a dead silence; then a voice cried, "Look out, the belt's off!"

"How do you know my name is Elia?" the youth asked the newcomer in sudden fear. Since the young stranger's arrival no one had called him by his name.

The other did not answer his question. Without looking him in the face he said, "Get down, Elia. It's my turn now. You go and rest."

"No!" cried Elia furiously. "No, by Christ, no! Get down, you little weed, or I'll throw you down!" He squared up to the stranger in a belligerent attitude; his chest was visibly heaving and the veins of his neck stood out. The people still kept quiet, even those who were busy attending to the belt.

Then the newcomer said firmly, "I told you to get down, Elia." And raising his head he looked him in the eyes. Then, unhurriedly, he touched him on the chest with his hand. Elia opened his mouth in terror as if he were seeing some dreadful vision that made him want to cry out. But he merely said, "Yes, sir."

Meekly and in silence he jumped down. The engine started up again, and once more its chatter filled the sun-drenched countryside. Then Silvano could restrain himself no longer. He sprang up and called out, "What's your name, young man?"

The unknown had already begun to load sheaves with incomparable skill. Without looking up he replied, "Emanuele."

Behold, I have created this world, or perhaps I should say rather that I believe it is my creation. So far in this story it is I who have given life to its men and women: a lonely priest who loves the past of his church more than its present, more than his flock; a young writer who lives in a wealthy household and suffers the pangs of love; a sensitive boy who killed his dog and saw it again in a mysterious vision; an illegitimate son whom a

(44)

stony-hearted woman drove from his father's deathbed. My chil-
dren; their thoughts are mine. I want to share their suffering,
weep with them when they weep, and laugh with them when
they laugh—for I brought them into the world, watched over
them when they were infants, breathed the breath of their
nostrils, and peopled their land; the Little Valley of God, our
country, our private universe. But if everything leads me to be-
lieve that these men and women, their emotions and desires,
their tears and their laughter draw reality from me, are created
by me, spring from me, and can never break away—I know well
that in saying so I am deluding myself, I know well that in
cherishing such a hope I am crazy. The truth is that my children
escape from me and I can do nothing to hold them back; I can-
not even share their suffering.

I knew Thee at once, Thou who dost snatch away my children
and draw them after Thee by the power of thine irresistible be-
ing. Lo, thy body is wasted and sick, thy breath cometh short and
fast, thy flesh is waxen, thy countenance emaciated, thine eyes
are hollow with weeping, thy lips are set, there is in Thee naught
but suffering and strife and death, and silent loneliness and
desolation; what then is thy power, why do my children leave
me to follow Thee?

Having instantly recognized Thee, all I can do now is to go
on with my story, go on creating. Set apart, for Thou wilt not
even let me suffer.

After an hour's hard work the youth who had said his name
was Emanuele called to the woman who was putting out bottles
to cool and asked for some wine. He drank a glass and then he
began to sing. Straightaway something entered into these men
and women toiling under the sun. This singing was a ray of
sunlight that melted the ice in their hearts.

For the first time since they had begun threshing they all
raised their heads and looked at each other with blissful faces.
They became aware that they were human beings and could
love each other. And suddenly they felt that a thousand ties
bound them together. And no one thought it strange. What then
had become of that deadly chill which had been freezing their

hearts? That was what each one of them was secretly wondering but no one knew the answer. And the world suddenly seemed to them quite different; some clapped their hands for joy and some smiled upon each other.

Signorina Carmela lifted her blue eyes from her ash stick. She sighed deeply, then said aloud, "Heavens, what a lovely day!" She tossed her stick to a maidservant. "You do it, Caterina." All of a sudden she seemed to feel a great longing to rest, to look at the golden corn from another angle, and just revel in the great glittering sun. Meanwhile the young workman on top of the threshing machine continued to sing.

Caterina said to the footman, "Tonight, dear, I'll wait for you in the barn."

The footman was rather ugly and had a little hump on his right shoulder. He asked anxiously, "And what about Federigo?"

"Oh, never mind about Federigo!" Caterina exclaimed. "That bull of a man. I'd send him packing any day for one of your smiles."

Silvano got up and stretched himself luxuriously. Why did I suffer so much last night? he asked himself. Barbara loves me, I'm sure of it. She loves only me. And he felt happy. The young stranger continued to sing.

A woman rushed onto the threshing floor, breathless and with her hair undone. "Is Patrizio there?" she shouted.

Patrizio was the leader of the commission that had been sent by the peasants' union. A full-blooded, resolute man. He came forward and said, "Here I am. What is it?"

"Run home quickly," she called to him. "Your wife is in labor."

"No? You're not joking?" Patrizio exclaimed. He waved his hand joyously to the company and dashed off. The peasants heaved a sigh of relief. Signorina Carmela said, "Heavens, it's really a glorious day." The young man was still singing on top of the threshing machine, under the great August sun.

Leopoldo came up to her with a certain diffidence.

"How is our mistress?" he asked with affection in his voice.

The lady smiled gaily. "Very well. And you, Leopoldo?"

"What about the division of the crop?" he asked, his head bent.

"He who sings has no cares, Leo," said Carmela in a bantering tone. "Why don't you ask the young man up there? He'll give you the answer as he sings, you'll see."

The man up there was Emanuele. The threshing machine was humming under the throb of the engine and the youth never stopped singing. Yet, goodness knows how, he heard these words. He turned round, looked down at Leopoldo, and replied with a smile, "What does it matter to me? Ask your mistress, my friend."

It took Leopoldo a little time to grasp this. Then his face lit up and he spat on the ground. He went back to Signorina Carmela and declared, "Lady, I've said it from the start. We'll go halves as we've done every year, as our forefathers did. What does our mistress say to that, eh?"

There was a strange smile on Signorina Carmela's face and a rapt, faraway look in her eyes. She had just come to a decision that made her feel free and happy. "Leo," she said solemnly, "do you know what I'm going to do? I'm going to make you a present of two sacks of grain; you understand, two sacks." Then, looking round the company, she asked, "Friends, what shall we do this evening?"

And after that they spoke grave and gentle words to each other, and men shook hands, and women wiped their eyes with the hem of their aprons.

Signorina Carmela heaved a loud sigh. Lord, how happy she felt!

(7)

Night on the Threshing Floor

AFTER darkness has fallen the Spirits of the Corn roam about where the wheat has been threshed.

The threshing floor is bounded on one side by the farmstead and on the other by shady trees—oaks, walnuts, and mulberries. Under the trees there are rustic stone benches so that the men can sit down during the midday siestas.

In the clear moonlight the threshing floor seems much bigger than it is by day. The moon goes down behind the roof of the darkened house, and its sleeping front, which a moment ago was shining like silver, now sinks into quiet shadow. Upon the ground, still in disorder after the day's labors, falls a mysterious gloom. In the silence of the night men and women are asleep at last. In the early hours of darkness the young folk were sporting amorously in the fresh hay and the rustling straw, chasing and tumbling each other without restraint. The old men, the gray-beards laden with years, stayed on at the supper table, smoking their pipes with flasks of wine for company, and murmuring, "Ah, if only we were young again!" Now all are asleep, dreaming of the day that is over. The only sound in the stillness is a dog baying at the moon.

It is when the threshing machine is at work that the Spirits of the Corn come forth from the ears of the sheaves it has engulfed. During the day they are not visible; they materialize at night, in the light of the moon, which colors them with soft hues. Usually they are paler than transparent shadow, but they may also be bluer than the sky, or as green as grass, or as yellow as sunflowers. There is no color in Nature's palette, no blanching beam of moonlight, that is not to be seen reflected on their aerial forms.

They dance on the deserted threshing floor, chasing each other between the mounds of newly threshed wheat. The dog goes on barking, the moon hides behind the house, the sleeping men and women dream of the past and the future. The cicadas sing in unbroken rhythm and oh! how tender is their song!

(8)

In Which We Read of Lovesickness

At five o'clock in the morning Silvano got up to write to Barbara. The valley was still deep in shadow but behind the peaks a vague light was growing stronger and the stars were slowly disappearing. It's no use lying in bed when I can't sleep, thought Silvano restlessly. Not without difficulty he lit the lamp that stood on the table and left his room. He felt a light but painful pressure on his stomach and his whole body was shaken by a trembling he could not explain. It's nerves, he said to himself as he passed through the deserted room. It's nerves—for men often fasten on simple words like these to explain what baffles their understanding and holds them in mysterious thrall.

The fact was that Silvano, without knowing it, was in the power of an Imp. During the night it had been crouching invisibly on his chest and it meant to stay there for good. It was a malicious roving Imp with a disposition very similar to that of mortals. And Silvano, who did not know that it was there, kept saying to himself, Nerves, just nerves. He thought it was the memory of Barbara that was disturbing him.

He had been in the Little Valley of God for several days now and he had not yet managed to have a talk with her. The occasions when he could have done so had not got him any further, either because he had been too shy to take advantage of them or because she had been inexplicably absent when he had called to see her.

(50)

I'm greatly to be pitied, he thought with exasperation as he moved about aimlessly in the sleeping house. Oh, curse my shyness.

He returned to his room and set the lamp on the table. The manuscript of his novel was there, wide open. He pushed it aside with a kind of resentment and put a large blank sheet in front of him. Then he wrote: My dear Barbara . . .

"My dear Barbara, do you know that I can't live without you? My nights are full of horrible dreams and my days are torture. Dear Barbara, I want to speak to you. Why are you so cold to me? What have I done? Damn it all, didn't I come here for you? Alas, Barbara, you can see what a state I'm in. Here I am using swear words even in a letter. . . ."

The constriction in his chest grew even more painful. He finished his letter and said to himself: As soon as it's daylight I'll get Gattino to take it to her.

Gattino wore a great fur bonnet which he set at an angle above his greenish eyes. They were very like the eyes of a cat and that was why people called him Gattino.* He was himself so sure that he was a cat and not a boy that often he miaowed. On the whole, though, he was happy; even a cat can be happy on this earth.

He handed Silvano an envelope and said hurriedly, "When I got there Signorina Barbara was still asleep. A maid woke her. She was very reluctant to do it, but I talked her into it. Then I gave Signorina Barbara the letter. Here's the answer." And he handed over the envelope with quite an air, for he could be a refined and well-mannered lad when it suited him.

"Thanks," said Silvano. "You're a nice little fellow." And he gave him ten lire. Gattino fled, miaowing as he ran. Silvano gazed at the envelope and murmured: "O God." For some time he held it in his hands; finally he brought himself to open it.

The sun had now risen and was lighting up the countryside with its golden rays. The first-awakened birds were singing in the woods and the juniper bushes glittered with dew. Trails of

* Little cat

(51)

mist were rising from the ravines and vanishing in the upper air. Another day was smiling joyously upon the earth. But Silvano paid no attention; he had just ripped open the little pink envelope and was fingering the scented notepaper. The letter said:

"My dear Silvano, there are some things in your letter that I haven't been able to understand. But since you must talk to me I will come. Expect me about nine o'clock, under the oak on the road that goes from Ca' d'Orso to the stream. You know, the place where we met the madwoman Clotilde and had such a good laugh over what she said about the mayor's motorcycle. Remember? She said it was his donkey and that he had cut off its legs out of spite. That was it, wasn't it? We'll meet just there, shall we? That's settled then. Good-by. Barbara."

There was a postscript.

"For heaven's sake, if ever you write to me again don't ask a child to deliver the letter. Surely you know that everyone gossips in this country. Whatever will people think now. . . ."

There's a simple answer to that, thought Silvano, they'll say we're in love with each other. And they won't be far wrong. At least, not so far as I'm concerned. This seemed to him as crystal clear as the sunlight that was now spreading across the whole countryside. I don't see what else people can say, he muttered to himself as he marched up and down his room. He tried not to let his eyes rest on the bedspread, which was embroidered with the words "Sweet Repose"—which rather got on his nerves. But what was there in his letter that Barbara hadn't been able to understand? His stomach was still hurting and in the hope of calming it down he lit a cigarette, but he found the taste of it so disagreeable that he flung it from him. Sweet Repose indeed!

He left the house and made his way toward the wood along a sunlit path. It was barely eight o'clock; he had more than an hour to wait. The air was warm and seemed to hold abundant promise of new life and hope; the grass was sparkling with dew and soaked his shoes, making them glitter. He abandoned himself to his thoughts and without thinking where he was going he reached the stream, then followed its course as far as a little lake. There he sat down on a fallen trunk, and again lost himself in his thoughts.

There's no doubt about it, he said to himself. I'm lovesick. The water was green and trembling and the willows that overhung it were reflected in its limpid depths. It must be ice-cold, he said dreamily to himself. He plunged a hand into it and found that it was as he had thought, ice-cold and light as air. Already a few dragonflies were darting about in the sunshine, and alighting on the tall yellow flowers that grew along the bank.

How does one cure such a malady? Silvano wondered. He was twenty-six and until now he had never been in love. Clasping an unknown woman in your arms wasn't love; no one would ever pretend that it was. Or again, who would claim that it was love to throw yourself upon the cold, unresponsive body of a woman whose thoughts were elsewhere as you fondled her?

Silvano was well aware of what was lacking in his experience as a lover; it disturbed him and made him incapable of the right sort of action. If Barbara lets me kiss her, he said to himself at one stage, that might cure me. But these were mere words. When he tried to give them a practical application how would he go about it? And would she allow him to kiss her? And . . . oh dear, oh dear, love was the devil. He felt more and more uneasy. The queer shakiness had come back and was now worse than ever. How cold the water was, how soft the sun! Damn love, to hell with it. Barbara, I'm trembling like a leaf.

This was because the Imp sitting on his chest was making fun of him. It was reading his thoughts and that was the reason for its merriment. Here was the true explanation of Silvano's shaking and trembling: the quaking mirth of the Imp. But he could not know that. Barbara . . . oh dear, oh dear.

He rose to his feet, set out again, and a few seconds before nine o'clock he reached the meeting place. Almost immediately the girl made her appearance.

She was wearing a dress with green and white stripes. Silvano went up to her and for several minutes they stood there without

(53)

saying anything. Every time he saw Barbara something broke in him and he could not utter a word; it was as if he had been knocked to the ground. And yet, within, there was clamor and confusion: Barbara, the sun, your green dress, Barbara, how wretched I feel, Barbara, I'm trembling like a leaf. (The Imp was still reading his thoughts and making game of him without mercy.)

"What's the matter with you?" Barbara asked in a low voice. "Why are you trembling?"

He managed to find his voice. "I don't know. Perhaps I have a touch of fever, Barbara."

Lightly she felt his brow. "You're not feverish, and yet you're awfully white. You look like a corpse. What's the matter with you?"

"Barbara," said Silvano.

The girl had been staring at the ground. Now she looked up. "This won't do," she said in a preoccupied voice. "You're sure you aren't ill, Silvano? Tell me, what's the matter? You can't speak—that's evident."

He fought to regain command of himself and drew a deep breath.

"That's better. I brought you here, Barbara, because I wanted to talk to you very seriously."

"Talk to me very seriously?"

"Yes. There are some things I want to get straight. I tell you . . ."

"But there's nothing to get straight."

"Things can't go on like this. Barbara, why don't you listen to me?"

"There's nothing to get straight," the girl said again.

"Nothing?"

"Nothing."

"But if I love you?" said Silvano.

She gave him a sidelong glance. "What do you want of me?" she asked with a shade of irritation. (The dim, muddied river again—it was flowing back upon her.)

"How should I know?" said Silvano sadly. "But I love you, Barbara."

(54)

She flushed. "You don't respect our conventions, Silvano," she murmured. At that moment she seemed infinitely far away from him and no longer bound to the earth. "You don't respect our conventions."

Then something happened. Deep within him Silvano heard a muffled sound that might almost have been a stifled sob; he was suddenly afraid of a danger that could not be seen; he felt limp and squashed, as though dominated by an unknown presence. His head drooped, and he murmured, "You're right, Barbara. Forgive me."

At that moment the mocking Imp who was seated on his chest put an invisible hand very firmly over his mouth and began to speak for him.

"I don't give a damn for your conventions!" he burst out angrily. "D'you know that I'm near the end of my tether, Barbara? Don't you think that seven months of this is long enough? It's seven months since the fatal day when I realized that I was in love with you. Seven months since that January night when I wrote you that letter and slipped it into the pocket of your black coat before I went away. Do you remember what I said then? Didn't I say I was in love with you? Well, I'm still in love with you, do you understand? My God, I love you, and I can't go on any longer."

She looked at him with stupefaction, gazing into his eyes. And those eyes clearly expressed a sudden furious determination. She had never seen him like this. He was standing with his legs set apart, firm as a rock, and his manner was truculent and aggressive; he would stop at nothing to get her. At first she was thunderstruck; then a feeling of weakness came upon her, accompanied by a weary but sweet anxiety about what he proposed to do. Almost against her will she said, "But there's the pact we made, Silvano, the pact between us."

Angrily he shook his head. "It's a pact that isn't a pact. It's childish, absurd. Why, we'd be the laughingstock of the valley if people got to know about it. You asked me to wait and I promised that I would. That was all, you can't deny it. Well, I've waited, and now what? There's a limit to everything. I love you, I love you, I love you. Must I keep on saying it? I'm at

(55)

the end of my tether, I want you. I love you. How long am I to wait for you? Ten years? Until I'm an old man? Until I'm dead? I love you, I love you, and I want you. I'm mortally afraid that someone will take you from me . . . and . . . O God, I love you."

"Please, please, not so loud. . . ."

"What's that you say? Not so loud? Am I to speak quietly when I'm eating my heart out? Oh Barbara, d'you know what I'm going to do instead? I'm going to kiss you. What do I care if people see us and hear us? I'm going to kiss you, my darling, I'm going to kiss you because from now on . . ."

"Quietly, Silvano. It will be dreadful if . . ."

"I don't give a damn for anyone. . . . You're the only one who matters to me. You, my darling . . ."

But at that moment the girl opened her eyes very wide and cried out, "There's someone between you and me, Silvano, I feel it." And she began to utter piercing screams that shattered the quiet of the morning.

(It was at that moment that the Imp jumped off Silvano's body and vanished, leaving him dazed and stupefied.)

Suddenly Barbara stopped screaming. Then, seized once more by a mysterious sensation of dread, Silvano looked at her for a moment as though he did not recognize her, and took to his heels.

Breathless, he reached the little tarn and stopped on its brink. He felt lonely and abandoned and he was a little sorry for himself. But he was hungry, his pain had gone, the sun was sparkling on the surface of the water—love could go to hell! He cried aloud, "It's time I had breakfast!"

He could no longer remember very clearly what had happened.

(9)

In Which a Blind Man Meets a Milkmaid and Loses His Virginity

To the north of the Little Valley of God is a very high mountain. The people call it just that: the Mountain. Shaped like a woman's breast and dark green in color, it rises between the cultivated terraces and divides two great agricultural regions. Oaks, chestnuts, and beeches clothe its slopes, and in some places there are pines and firs. Amid its solitudes live woodcutters and charcoal burners. It also shelters fugitives from the courts of justice on the plain—men who have accounts to settle with the officers of the law.

Gio was neither a woodcutter nor a charcoal burner and he had never committed any crime. But he was blind and he had no one left in the world except an old dog called Portovallo. He lived in the woods with his dog, and inhabited a stone house that was falling to pieces with age and overgrown with vegetation. Crouched on the threshold, he spent his days making baskets and hampers of withes, which he did with consummate skill. While he worked he was in the habit of talking in a low voice to his dog.

Now this blind man was twenty-five years old and you are to know, reader, that for the past ten years, in the midst of his loneliness, he had been tormented by a craving for love. One day he accidentally became aware of the existence of a milkmaid who looked after five or six cows and regularly drove them to a pasturage on the slopes of the mountain. He could not tell what she was like in appearance but quite suddenly he pictured her as incredibly beautiful. Not knowing of any other way in which he could declare his love he fashioned himself a reed flute and one fine spring morning he went whistling down the mountain to meet her.

At first she laughed at him; then, when she came to inspect him more closely, she realized that he was strongly built and good looking. She was already thirty and she wanted a lover. She flirted with him for some time until one night she had a dream about him. It was a confused dream in which she kept seeing his legs and his muscular arms. And she dreamed of much else besides. The next morning when he made his appearance as usual, whistling merrily, with his dog trotting at his heels, she said to him, "Lie down beside me on the grass."

And what followed was her doing, not his.

The dog Portovallo looked at them in silence and did not interfere.

It was in the spring that all this happened; summer with its quivering heat was still a long way off.

Some months later the milkmaid realized that she was pregnant. At first the shock of it made her furiously angry with Gio. In her rage she called him all sorts of names—scoundrel, idiot, wretch—and showered curses on his father and mother. Then she began to cry and made up her mind that the child would never be born.

She wanted to tell the blind man of her condition. Back she went to the wood and found him near his green tumbledown house, with Portovallo by his side. When he heard her step he got up and called her by her name.

"Fidalma!"

She laughed bitterly and went up to him.

"I'm pregnant," she announced.

At first Gio did not understand; he had been blind for twenty years and he had always lived by himself. He opened his mouth and said, "Eh, what?"

"Pregnant," she repeated. "I'm going to have a baby. And it's your fault—you've done this to me."

(58)

"Fidalma!" said the blind man. There was a short silence and then he asked, "When?"

The girl burst out, "You beast, you pig, you took advantage of me!"

She began to cry. "Oh, it's awful," she sobbed. "I must have an abortion."

Gio groped for Portovallo's head. He did not understand what she was saying, but he guessed that it was something frightful.

"What does that mean?" he asked.

"A lot you care!" the milkmaid retorted. "It doesn't mean anything—except that the child won't be born."

"And who will kill it?" demanded Gio, trembling with anger.

The woman was rather alarmed.

"I don't know. . . ." she muttered.

Then she made off, leaving him by himself. He began to play his flute and he fell into deep thought.

It was the middle of the afternoon, and the sun was still high in the heavens. The evening came, and then the night; at last the moon rose and the Mountain turned the color of snow. Gio went on playing his flute, and he was thinking hard.

Next morning he whistled to Portovallo, and guided by the dog he made his way to the cabin of a herd who lived in the neighborhood. He gave him a dozen wicker baskets, and asked for some *ricottas* * in exchange.

"Good heavens, Gio," said the herd, "you look very queer this morning."

And as the blind man did not reply he persisted, "Do you know that you look ill?"

Gio made an impatient movement.

"I didn't ask you what I looked like, did I?"

"No, no, certainly not," replied the herd. "I was joking, Gio."

The truth was that what he read in the blind man's face was enough to make him tremble; and so he was glad when he saw Gio making off with his basket of *ricottas*.

"Oh, Gabriel," he said aloud, "when will you teach me to mind

* *Ricotta:* cheese made of boiled cream. Found in many parts of Italy, especially in country districts.

my own business?" The herd was a bit of a philosopher and he had a habit of carrying on conversations with invisible companions; at that moment he had been having a talk with a mighty archangel.

After an hour's walk Gio reached the milkmaid's house; she lived there with an old aunt who had a notorious reputation in the Little Valley of God. When Fidalma saw the blind man she came out on the doorstep in a state of extreme agitation.

"I've brought you these *ricottas*," said Gio calmly.

"Yes, but you should never have come here. What on earth did you come for?"

"Listen to me, Fidalma," said the blind man, and there was a note in his voice that reduced the woman to silence.

Then he began to question her.

"Must you really kill the child?"

"Yes," she said faintly.

"Why?"

"Gio, there's something I must tell you," she murmured. "I'm betrothed to Fanuel the charcoal burner. I have no one in the world, I must get married. That's all, Gio."

The blind man bowed his head. "All right, Fidalma," he said. He drew her to him and took her in his arms. The house stood in a deserted spot; there was no one to stop him. The woman did not resist and she even yielded herself gently to his caresses.

"But I love you so much," he told her, "and the child too."

"I know, Gio," the woman answered, "and yet I must marry Fanuel. You do understand, don't you?"

"Why must you? Who's forcing you to marry him?"

"No one. Who could force me to do it?"

"Well, then . . ."

"I can't go on living like this."

"What do you mean, like this?"

"You call this a life? Well, it isn't. Looking after animals, never getting a proper meal, living in rags, not knowing where to turn, being treated like dirt, just existing . . ."

"You have this house."

". . . not having anything you can call your own, not one single article that you can say is yours, not even a bed, not even

(60)

a comb. I'm thirty, Gio, and the house isn't mine, it's my aunt's."

"You have your aunt Marion."

"She can hardly bear me, she doesn't even notice whether I go or stay. I've no one."

"But you have me. You don't love me?"

"Yes I do."

"Well then, why don't you come and live with me? We could live together, we could be together always."

But the milkmaid put her hands on the blind man's eyes. "Gio," she murmured.

He understood and said, "All right, Fidalma. Oh my darling, darling Fidalma." He drew her close to him again and rocked her in his arms and kissed her face. He realized that she was crying, for he could taste the salt tears on her lips.

"Is it really necessary?" he said again. A nameless terror, something like an approaching wave of panic, drove him to put the question again and yet again, to go on asking it.

"Is it really necessary for you to marry Fanuel?"

For the second time she laid her hands on his eyes.

"Yes, Gio."

Then, gently, he put her from him.

"When are you thinking of getting rid of the child?"

"One of these days, no doubt. But that isn't the way to talk, Gio; it isn't a child. It's only a lump of flesh, it hasn't got a soul!"

"I want to ask you one thing," said the blind man. "That lump of flesh—put it in a box and bring it to me on the Mountain."

And something turned over inside him.

"Listen, Fidalma. If you don't do as I ask, as sure as there's a God in heaven I'll tell Fanuel everything!"

The woman said, "All right, Gio. I'll bring it to you."

It was toward the end of August that this happened and when, a week later, the milkmaid brought a well-wrapped parcel to the Mountain, it had an acrid odor of flesh and blood.

But Gio had already fashioned a little oak box. He put the parcel inside without opening it for, being blind, he could only imagine what was in it. He covered the little chest with flowers and buried it close to his house. Then he knelt down and bent his head until his brow touched the ground.

"Sleep," he murmured. "Sleep, sleep. . . ."

He sat down on the ground beside the grave, and fondled his dog's head. After a while he began to play his flute.

(10)

In Which Professor Silvano Visits a Fallen
Woman to No Purpose

THE heat of August, which makes men limp, stirs the blood of women. Not that there was any need to invoke these wise sayings where Maddalena Amato was concerned. I don't know precisely to what extent her behavior was governed by the seasons in their swift flight across the face of Time's relentless clock. The fact is that she sinned a great deal; it could even be said that she had no other occupation. I can't tell you either whether she sinned from carnal desire pure and simple or from some other cause. She lived alone and had neither a family nor any close relations. She was a good and gentle young woman, and it may well have been that she did what she did out of kindness of heart. She was twenty-four years old; tall, strong, and healthy. She lived in a little house among flowers, chickens, and sacred images. Her door was always open, and the men of the valley could go to her at any hour of the day or night. She was a friendly woman with refined manners; she smiled upon all human creatures, as upon all terrestrial things, and she could never say no.

In the Little Valley of God the men said they knew of nothing in the world more beautiful than her smile. Maddalena had big pearl-gray eyes, utterly honest, and golden lights could be seen in them when she smiled. Her smile was frank and sincere and —above all—innocent. The men were in the habit of giving her presents after they had been to see her. But even if they had given her all the fields and woods and houses of the Little Valley of God they would never have been able to repay her for that smile of hers.

It could not be said that Maddalena Amato's smile was in perfect harmony with her body. You will often find, as a matter of fact, that two senses or two organs belonging to the same person are irreconcilably opposed. Maddalena's body aroused in men the sharpest appetites, the most tormenting, burning, and mysterious passions. And her smile calmed and soothed them, made them feel at peace with the world, persuaded them that—say what you like—the earth is a good mother and we her children are all brothers; it inclined them to a chaste way of living, to innocent thoughts.

Countless stories about this were told at the Shop, where the tales that went round made up a chronicle of life in the Valley, past and present. Especially striking among the more recent of these was the story of Maddalena Amato and the monk Giocondo.

"Hearken, ye children of men, to what befell a monk whose name was Giocondo. Are ye listening, brothers? The monk Giocondo lived in one of the monasteries in these mountains. One day he saw Maddalena Amato's body and he fell head over heels in love with her. Don't ask me what it means to fall madly in love with a woman; we all know, the whole world knows. So you can well imagine what a frenzy the monk Giocondo was in, and how desire burned in him, and what secret agonies he endured in his cell. Brothers, the flesh triumphed; can you wonder at it? The flesh triumphed, and he went to Maddalena Amato's house, and he lay with her a long time, and he loved her with all the violence of a man who for years has kept away from women. Then—brothers, are you listening?—came the dawn, came the daylight; the monk was exhausted, he sank into a deep sleep, but the sun roused him from his slumber, and close to his face he saw Maddalena's smile, he saw her frank, calm, innocent smile. And looking upon that smile the monk Giocondo screamed out, he screamed out like a lost soul: O God, Thou hast forsaken me, O God, what have I done? He screamed like a bitch whose whelps have been taken from her—and then came

(64)

Repentance. The monk Giocondo went back to the monastery, he took stick and knapsack, and departed to China, where he died a martyr."

That is the story as it was told at the Shop during the midday siestas—the story of the monk Giocondo who knew only one woman in the world, and thought of her all his life long.

But enough of the melancholy past; in the long run we people of the Little Valley of God are really only concerned with the present, and it's the present alone that matters to us.

Well then, it came about that Silvano felt the smart of love's arrows flaring up again, more painful than ever, after a momentary respite from the torment which, as we have seen, had kept him awake all one night. He felt extreme discomfort; however, knowing that this was not a case for a doctor, he thought the best thing he could do was to go and ask the advice of young Otello, a close friend of his who had a wide experience in certain matters. Otello listened thoughtfully to what Silvano chose to tell him, and then tapped him lightly on the shoulder.

"There's one thing you're in need of," he said. Otello was a youth of medium height, with slightly round shoulders; he had clear-cut features, a smooth complexion, and very white hands; he was skeptical and fastidious, very reserved but capable of warm friendship. Women adored him.

"What's that?" Silvano asked.

Otello looked at him steadily.

"A woman."

"But I'm in love," said Silvano, rather surprised.

"Exactly, my dear fellow. You need to sleep with a woman, that's what I mean. In certain cases it's a miraculous cure." Otello was in a position to defend this theory with complete assurance since he put it into practice himself every day of the week.

"You think so?" said Silvano. This conversation was shaking him a little.

"I'm sure of it, my dear fellow," the young man said with conviction. He was fully experienced; he knew what methods to employ.

"And where am I going to get hold of her?" Silvano said next.

(65)

"Get hold of whom?"

"The woman. Didn't you say that I must find myself a woman? Where am I going to get one around here?"

Otello began to laugh. "Isn't there Maddalena Amato, my friend?" And with these words he dismissed Silvano, for he had to receive a delegation from the peasants' union.

Maddalena Amato lived in a little house at the back of the church of San Sebastiano. Her mode of life being what it was, the priest had tried to get her away from the sacred precincts, and he had even fired some very pointed remarks at her in his sermons. But he had been forced to moderate his zeal as a defender of public morals in order to stop crowds of men from forsaking the church services and openly plotting mischief against his person. The fate of Maddalena Amato was of deep concern to countless bachelors in the Little Valley of God and to quite a number of married men. Nevertheless, Don Marcello successfully withstood all external pressure until one day Maddalena, meeting him face to face, did not smile at him. It was then that the priest decided to let well enough alone, consoling himself with the thought that the ways of God are inscrutable. It was in fact common knowledge that men going to visit Maddalena and finding that she had someone with her would drift into the church and say their prayers while awaiting their turn.

When Silvano arrived, Maddalena Amato was busy poaching two eggs for her evening meal. She was wearing a summer dress of white linen, and she dropped him a little curtsy in the manner of bygone days, for she understood the graces of life and she had breeding.

"I've been sent by Otello," said Silvano. It was the first time he had been in the house and he felt a trifle embarrassed.

Maddalena said to him, "Sit down, Professor. You don't mind if I finish my dinner?"

"Please do," said Silvano without looking at her. He sat down on a chair.

It was evening and the swallows were dipping and twittering over the road nearby. There was a clucking of hens, a child could be heard calling to its mother, and far away a dog was barking. Familiar sounds, full of a strange impression of peace.

Silvano listened to them in silence, then declared, for the sake of something to say, "We're in for a change of weather."

"How can you tell?" asked Maddalena.

He gazed at her with an absent look. "Because the swallows are flying low."

"Let's hope it will rain," said Maddalena. "That wouldn't do the gardens any harm."

"Let's hope it will."

She finished eating and got up rather hurriedly. She put the dirty plate under an old stone tap, set the table to rights, and placed a bowl of flowers on it. Then she turned to Silvano.

"You know my name?"

"Of course," said Silvano. "You're called Maddalena."

When they were in her little room and had closed the door, Maddalena sat down on the bed and began to weep silent tears. Silvano looked at her for a moment; then he asked her in some concern, "What's the matter?"

The woman lifted her tearful face. "I don't know," she said. "I feel I want to cry."

"Does this often happen?" Silvano didn't know what to say. He stood rather stupidly beside the bed and felt a growing uneasiness.

"Excuse me," said the young woman. "It never used to affect me like this."

"Really?"

"I assure you it didn't."

"And now it does?"

"Yes."

"Very odd." Then Silvano asked, "But perhaps something has happened to you?"

Maddalena began to look at the bedspread and the usual lettering: Sweet Repose.

"Why don't you answer?" Silvano persisted.

"I believe I'm in love," she said. And she was clearly a little ashamed of it.

Silvano smiled faintly. "So you're in love too, are you?"

The woman also smiled and her eyes shone. "What, you mean you're in love?"

(67)

"Yes, I'm in love too."

Then she made room for him on the bed beside her. "Let's console each other," she said.

But when they had consoled each other, Silvano, who was lying quiet and thoughtful, opened his eyes and said, "I feel just as I did before. Rather worse. This time Otello has made a mistake." Then it struck him that he had been impolite to the woman, and he added with great sincerity, "Oh, it was magnificent. Only . . . I still feel very restless."

"So do I," Maddalena confessed.

"Perhaps it's because we're too much in love."

The woman bowed her head. "Perhaps," she agreed.

Then Silvano asked, "But whom are you in love with?"

She made no reply.

"You really won't tell me?"

Maddalena drew the sheet over her white bosom as if she were not allowed to pronounce the name while her nakedness was exposed. Humbly she covered herself up, and it was only then that she said, "With a newcomer, a young man whose name is Emanuele."

(11)

Another Story of the Little Valley of God and the Wide World

DETTO BANTI was gazing now at the letter and now at the police sergeant who stood before him, tightly buttoned into his uniform. The sergeant had red cheeks and legs that looked as if they had been riveted into his leggings. Detto Banti said to him, "Do sit down, sergeant."

The policeman sat down, and as he took a chair he let out a sort of whistling sound, like the hiss of a balloon going flat. He removed his cap, laid it on the table beside him, and without taking his eyes off it began to nurse it in his hands, gently, as if he were afraid of damaging it. "The trouble is, I know him so little," he said, without looking up. "The sergeant who was in charge of this station before I came said to me just before he left, 'If you are in any difficulty, go to Signor Banti. Signor Banti is a man who's worth his weight in gold.' These were his very words."

"Have something to drink, sergeant," said Detto Banti.

"A man who's worth his weight in gold," the sergeant repeated. He drank the sweet wine that the other had poured out for him and brushed his hand over his mouth like a schoolboy.

Detto Banti looked at the letter once more, then he took off his spectacles and very carefully folded them in half.

"I'd much rather not," he said.

"It's a favor," murmured the sergeant.

"True enough."

"I'm asking you to do it as a favor," the sergeant persisted.

Detto Banti got up and strode across the room. He sat down in the ingle of the fireless hearth, then got up and went to the window. On the wall there was an image of the Madonna of Pompeii. He looked at it a long time as if he had never seen it before. "I've known Gallo for twenty years," he said at last.

"Yes," said the sergeant.

"Twenty years is a long time," said Detto Banti. "People get to know each other quickly in this country. I'm a butcher and he's a charcoal burner. This boy was his only son. D'you know what I've been thinking? I'd rather be punched in the face than asked to break such news to him."

"It's a favor," the sergeant said for the third time.

Then Detto Banti said to him, "Very well, I'll do it."

The sergeant took his leave and Detto Banti went out. It was already after six and Gallo would be coming down before long. Shadows were lengthening on the Mountain; as he passed the stable he heard the mules stamping in the straw.

He crossed the road and took a path through the middle of the fields. Suddenly a strong smell of frying was wafted to his nostrils. That must be his wife cooking his supper, Detto said to himself. For Gallo was fond of fried food and his house was quite near.

A bad business, Detto Banti said to himself, a bad business. He had the telegram in his pocket, folded across four times; it was the sergeant who had meticulously doubled it over. Poor Bruno, said Detto. Poor Bruno. The path was quiet and peaceful, and the odor of frying had dispersed. The telegram said: INFORM FAMILY SUICIDE PRIVATE BRUNO ANDREANI. It was signed by the colonel. It also said: LETTER FOLLOWS. And the letter was here, in Detto's pocket, likewise folded across four times. What possessed the sergeant, why did he have to fold everything in half?

Poor Bruno. . . . The path was steep, but up here by the fountain it widened into a mule track. I'm bound to meet him,

Detto said to himself. He'll come, he'll come. And he could almost imagine what would follow.

He heard a clattering of hoofs and saw Gallo coming down, holding his mule by the bridle. He was a thickset man with a frank but toil-worn face, black hair and a black complexion; he wore a black smock over black corduroy trousers. The mule was laden with two sacks of carbon, slung on each side of the saddle. All the exposed parts of Gallo's body were black with carbon.

It was not until he was beside Detto that he raised his head, though he had probably seen him waiting below. "Hello," he said, and even his voice was weary. "Hello," said Detto, and looked at him without moving.

The mule stopped. "What are you doing here?" Gallo asked. Detto began to stare at the ground; then he pulled his spectacles from his pocket and fitted them carefully to the bridge of his nose, without lifting his head. "I'm looking for something I've lost," he muttered. "I've been searching for it a good half-hour and now it's getting dark." He straightened up and averted his eyes. "Goodness me, how quickly the light fades."

"You're going down?" asked Gallo.

"Yes."

"Good. Then we'll go down together." The sun had vanished but it was not yet quite dark. There was a great stillness, and the mule's shoes sent pebbles rolling down the path.

"It will soon be winter," said Detto with a preoccupied air. He was walking on the very edge of the path and he was afraid of slipping and falling. Gallo walked on the other side of the mule.

They stopped when they reached the first houses. Gallo moved calmly round the animal and put a hand on its neck. He was now very close to Detto; his breath smelled faintly of garlic. It was impossible to see his eyes, but Detto could imagine them. They must be wide open and full of misgiving.

"It's something to do with my son?" he asked suddenly.

His voice was laden with fear. It was not like Gallo to say "my son"; usually he said "Bruno" or "my boy." Detto noticed the difference and was so moved that he could not speak; he stood in front of him with downcast eyes. For a moment neither of them stirred. Then Gallo turned round and slapped his beast two or three times on the neck. "Hup!" he said, and the mule made its way toward the stable. When it was inside he unloaded the two sacks. Detto watched him and managed to say, "Come to my house when you have had your supper." And he went off without waiting for Gallo's answer.

"I don't want anything to eat," Detto said to his wife. "Clear out." Without a word she left the house. She'll probably go and sit with the neighbors, he told himself. And for the first time in his life he was overcome by a feeling of loneliness. He took his beret and set off for the charcoal burner's house.

He planted himself near a lighted window and called, "Gallo, Gallo!"

After a moment Gallo made his appearance. "What is it?"

"Come to my house, I'm alone, my wife has gone to sit with the neighbors."

The other man did not reply immediately; he stood at the window without saying a word. In the kitchen Detto could hear the usual bustle of women going to and fro after supper, clearing away and washing up. "Come round," he said again, but in a faint voice. He was thinking of a woman. . . .

"All right," said Gallo. "I'm coming."

"Come to my house," said Detto.

They entered the room where the sergeant had stood only a short time before. Detto lit the lamp; he wasted several matches because his hands were shaking. The charcoal burner seemed very pale; he remained standing but he put a hand on the table to support himself.

"My son," he said.

"Your son," Detto repeated.

"He's dead."

"He's ill," said Detto.

"No."

Detto was silent.

"He's dead," the father said again, almost angrily. "I know quite well he's dead. Why don't you say so?" Then he began to tremble.

He stood in the kitchen, beside the table, leaning upon it with one hand, and the lamp Detto had put there began to sway; huge shadows rose up and climbed the walls, filling the room with an extraordinary tumult of light and dark. The trembling that shook Gallo did not affect all his body but each of his limbs in turn; first the right arm, then the left, then one leg, then the other; and each spasm produced a corresponding movement of the table, set the huge shadows dancing on the walls. He did not utter a word, and yet a muffled sound came from his lips, like the toneless murmur of a worshiper telling his beads and making responses from the back of a church. This lasted for several minutes. Then Gallo stopped trembling and sat down on a chair. "Tell me about it," he said to Detto, who was pale and bathed in perspiration. He spoke in a humble voice, the voice of a frightened child.

Detto Banti fumbled in his pocket and produced the colonel's letter. He went over to the lamp and began to read.

On the last Tuesday of the month the captain had paraded the men of the company on the barrack square. He gazed at them for several minutes in silence and then announced: "Orders concerning the departure of those of you who have completed your military service have now been received. The quartermaster will give you fuller information. All I want to say is that the colonel wishes us to carry on as usual. There are to be no demonstrations." He gazed at them again before ordering them to fall out. As they obeyed the command he added, "You're glad to be going?" He was a rather stout man with a pale face, always closely shaved, and very black hair that glistened with brilliantine.

Something like a ripple of hollow laughter could be heard, though none of the soldiers ventured to reply directly. "I understand," said the captain. "I quite understand."

He stared hard at them again (it was a trick he had) and then spoke to the sergeant. "Tell Private Bruno Andreani to come to my office." With that he left the square, marching away with his ungainly stride.

Private Bruno Andreani entered the room and stood to at-

(73)

tention. He was of medium height but very strongly built, with a red face, black hair, and wide-open eyes. He was like a young bull and that seemed to please the captain. "How goes it, Andreani?" The soldier made no reply. "Look here," said the captain, becoming insistent, "you've got to pull yourself together, Andreani. Stop behaving like an idiot, my boy, and tell me what's the matter. What's wrong with you?" He seemed to have dropped his habitual reserve.

"There's nothing wrong with me," the boy said at last.

The captain began to examine his nails, which were white and carefully manicured. "Have you a match?" he asked. He lit a cigarette and flung himself into a chair. "That's not how you address an officer, Andreani. There's nothing wrong with me, *sir*. And anyway it isn't true."

Once again the soldier made no reply. He was very pale and he kept staring doggedly at the floor. His dark-skinned legs, strong and muscular under his short trousers, were visibly trembling. Raising himself on his elbow behind the table, the captain asked sharply, "Women?"

"Yes," said Bruno Andreani without looking up.

"I thought as much," said the captain. (In the report which accompanied the colonel's letter he had written, "I had guessed what was wrong and for a long time I had been keeping this man under observation; he had a look that I didn't like.") "I thought as much. Women are the cause of all the trouble with you fellows." There was a faint note of cynicism in the captain's voice. "Who is it?"

"A girl."

"Local girl?"

"No."

"Well, where does she come from?"

"From where I live." ("This also corroborated my information. The men have few distractions in this small isolated country and the girls are not too friendly. We soldiers have very little contact with the civilian population.")

The captain looked at the boy and then eyed his legs. "You're a strong lad, Andreani. Are you fond of women?"

"Yes"—and he reddened.

"Tell me, have you got her into trouble?"

"It's not that."

"What is it then?"

The lad made no reply. "Come along, I want to know," the captain persisted. "Have her parents raised objections?"

"It's not that."

"Well, what is it?"

"She won't have anything to do with me," the boy said in a low voice.

The captain looked at the ceiling. Someone appeared on the doorstep. "Clear out!" the captain shouted to him. "Can one never get a moment's peace in this damned office?" Then he leaned on the table with both hands. "It's tough luck, Bruno." It was the first time he had called him by his Christian name. "Has she written to you?"

"Yes."

"What sort of girl is she?"

"She's all right," the boy answered.

"It's tough luck," the captain repeated. And he went on, "Listen to me. . . ."

"It's that chit of a girl," the father said without moving from his chair.

Detto sat down beside him. "You must be brave, Gallo." At a loss to know what to say, he was in a hurry to finish reading the letter. "You must be brave."

The father did not seem to have heard; he was looking fixedly at the lamp. "It must be that girl, I knew it straightaway. She's taken my child from me, she's killed him." But he said this without heat, in a tone that was almost indifferent. "Oh, this Little Valley of God!"

"Shall I go on?" Detto asked. "It's the same everywhere, you know."

"Yes, go on," said Gallo in his flat, dead voice.

When Bruno left the barracks it was almost dark. The sentry turned to him for a moment. I daresay he's surprised to see me go out at this hour, the boy thought; the others will soon be

(75)

coming back, the corporal was just getting ready to sound the bugle. It's nearly nine o'clock. And this put him in mind of the old watch he had left in his kitbag, wrapped up in blue paper on which he had penciled the address of the girl he loved. It will be something for her to remember me by, he thought with a rush of tenderness. Even the pain at his heart had gone, along with the horror and despair that had overwhelmed him during those interminable hours of darkness that now seemed to be slipping away into an unreal past.

He could truthfully say that he felt no resentment against anyone. He passed through the iron gate of the barracks, and almost at once he turned to the right and began to follow the wooden paling. He was walking on soft grass, and this gave him an indefinable sensation of pleasure. It had been the same on those mornings when he had taken the path through the woods with his father and the mule. How glorious it had been then to trample the fresh springing grass or the dead leaves heaped up by the passing seasons! No, truly, he bore no one any grudge. And anyway, whom could he blame for what had happened? This thought preoccupied him for several seconds. He could now consider it with absolute composure.

He walked slowly with his head bent and his hands in his pocket. He had no wish to smoke and indeed the very idea of lighting a cigarette at such a moment made him smile. Whom can I blame for this? he asked himself again. Lina? No, I certainly can't blame you, Lina; why should I bear you any ill will? It isn't your fault that you can't love me. Perhaps you played with me a little, but girls of your age do that sort of thing, don't they? There was a time when you even tried to love me. Is it your fault that you didn't succeed? No, it's all my fault. First of all because I oughtn't to have fallen so deeply in love with you. Secondly, because I ought to have resigned myself to giving you up when you began to say no. Now it's too late, I just can't give you up now. This has been going on for two years, Lina, and two years is a long time. Two years, my darling, and in those two years I've thought only of you. Every time I've had something good to eat I've thought of you. Every time I've said my prayers in the evening I've thought of you. Every time I've done a good job of work, I've thought of you. Every thing I've done in those two years I've done for you—you were my inspiration. How could I go back now and do the same things, eat the same food, smell the same scents, see the same people, do the same jobs—all without you? Oh, Lina, I certainly mustn't blame you—you or anyone else. This is my fate; I was born under an unlucky star.

He was still walking along the wooden fence, thinking of his childhood, of his father and mother, and the Little Valley with its timbered slopes. I wish I had never seen her! he said to himself. I wish I had never gone to the dance that evening! But immediately something within him rebelled and said: No, she was worth knowing! Better to die having seen her than to live without knowing anything about her, without having loved her. Of that he had no doubt at all, and this certainly brought him fresh comfort.

He felt neither pain nor fear nor remorse. He left the paling behind and walked into the countryside. It must be a little before nine o'clock, he thought. At home they will be sitting round the table. For a moment it seemed to him that his nostrils were filled with the smell of cooking that came from the family kitchen when his mother was frying pimento and the window stood wide open, with the silvery light of the moon shining down upon the mountains of the Little Valley of God.

Thinking these thoughts, he reached the railway line. He climbed onto the graveled bed and walked a few hundred yards between the rails. There was a vast shadow around him and the moon was climbing among the stars. The grasshoppers chirruped, and the sweet-smelling night scents of mint and flowering juniper came to him on the light wind. At last he saw the black mouth of the tunnel.

Then he bent down and began to pluck up the grass that grew here and there beyond the metals; he gathered great handfuls and tucked them under his left arm. He made a big bundle, penetrated a little way into the dark tunnel, put it on a rail, and stretched himself out on the ground, with his head resting on the grass. It was cold and damp, as if it had just been soaked, and it had a faint but persistent fragrance. Bruno

(77)

kept his eyes open and gazed at the blackness that stretched over his head. And he could think of nothing, for from now on he had no kinship with any living creature. He could only murmur, "Lina, Lina." The pebbles under his body were cold and sharp, but he never stirred, he heard nothing, not even the rumble of the approaching train.

I dedicate this chapter to the memory of Bruno M——, a soldier who took his own life because he was in love with a girl who did not love him. He was a lonely boy who never said much. No one will ever know what he must have suffered. After he had killed himself people spoke ill of him. They said that a man does not kill himself for a girl, and that if he does he is a coward and a fool. But you were neither a coward nor a fool, Bruno. These things can happen to any of us, in the Little Valley of God and elsewhere; and if people speak ill of you, Bruno—well, what does it matter?

(12)

"Scherza coi fanti . . ." *

IN this blazing summer the landowners and factors of the Little Valley of God said that the Lord was doubtless angry with the world. The unrest among the peasants rose to such a pitch that these gentlemen, though peace-loving by nature, were driven to carrying all sorts of weapons in their coattails. Those who felt most strongly about it declared that they would let themselves be massacred in the farm courtyards rather than yield the smallest percentage of the profits beyond the share to which the leaseholders were entitled under the old law that had operated for so many generations. It was usually the women who suffered most from this state of affairs; as the men lost interest and abandoned themselves to dissipation, the despair of their womenfolk correspondingly increased. The men, for their part, did not fail to unburden themselves in the arms of Maddalena Amato; rich or poor, landowner or peasant, they all poured out their secret troubles. And for all she had words of comfort, being naturally disposed by the prompting of her warm heart to tell each one of them in turn that he was in the right. She was besides convinced that there was no one in the Little Valley of God who wasn't partly right and partly wrong. From which one can conclude that if Maddalena Amato had cherished politi-

---

* *Scherza coi fanti, non scherza coi santi;* "Joke with men-at-arms, joke not with saints." Old Italian proverb. The allusion is to the respect with which holy things must be treated.

cal ambitions she would have solved the problem of the lease-holds and risen to Parliament; being merely a woman, she dispensed consolation in her maternal way to all who visited her, and did as much good as she could.

Gastone Ferro declared war on his tenants. In all the Valley he was the only one to declare it without reserve and wage it openly. He was a young man, a little below middle height, with curly hair and glowering eyes. He had muscles like whipcord and he used an old red motorcycle to visit the seven properties in which he was interested. He had no fear of anyone, not even of the Devil—or so it was said.

At the last local election he had stood against the peasants' candidate. This was Angelo Tani, a hard, harsh, plethoric man, eaten up with vanity. Once, for a wager, he had felled a calf with a blow of his fist. When the ballotbox was examined after the vote it was found that on one of the ballots somebody had written: "Down with Angelo Tani—he's a stupid boor whose wife deceives him." The clerk trembled when he had to show him the ballot. But Angelo Tani took it calmly and even smiled. Moreover, when he was elected mayor his first official act was to commandeer the ballot, which he put in his pocket.

Three days later, while the great Valley fair was in progress, he said loudly, "I'd very much like to know who wrote that"— and he produced the ballot. Gastone Ferro was busy selling a calf. He raised his eyes from the animal's teeth and said, "I did." The new mayor looked at him for a moment, then he folded the paper and put it in his pocket without a word. Nor did he ever refer to the matter again. From that memorable day the people of the Little Valley never called their mayor by any other name than Boor-Cuckold, when he was out of earshot, naturally. Furthermore this incident in no way diminished his popularity with the electors; perhaps it even made him more popular.

A delegation came specially from the Town to stir up revolt among the peasants. For some days oratorical fury, false promises, and presumptuous ignorance honored the humblest dwellings with their presence and inflamed minds that were usually resistant to every kind of political propaganda. So much so that

(80)

the peasants spat in their hands and cried with one voice, "As sure as there's a God in heaven the landowners aren't going to get away with it this time!"

Of all those who were involved in the dispute the most violent, the least amenable to reason, was the farmer Simone Lamorte.

Three days before the threshing (which, in the Little Valley of God, does not take place before the month of August, because of the altitude), Gastone Ferro summoned his tenants to his house. Without inviting them to sit down he asked them point-blank, "What do you intend to do?" The peasants began to whisper among themselves without arriving at an answer. Finally Gastone Ferro lost patience and said, "You might take your hats off, you swine! Where do you think you are? At the Shop?"

Cowed by his tone, they all took their hats off. Then Simone Lamorte went forward and said, "We will do as the others do, landlord."

"What others?" demanded Gastone Ferro, and his eyes widened.

"The comrades."

"Don't know them! Who are they, these comrades? They're yours, not mine. Don't talk in riddles, speak plainly, will you?

"You know quite well who our comrades are," said another.

"I tell you I know nothing about them! I don't concern myself with other people's affairs. You give me enough to do as it is. I have to consider you at every turn."

"That's true of us too," retorted Simone Lamorte without looking at him. "We have to keep thinking of you all the time. And it goes against the grain."

"Oh it does, does it?"

"It does indeed."

"So when you bring me my share of the harvest—my cheese, wool, eggs—you don't do it willingly?"

"No indeed."

"Is that true?"

"Yes, it's true."

Gastone Ferro did not reply immediately. Then he asked,

"Well, what about it?" and there was a smile at the corners of his mouth.

"What about it?" rasped Simone Lamorte. "It's this little matter of sixty per cent."

The landowner reacted as he had done when the men came in.

"To hell with you," he shouted. "Get out, you swine!"

They filed out without a word.

That same evening Gastone Ferro went over to the offensive and launched an attack. With a bodyguard of two trusted servants, armed to the teeth, he paid a visit to each of his farms. Each time he summoned the head of the house and made the man come with him into the fields. One by one he counted the tomatoes climbing along the wires. He calculated the exact number of peaches that might be gathered from this tree and that. Nothing escaped him; he examined and took note of everything. And after each inspection he said loudly, "I'm going to teach you a lesson, you insolent swine! You'll see what's meant by a leasehold farm." Then he went off, leaving the peasants in a great state of alarm. What's he up to? they thought. Someone asked Maddalena Amato, but she merely advised them to put themselves under the protection of some saint or other. She was very devout and as she was particularly attached to St. Rita she added more specifically, "Under the protection of St. Rita, for instance."

The first of the tenants to take up arms was Simone Lamorte himself. He kept rubbing his hands and exclaiming, "We'll give that fellow something to think about! We'll teach him!"

The night before the affray he went to the hayloft and pulled out a sub-machine gun. He put it conspicuously in the kitchen, hung on a nail. This happened at a time when the Government was much too busy to make a check of the firearms in private hands. That explains why, on the night when the farmer was getting his machine gun ready, Gastone Ferro was lubricating his Colts with pure oil—and giving them plenty of it. He too was rubbing his grease-covered hands and saying, "I'll teach him a lesson, the dog!" From which it will be seen that identical

(82)

thoughts can spring up in the minds of men who are poles apart.

Gastone Ferro's mother was a thin, pious lady who always had a grumble about something. She had been a widow for years and her life fell into a routine which she never varied. She divided her day in half; in the morning she stayed at home and prepared her son's meals, in the afternoon she went to church and poured out her troubles confidentially to the Lord or to His authorized representative, Don Marcello. In these troubled times a new cause for anxiety had been added to her day-to-day worries —the attitude of her son Gastone, which she found mysteriously stubborn. She went to the priest, told him what she had on her mind, and asked for his help. "It will be a real massacre," she said. "The farmyards will be running with blood—you mark my words. My son means to use violence. You must dissuade him."

Don Marcello could in fact have done it. However, besides being a priest, he was a landed proprietor, and he could not but approve of the firmness with which Gastone Ferro was handling his own affairs. He shook his head and tried to prevaricate.

"Do you think he's really prepared to go to extremes?" he asked.

"My son? He certainly is. He'll let nothing daunt him, and that's the truth. You know what he is, *reverendo*."

"Oh yes, I know. You've tried to speak to him?"

"Of course. Good heavens, the trouble I've had!"

"You had no success?"

"None, Don Marcello. These things only happen to me. He just smiled while I was talking to him. He listened to me and he went on smiling." At this point the old lady was assailed by a kind of doubt. "That's just how people treat lunatics. Does he take me for a lunatic, do you think?"

"I don't think so," said the priest. "I think a smile can be a sign of natural determination in a man. Gastone is a man of strong personality. I like him very much." And he really did feel a growing admiration for the young landowner. "Dear Gastone," he murmured.

(83)

"Yes indeed," sighed the old lady. "And now what?"

"I'd rather see what I can do with Simone Lamorte," said the priest.

He found Simone sharpening the blade of his scythe on a grindstone and smiling angelically as he applied himself to the task. He was a little fair-skinned man with sharp features.

What has he got to smile about? Don Marcello asked himself, rather shocked. Everyone's smiling; what is there in the air that's so amusing?

"I'm getting ready for tomorrow," the peasant told him, with undeniable sincerity.

"I'd like a word with you," began the priest.

Simone showed him into the kitchen and offered him wine. The priest shook his head.

"Thank you, I don't drink."

"What do you mean, you don't drink? Of course you do," the man answered curtly. On his little yellow face a smile could suddenly become a scowl.

"Sometimes, but not . . ."

"Why not now?"

". . . not between meals. I don't drink between meals, Simone."

"As you please," said the man. "Well, what is it?" His tone was forbidding.

The priest was a little frightened, but with an effort he pulled himself together. "I'd like to talk to you about tomorrow," he said, stammering slightly. Why hadn't he accepted the wine? "You all know your master; you wouldn't like anything to happen to him."

"Speaking for myself," said the peasant, "I haven't got a master."

"For God's sake, Simone. The Little Valley of God is a peace-loving country."

"Why don't you mind your own business?" Simone asked.

Don Marcello's fear was growing; he became aware of this and it made him put on a bolder front.

"What you're going to do isn't right, Simone."

"And what am I going to do?" The peasant was small of stature but he stood up to the priest and led him on.

"You know. You want to break an old agreement. Render unto Caesar the things that are Caesar's. That's what your fathers did."

"I don't give a damn for our fathers," the man said. "And let me tell you something. I don't give a damn for your fathers either." He pronounced the words with such scorn that for a moment the priest forgot to be afraid. He flung his arms wide and cried; "Careful, Simone. If there's blood spilled it will be on your head. I don't say that to—"

"You make me laugh! That's really funny, that is," sneered the peasant. And what he actually said was not "really" but "weally." For Don Marcello could not pronounce his r's. He had never been able to overcome this speech defect and it had caused him much secret humiliation.

Now a great wave of anger swept over him. The blood rushed to his face and for some moments he was afraid he was going to faint under the stress of the violent emotion that had been roused in him. He went to the door and shouted, beside himself with fury, "You wretch, you wretch, you'll be sorry for this!"

His cry had brought Simone's wife running in and as he went out he heard the man shouting to her, "I'll be sowwy for this, wetch that I am!"

(13)

A Diary Typical of the Writer

THE most convenient way of getting some inside knowledge of the events that occurred in the Little Valley of God during the summer we are speaking about is to cast an eye over a diary kept by young Maddalena Amato. It was her habit to jot down in it a record of everything that had impressed itself most strongly on her heart and imagination. She had begun it in her early teens; at that time her family was in comfortable circumstances and she was a pupil—much liked by the nuns—at a smart boarding school in town.

Evening, August 8th

I got up at dawn. That was because I had been awakened by a ray of sunlight coming through the window and tickling my cheek. There was a little wind and I noticed with pleasure that it was laden with the scent of horse chestnut. I went straight out and fed the hens. There is one that really seems to know me. You wouldn't believe how delighted she is when she sees me. I call her Esther.

While I was doing the housework I found a photograph on the floor. It was a photograph of a girl with a sweet, gentle look. She seemed to have blond or at any rate chestnut hair. That type of girl would be just right for Silvano Perri; which makes me think that this photograph must have dropped out of his wallet yesterday evening. He's a good boy, Silvano, though extremely shy and quiet. When he comes back I'll try to talk to him about it. He's a little standoffish to begin with, but afterwards he confides in me very freely.

This photo must be his. My only other visitor last evening was that old Simone who wears waistcoats of every color under the sun. He stayed an hour. The subject of the photograph isn't the kind of girl to give snapshots of herself to a man like him.

Then I gathered zinnias in the garden and I went to church. I arranged them in vases and sat down on a bench to look at them.

Evening, August 10th

I've put aside the vest I'm knitting for little Mafalda. She'll have need of it next winter. As soon as I've finished writing these lines I shall go to bed. It's already late, at least for me. A warm scent of jasmine is coming in through the open window, and in a little while the moon will rise.

Today young Avre came to see me at last. He turned up in the very middle of the day, just at the time when the heat makes everyone want to lie down and rest. He had a furtive smile and he was as red as a peony. At first he tried to put on the airs of a grown man; then he changed his tune and confessed that he had never been with a woman. I had realized that immediately, but I didn't tell him.

He was very nice, apologized profusely, and promised to bring me game.

Tonight he came back, bringing a basket. There was a wonderful cream cheese inside it, covered over with chestnut leaves. While I was thanking him he again seemed extremely embarrassed.

As I was knitting just now, I looked at the sky and I started thinking. It seems that when you see a shooting star you must make a wish, and that wish is always fulfilled. So I wished that the young stranger would come to me, the young man they call Emanuele.

And now the moon is rising.

Evening, August 15th

Last night I dreamed of Emanuele. He was close to me and I was looking at him. And I cried and cried.

This morning poor Lucia, who is a widow, came in search of me. Poor old woman! She didn't tell me, but I think she was hungry. I gave her the butter Clementino brought me yesterday evening. Clementino is a boy who pleases me very much—he's gentle and well brought up. He only stayed half an hour; he must have understood that I had a lot to do.

The fact is that I have to go to Simone Lamorte's funeral. But as I'm rather tired at this late hour I won't speak of it until tomorrow morning.

Morning, August 16th

I said I would write about the burial of Simone Lamorte and I'm keeping my promise. The ceremony was most impressive. Many people joined in the singing and the bier was covered with a red flag. But I didn't see Don Marcello, which surprised me, naturally enough. Later on, I learned the reason at first hand from a cousin of the dead man, Andrea Moro, who came round after the funeral. He's a man verging on thirty, very strong and, I think, rather violent. Just the opposite of poor Simone Lamorte, in appearance at least. And that has set me thinking of Emanuele, who must be so different.

Later, Andrea Moro told me the story of the farmer's death. Simone had been struck on the right temple by a cart shaft. His wife and two other women were there. He had taken the cart from the shed and was dragging it behind him on a slope. For some unknown reason he lost his balance, the cart ran away, and the pole swung round and hit him violently on the head. He died on the spot. This happened a few moments before the threshing was due to begin. The workers had to go home again. Among them was Emanuele.

It's said that Simone Lamorte was killed by the curse Don Marcello had laid on him.

Evening, August 17th

A visit from Signor Gastone Ferro. Rubbing his hands, he said: You heard what happened to that————? (Here he used an ugly word which I won't repeat.) He seemed quite delighted. I thought it horrible of him and I didn't hide my disapproval. He laughed in my face.

(88)

The pigeon's eggs have hatched. The little ones are really rather touching, all skin and beak, with mouths that gape for food the whole time, as if they could never get enough to eat. Papa and mama strut before the nest and look ever so proud of themselves.

Three young men came during the evening: Davide, Fiordaliso, and Max. They seemed rather drunk and I had some difficulty in getting them to go. Come to think of it, there's an excuse for their behavior. This leasehold question is getting everyone down; people don't know where they stand and keep changing their ideas to suit themselves.

Andreino Cirri, who is serving in a big seaside town, has sent me five hundred lire in an envelope with a little note: Pray for me. I thought he might be in danger, and I gladly did what he asked. Poor Andreino! We grew up together, and I haven't forgotten the day when he cut off my hair as a joke. I was ten at the time, and when I looked at myself in the mirror I dissolved into tears. I think he cried too.

I know what I'm going to do with the money he has sent me. Three hundred lire to get my shoes resoled; I'm thinking of giving the rest to old Lucia, who is very hard up, though she doesn't admit it.

Cirri's letter made me think of poor Bruno who committed suicide in a distant country because he'd had a disappointment in love.

Evening, August 19th

It seems that Gio, the blind man, has gone out of his mind. He spends his days playing the flute in front of a stone. People are saying that his heart is buried under the stone and that he'll have to stay there till he dies.

This evening Don Marcello went to Benedetto Anile's to sprinkle holy water. I was told that he tried to drive out the Demon that's taken up its abode in the widower's house. There have been manifestations—noises of various kinds and mysterious voices.

Three days ago I saw Emanuele go past on the road as I was looking out of the window. Three long days . . .

(89)

Afternoon, August 20*th*

This morning I rose very early to go to church. I vowed that I will climb the steps of the Great Sanctuary on my knees if Emanuele comes to me.

When I got back I noticed that the last magnolia bud had opened. Am I to take that as a good omen?

Evening, August 21*st*

Today is my birthday and I've made myself some syrup *frittellas.**

* *Frittella:* spoonful of dough, kept moist and fried on the stove with oil or fat.

(14)

In Which We Hear of a Plot Hatched by a Decent Fellow and a Fallen Woman

WHEN a man is enduring the pangs of love, anyone who tries to console him only succeeds as a rule in adding salt to his wounds. You know what happens, don't you? We will suppose that the victim and his comforter are walking along a deserted road. The sun is going down; on either side of the road wave crops ripe for the sickle, and the fires of the sunset blaze overhead in a glory of crimson, orange, and gold. If there has been a little rain the scene takes on a beauty beyond words; the grass is verdant upon the slopes, sounds echo in the glassy air, and the poppies are a dazzle of scarlet among the blond ears of the wheat. With the friend who is trying to help him at his elbow, the lovesick man follows a track that gradually grows fainter until it loses itself in open country. Sunk in the depths of grief, he walks on with downcast eyes, and at this hour when life for him is so full of sadness he is incapable of enjoying the delicate charm of Nature. And yet the bells pealing in the steeples are calling to each other across the evening sky and waking answering echoes with their clamor; the swallows are wheeling in the blue vault of heaven; and from the damp earth rises a sharp scent of manure and wild herbs. The comforter too is silent; perhaps he is cogitating what he ought to say and preparing the opening words of his speech. Suddenly he lifts his head.

"Listen . . ." "What is it?" asks his lovelorn companion in a faraway, indifferent tone. The comforter has decided to take the bull by the horns. "Listen, I hate to see you in this state! I tell you . . ." "In what state?" "Oh, God, don't look as if you can't guess what I'm driving at. You hardly say a word, you're worrying yourself sick, you look half dead. Now listen to me . . ." Farther away than ever, his friend interrupts him again in the weary voice of a man who has abandoned all hope. "But what do you want me to do?" "How do you mean, what do I want you to do? Listen, you're all wrong about this. That girl isn't for you. She's a silly little thing, haven't you realized that? She doesn't love anyone, she's a complete scatterbrain. Listen, why don't you go after someone else? There are so many women . . ." And so on, and so on, until the lovelorn one reaches a stage where he either starts screaming or bursts into sobs. And as that sort of treatment only makes the pain harder to bear, the sunset is utterly wasted on them; it might as well not exist, for all the notice anyone takes of it. Now that was pretty much what was happening to Professor Silvano at this time when he was tasting the bitterness of disappointment and wounded pride through his failure to make any impression on young Barbara.

Yet Silvano could boast a wide circle of acquaintances round about, whose relations with him were highly flattering to his self-esteem. In spite of his youth and the fact that he was not a native of the country, a great many worthy inhabitants considered it an honor to be counted among his friends. Perhaps it was just because he was not a native; his foreignness was a valuable attribute thanks to which he could avoid getting entangled in the web of local gossip. If people did bring him into their conversation it was only to speak well of him. The men liked him because they could not see him competing successfully for the favors of the girls, and the women, perhaps because of his natural reserve, were secretly fond of him. During his stay in the Little Valley of God Silvano was receiving many love letters, under cover of subterfuges that were patently obvious. He read them with a solemn face and then arranged them in his black wallet; he did not show them to his friends, he did not make fun of his correspondents, and he did not allow himself to get conceited.

He thought it natural that certain girls should feel sympathy for him and that he ought to behave as if nothing had happened. He lived discreetly, writing his stories, roaming about the woods, chatting with dogs and the people he met on his walks, contemplating the beauties of Nature and hardly ever tiring of them. His passion for talking to dogs was one of his main preoccupations; he gave himself up to it with especial delight when the dogs were strays, for he was inwardly convinced that these animals had a sound knowledge of the world. Underlying all this, of course, was his love for Barbara.

To return to our story: I must now tell you that Otello had been forced to admit, not without embarrassment, that the advice he had given his friend had not produced the hoped-for result—far from it. Silvano said little and had the worried look of a man who is secretly enduring agony. When he did speak he liked to speak in solitude. One morning a peasant working not far away had heard voices raised in a bitter argument about matters so complicated that he had not been able to understand them. His curiosity had been roused and he had tried to identify the speakers. Imagine his astonishment, not unmixed with fear, when he realized that Silvano was having an argument with himself or with someone who was not visible to mortal eyes. In the Professor's talk the same word kept recurring: Torture, torture. The peasant had carried his tale to the Shop and Otello had listened with close attention. He wished Silvano well and was distressed by his sufferings; so he decided that he would try to put an end to them. One morning he went to Maddalena Amato's and began asking her questions.

To all of them she replied, "He's in love, he's smitten; there's nothing one can do about it." Then she sighed and added compassionately, "Love is a terrible thing!"

Otello gave her a sideways glance and then talked to her for a long time. Maddalena listened with interest; at last she promised, "All right, I'll do what you ask. Let's hope it will work out for the best."

She found that the trouble she went to on behalf of the poor lovelorn young man helped to alleviate her own lovesickness.

When Silvano returned to Maddalena's house (he was now in

(93)

the habit of making frequent visits to her), she adroitly brought the conversation round to the topic of love. With tact and skill she talked of the sufferings of those who love in vain. Finally she exclaimed, "You must suffer a great deal, Professor."

Silvano told her that in fact he was suffering agonies.

Then Maddalena pretended to get angry and cursed the girl who was making such a highly respected young man so wretched.

Silvano begged her to leave well enough alone and speak ill of no one. The fault was entirely his. Besides, he said, there is no armor against fate; instead of rebelling and cursing heaven the strong man must bear his cross with firmness and equanimity. In such cases he even has a duty to cherish the memory of the beloved.

"But perhaps she isn't worthy of such devotion!" cried Maddalena at this point in Silvano's harangue. She was in the act of laying the table, for the Professor had got into the habit of staying for a meal each time he paid her a visit.

"Who?" he demanded vehemently. But Maddalena was in no way disconcerted.

"I'm speaking of the girl you love, Professor. And I was saying that perhaps she isn't worthy of such devotion."

Silvano retorted somewhat abruptly, "But my dear Maddalena, you don't even know her. All I need tell you is that she's a jewel of a woman whom I regard as altogether above suspicion. The fault is mine, and mine alone."

"I very much doubt it," said Maddalena, who was kneeling on the stone hearth. "There!" She cracked two eggs and dropped them gently into the boiling water.

Silvano told her that he would be very glad if she would change the subject of conversation. Since she did not know the object of his affections her suspicions were uncalled for and distasteful, to say the least, and didn't she think it would be better if she kept quiet about them? Hoity-toity, said Maddalena. But Silvano kept on and declared that he was not at all in the mood to sit there and hear the girl he loved insulted. Any provocation of that sort and he would be on the warpath. Maddalena did not open her mouth until she had turned the eggs. Then she said, "All the same, people have been talking."

"Let them talk as much as they like!" retorted the Professor. "Isn't that about all they're good for? Let them talk. The girl I love is without stain, and a lot of idle gossip isn't going to tarnish her reputation. Besides, they don't even know who she is," he added with a certain bitterness.

It was not until he had pushed away his plate that Maddalena said, "It's possible that the people here don't know who she is. It may be that I don't know myself. But if she's the girl I have in mind, then I would advise you to give her up, Professor. Because," she added gently, "if my guess is correct (I may be wrong and I sincerely hope I am), then you have been tricked and deceived. What I mean is that she's on the best of terms with young Gustavino, as everyone knows."

"Bitch!" cried the Professor, and he dashed out of the house. He never used bad language, and such a word on his lips was equivalent to a tremendous oath.

"Poor man," Maddalena said later to Otello. "He was terribly upset."

Otello was thinking that if it didn't rain the chestnut crop would be ruined. "I'm glad to hear it," he said with zest. "At that rate he's going to learn sense, the idiot!"

"He among you that is without sin . . ." A Dream

Flowers and leaves tremble gently as the light wind passes over them, dragonflies dart above the water with a quivering of green and azure wings, the water chuckles among the white pebbles, the full heat of the midday sun falls upon the jaded earth. Behold the deep blue of the sky, the blaze of sunlight on fields and woods. Hark to the bellowing of a cow; at this hour of the day 'tis an awesome sound. Will it wake him, think you?

His head is pillowed on his arm, his chest rises and falls, everything within him is peace and tranquillity, and there is a smile upon his face. Who knows what dreams are his? Perchance, Silvano, thou dreamest of Barbara? Oh wake not, Silvano, this pulse of the universe is so calm and gentle. Wake not, Silvano, thou who dost slumber in the shade of the trees, on this burning noon!

A shudder of anger ran through the Little Valley of God when it was known that Elena Amadio's brother had got her with child. He had been found hanging from a rafter in the loft. In a note he had left for his father he confessed that he could not control his guilty passion for little Elena and had decided to kill himself. The note went on: "Take pity on her! I and I alone am to blame. Father, when I ravished her she was a virgin. I took advantage of her youthful innocence. Let the child be called after me." Old Giuseppe screamed aloud with grief, threw himself on the ground, and wept the whole day long. "O God, O God, kill me too, put me out of my misery!" But he did not lay a finger on his daughter, nor did he say one word to her.

It was the people of the Little Valley of God who pronounced judgment and decided that Elena Amadio had no right to live.

Two days had gone by since the suicide's body had been found, two days since the neighbors, in voices trembling with indignation, had spread the news about the countryside. So loud had been the sound of Giuseppe's lamentation that any attempt to cover up the truth would have been vain.

And so this morning dozens and dozens of men and women from every corner of the Little Valley of God were converging on Giuseppe Amadio's house, eager to put his daughter to death. To all appearances the bands advancing pellmell along the white roads of the valley were filled only with a shuddering horror of incest and a determination to exact vengeance for this breach of the immemorial laws of procreation. So you would have thought until you looked at them more closely—looked at their eyes and hands and their hair glistening in the sunlight, looked at their eyes and their hands and their screaming mouths. Then you would have seen that these were men and women blind and deaf to the vast sorrow of the world. What were they in truth, these avengers of transgression? There was a thief and there a sadist forever seeking the gratification of his perverted desires. There was a ruffian and there a man who slept with his mother; there was a villain who had squandered a poor widow's savings and there a starver of orphans left in his care by a stupid father. There was a man who had been made bankrupt five times over. The woman striding in the van was a prostitute at heart, her companion an old maid who dreamed of unspeakable orgies. Behind them came a woman who vented her lust on a dog, another who was fond of kissing adolescent girls, and a third who was trying to make away with her old mother. There they were, the men and women who had taken it upon themselves to exact vengeance for sin. Without doubt the indignation seething in them at the thought of Elena Amadio's transgression had dulled their own feelings of guilt and the memory of their own wickedness.

(97)

Marching at the head of this fierce, shouting mob was Piero della Giovanna: tall, disheveled, gesturing as he talked, and foaming at the mouth.

What disturbs his dreams? Fiorella, what disturbs his dream? Piero della Giovanna—Fiorella, what disturbs his dream? Maddalena, the whiteness of your flesh. . . .

Hearing the murmur of the crowd and realizing what it intended to do, old Giuseppe Amadio resolved to protect his daughter. He made her take refuge in the cellar, where she cowered white as a sheet and more dead than alive. Then he barricaded the doors of his house and sent two of his menservants in opposite directions. "You go and fetch the carabinieri," he told one of them. "You go to Professor Silvano's," he told the other. "Say that they must come at once—we're in great danger." But the three carabinieri of the Little Valley of God had gone off to the town for the day, and as for Silvano, all the messenger could do was to repeat over and over again, "Hurry, hurry! Run, Professor!"

When Silvano reached the Amadios' house and found it in a state of siege, he was a little frightened by this mob in the courtyards. Men and women had taken up positions outside the three main entrances and it seemed that they had no intention of going away. Time dragged on, the sun was high in the heavens, and the countryside lay scorched under the flaming August sky. But fiercer flamed the indignation of those avengers of sin.

And now Piero della Giovanna was about to speak. He climbed on a boulder, raised his hands for silence, wiped his mouth, and began: "We talk of Sodom and Gomorrah, cities of iniquity. But where are Sodom and Gomorrah now?" At these words the crowd went wild; the men howled, the women beat their breasts; if they had not known the sort of man old Giuseppe was they would certainly have tried to break down the doors. But they knew him; they knew that when he swore an oath he kept it. A few minutes ago he had declared that he would shoot the first man to advance a foot under the walls of his house. And he had

added, "I swear it on my son's dead body, which is still warm!"
Then he had taken up a position behind the open window, with
his gun leveled at the crowd. His son's body had been cold for
two days and lay stiff in a chestnut coffin; nevertheless the oath
held good and the people knew that very well.

Silvano was now close to the house. He saw that he would
never be able to get in, and this worried him. He was also a
little afraid. Why did they make me come here? What can I
do? But he felt deeply sorry for the child Elena; with pity in
his heart he thought of her pigtails, her thin legs, her narrow
chest. Oh Elena of the gray eyes! What have you done, Elena,
what have you done? And a great wave of compassion rose
within him.

Something must be attempted. He went up to Piero della
Giovanna and asked him, "What's happening here?"

Piero pointed toward the house. His eyes were dry and luster-
less, his black hair was tumbling about his neck. "The curse of
the Lord has fallen upon this house!" he cried. *Veniat mors
super illos, et descendant in infernum viventes.* O Sodom, O
Gomorrah!" The crowd pressed round him in silence; for a moment no one uttered a word. Then a woman began to scream;
she did not know what Piero had said, she did not know the
meaning of his words; nevertheless, the sound of his voice was
enough to make her shriek hysterically. Someone picked up
stones and began to hurl them against the silent house.

"But what's going on?" Silvano asked again. Something must
be done. He must play for time; perhaps those wretched carabinieri would turn up. Once more he asked, "What's happening
here?" And turning to the carpenter he called him by his Christian name, "Piero." He had always hated him; he detested his
blank fanatical gaze, the white foam on his lips, his long dan-
gling hands. But he went on questioning him, "Piero, Piero. . . ."

In a loud voice Piero said, "A slut of a girl lives in sin with
her brother. They share the same bed, they come together in
passionate embraces, they thrust their tongues into each other's
mouths. Horrible is their lust; Satan holds carnival in their bed.
And this goes on for months, for years; the same fondling, the
same lascivious kissing. Then one day the girl finds that she is

(99)

pregnant. 'I'm going to have a child,' she tells her brother cynically. And he kills himself. He takes a rope, fastens it to a beam, slips it around his neck, and hangs himself. But she's still alive; she eats, she breathes, she's still alive!" And Piero buried his face in his great swarthy hands. "Sodom and Gomorrah, O Sodom and Gomorrah, she's still alive!"

"But what do these people want, what do they mean to do?" asked Silvano in a frozen voice. He was afraid and he was trying to cover up his fear. Nevertheless he felt that his terror was growing and that presently it would get the better of him. "What does this mob want?" he asked again. Oh Elena, my poor child!

Hard, weary faces pressed round him. A woman cried, "We want to kill this girl, do you understand?" She was fiery red and her hair hung down in loose strands. Silvano noticed that it had a greasy shine; perhaps she rubbed in olive oil when she was combing it. Keep calm, keep calm, he said to himself. Don't lose your head. These hysterical people must be quieted down. He raised a hand with that idea in mind, then realized that he was repeating Piero's horrible gesture, and drew it back. "Yes, I understand. But have you thought of what you are going to do? You must, you must . . ."

At that moment one of the windows of the house was abruptly flung back and old Giuseppe's wrinkled face, convulsed with rage, appeared in the opening. "Hold your tongue, you whore!" he shouted to the woman. "Mind your own business; I don't meddle with yours!"

Then Piero broke into a shout, picked up a stone, and hurled it against the house. Muttering threats and curses, the old man withdrew and slammed the window. The mob brandished their fists at the sky and raised a horrible yell.

And then Emanuele arrived, with Maddalena leading him by the hand.

Maddalena, the whiteness of your flesh. Maddalena, the whiteness of your flesh. You have undressed beside the bed (I am watching you), you have cast away your clothes—oh Maddalena, your white arms! Standing at your side I look at you, Maddalena.

(100)

Your bed is like a threshing machine. What can you do? asks the driver. I can feed the sheaves, I can do a little of everything, I'm a peasant too, you know. Oh Maddalena, how sweet and clean your flesh is, what a fragrance of lavender comes from you! Yes, Elia. Isn't there Maddalena Amato? Look out, the belt's off! And then he begins to sing. Do you often cry? Excuse me, this has never happened to me before. But who is it, won't you tell me who it is? Yes, a young man called Emanuele.

There was a faint smile on Emanuele's face; he seemed to be miles away from this troubled world, wrapped in secret thoughts of his own. Maddalena, too, was smiling gently; but in her smile there was a suggestion of happiness, a sort of fierce joy that had its source in pride and grief.

And so, hand in hand, the man and woman made their appearance before the brutal, yelling mob. Emanuele left Maddalena and walked toward the house. He walked like a man in a dream, seemingly in obedience to a superior will, distinct from his own. His face was pale, his hands were white against his dark clothing. Silvano looked at him and was racked by the thought that if he went toward the house he would be stoned. The stones will hit him. . . . The idea was agony to Silvano, and once again he was seized by a feeling that he had seen this man before. But when and where? Emanuele continued his advance, moving stiffly and almost automatically, his face pale, his hands white and motionless by his sides. If he takes another ten paces—another eight paces—the stones will hit him. Stones, sun, dried-up earth . . . The thought of the stones striking Emanuele—but where and when have I seen him?—made Silvano feel sick. His head began to go round and a terrible anguish gnawed at his vitals. They're going to strike him now with their stones—these bullies, these thieves, these perverts, these bankrupts, these adulterers, these female lechers, these harpies with their sterile lusts and their hunger for male flesh—they're going to stone him now. Oh, if only I could hate them! And that was what was so strange about the spiritual upheaval that was taking place within him; his whole body was tense with hate, there was hate in every breath he drew, and hate tingled in every

(101)

fiber of his being; and yet *he could not hate*. He could not hate; this mob that was still hurling stones against the silent house, these men and women with their hard, contorted faces, dumbly preoccupied with what they were doing, this mob had somehow become remote and unreal, and his hate could not touch it. Though it sprang from the inner recesses of his being, from the limbo of his subconscious mind, Silvano's urge to hate was being nullified and swallowed up by a mysterious force, as the whirr of an insect is lost in the eternal silence of space.

And at this moment, in a sudden flash of revelation, Silvano understood that this inability to hate was Emanuele's doing. There was no longer any doubt, it was Emanuele who was making his hatred ineffective, Emanuele who was reducing it to naught. And a feeling of exhaustion came upon Silvano, oppressing his already overburdened spirit and adding to his sickness of heart. . . . In silence Emanuele went forward and in silence the crowd kept up the hail of stones. Whenever Piero della Giovanna hurled a stone he gestured wildly with upflung arms.

And so Emanuele came within range of the heavy, unrelenting shower of missiles. But he did not stop; who indeed could have stopped him? His face was hidden from the crowd; he kept his eyes on the ground, and there was a deep significance in his lowered gaze; it seemed an expression of conscious meekness. And lo! *not a stone struck him*. The fierce heat of the sun beat down, everything in the world was either intensely white or deeply shadowed, the grasshoppers chirped on, the crowd continued to hurl stones in the heavy stillness; *but not a stone struck him*. Maddalena watched with her great wide-open eyes, and *not a stone struck him*.

He reached the door of the house and touched it with his hand; it opened, he entered, and immediately it closed behind him. A scream of fury rose from the crowd, the hail of stones grew heavier: where had they gathered so many stones, these avengers of transgression? Piero della Giovanna mustered all the strength at his command and roared out, "Courage, my friends, courage! God is on our side!"

Then the door opened and Emanuele reappeared, holding little

Elena by the hand. He signed to the crowd of men and women, and all at once they stopped hurling stones. A cloud passed across the sun, the heavens darkened, and something vibrated in the motionless air.

Hush, why is that dog barking? Hush, for I have to tell now of something that had to come to pass. Emanuele was about to do again what he did hundreds and hundreds of years before we were born. He had to show these men and women that he could repeat the miracle—he who can do all things, for whom time does not exist. And, having recognized him, I am not now bound to respect the stupid logic of natural events, as a storyteller is required to do. Hush, let Silvano sleep beside the brook, let him dream. For while he dreams I can tell of something transcending the logic of this world that came to pass through the power of a great Presence that knows nothing of logic. May the cicadas sing sweetly for him, may the endless barking of dogs disturb him not, may the murmur of the water among the pebbles sound gently in his ears, may the flight of the summer-winged dragon-flies trouble him not. Hush. . . .

The people were struck dumb with stupefaction. Something had suddenly paralyzed their power of speech and movement, and not a voice echoed in the countryside. Emanuele stood for a moment on the doorstep and then, still holding Elena by the hand, he moved forward from the door. At that moment there was such a supernatural silence upon the land that Silvano thought: Death has begun his reign. Stirred by a mysterious wind, the leaves shivered mournfully on the trees; there was no other sound under the livid sky. Emanuele said, "Brothers."

No one answered; for what answer could there be? Then he let the child go, and flinging herself on the ground she covered her face with her hands. He moved a few paces from her and began to write in the sand, withdrawn from the rest of the world. At last he looked up.

"What do you want with this girl?"

No one answered. Elena Amadio was prone on the ground, her yellow hair loose about her face; she raised her thin hands as if to defend herself, and her legs twitched; she was obviously weeping. Elena Amadio, what have you done, Elena Amadio? Silvano's heart swelled with a sudden tenderness; he was close to tears. Elena, my child, why is it that I cannot weep? And he remained alone in the middle of the courtyard, without stirring, trembling a little and crushed by a feeling of helplessness. And then, once more, Emanuele's voice broke the silence.

"Do you really believe there is any man or woman among you who has the right to cast a stone at this girl?"

He resumed his writing in the sand. A new sense of peace spread over the earth, and from the crowd rose a kind of sigh, a murmur running from mouth to mouth; then the men and women drifted silently away, each burdened by the weight of self-revelation. Emanuele himself seemed weary. He said to Elena, "Go back to the house, my dear."

He walked away. Slowly, Maddalena followed him; her head was bowed, and she seemed troubled and preoccupied.

(16)

About a Noble Lady Anxious to Get
Her Daughter Married

MANY and diverse are the invitations, the polite subterfuges, and the transparent allusions that proclaim the natural agitation of a mother with marriageable daughters when she discovers that in the neighborhood, or even in a corner far removed from her abode, there is a young man who might make a suitable match for one of her girls. By such means, and by others that cannot be avowed, she seeks to rivet the said young man's attention on the charms of her offspring, while doing her best to withdraw it from other people's daughters. She engages in a desperate and pitiless battle, waged with smiles and small talk, with little social stratagems and some secret tears. It happens everywhere, I think; and during this blazing summer it happened in the Little Valley of God.

The day seemed full of splendor to Donna Teresa Conelli when, on her return from a journey, she heard the news that Professor Silvano was back in the valley. She noticed that the birds were singing in the trees and that the sky was frilled with dainty wisps of white cloud. But she was too energetic a woman to waste time in contemplation of the universe. A sudden determination seized her. Throwing out her ample bosom she turned to her daughter and said, "Wake up, you little idiot! This is the moment that will decide your fate."

Vitality was as lacking in young Carola as it was superabundant in her mother. Without moving from the basket chair in which she sat she turned her long pale face to the half-open windows. It was because of this face of hers that she had become known in the Little Valley of God as the Horse. The Horse now heaved a sigh, as her habit was, and asked, "What are you talking about, Mama?"

The people who had called the daughter "Horse" had bestowed the nickname "Penguin" on the mother. Donna Teresa Conelli, otherwise the Penguin. No doubt this was because she was fond of wearing white shawls with her black dresses, or possibly (who knows?) because when she walked abroad she pulled in her stomach—it was flat anyway—but threw out her regal bosom as much as she could.

She was the only daughter of a colonel, and it was said that she had been brought up to the sound of bugle calls, amid charging cavalry and marching regiments. From her youth she had known the intoxication of wild gallops under a burning sun, with a whole squadron of cavalry thundering breathlessly behind her at full tilt, in a confusion of shouts, words of command, and martial cries. All this took place on the borders of the Little Valley of God, where it opens out into the wide, spreading plain, at a time when other little girls of her age were studying French with their governesses or, after much persuasion, playing "The Virgin's Prayer" on the piano at family gatherings. Then the colonel's daughter made the acquaintance of the young Marquis Defendente Conelli. He was fair-haired and shy and it was she who, one evening, told him she was in love with him and wanted to get engaged. Don Defendente agreed. At the end of six months Teresa made up her mind to get married; she communicated her decision to her fiancé, who again raised no objections. After their marriage they took up residence in the castle which the Conellis owned in the Little Valley of God. Such was the woman who had been nicknamed the Penguin—perhaps on account of her black and white clothes, her stiff carriage, and her determined businesslike manner.

"Silvano is here, stupid," she said to her daughter. "Are you going to let him slip through your fingers once again? You're twenty-three, remember. You've got to find yourself some sort of husband—your father and I insist on it. Do you think we're going to let you turn into an old maid?" With her soldierly stride she marched over to the writing desk. "If you do, my pet, you're greatly mistaken. I've decided to drop Silvano a line and ask him to dinner. And we've got to have him here soon—not later than tomorrow evening."

As a rule young Carola did not open her mouth when her mother was speaking. It was a family regulation. Her father himself could not but approve of it. This time, however, she waited until her mother had spoken her mind and then said, "The Professor has taken a great fancy to Barbara, Mama."

Donna Teresa had begun writing in her firm hand and she did not even raise her eyes from the paper. "He can take a fancy to whoever he likes. I'm personally quite convinced that this professor is a young man with his head screwed on the right way— he'll know where his interest lies. Barbara, that chit of a girl! Why, she hasn't a quarter of the dowry your father and I have decided to give you!"

Then she pressed the bell and rather scornfully handed the maid the note she had just written, with instructions that it was to be taken to the Professor.

"In any case I'll go to Ca' d'Orso and have a talk with Donna Elena. That dear old woman! One needn't hide anything from her."

From time to time the goddess of Chance forgets that we human beings exist and it's then that we live free and happy lives. On the other hand there are occasions when she does nothing but busy herself with our affairs. At this particular period she seemed to be giving all her attention to the case of Professor Silvano.

After a hard struggle with himself he had decided to go in person to Ca' d'Orso, and as he was getting near the house he had to fall in with Donna Teresa Conelli, who was placidly coming along the road in a pony carriage. Dressed in white and black as usual, she was in the act of lighting a long cigarette with a gold tip. She offered him one, having greeted him effusively, but he declined on the pretext that he had had nothing to eat since morning. To which she replied, after making room for him beside her in the carriage, "What's that? You've had nothing to eat? But it's five o'clock in the afternoon, Professor!"

Silvano did not think this an opportune moment to go into the pranks that love was playing with him; and so he made up a white lie and told her that he had been rather out of sorts.

Donna Teresa immediately displayed the liveliest interest in the seat of the trouble and wanted to know if he had now recovered.

He replied that off and on he had been getting spasms of pain in his stomach—just as if it were being pounded by galloping horses.

Donna Teresa appreciated the force of the comparison, but deduced from it that the Professor must have eaten something that disagreed with him.

"I don't think we can blame the sun for this, like those stupid countrywomen who believe it's the sun that causes stomach-ache. Have you any idea how they claim to cure it? I'll give you three guesses, Professor. Come along now, say something."

Silvano said that really he had not the remotest idea. If she would be good enough to tell him. . . .

Donna Teresa smiled with satisfaction.

"You'd like to know. All right, listen. They take a fowl, wring its neck, cut out the entrails and burn them. Then they put some wine with the ashes, and they make you drink the mixture. Well, I ask you! That isn't the sort of remedy I'd advise you to try!"

Silvano declared that it was all very interesting, but he hadn't the slightest intention of trying old wives' cures.

"Black magic, you mean!" exclaimed the lady, giving her horse a prod. "This is something very different from an old wives' cure. It's witchcraft, and no mistake. But tell me, did you receive my little note?"

"What little note?" asked Silvano. "No, dear madam, I haven't received any note."

"Then you will," exclaimed Donna Teresa with conviction. "Just an invitation to dinner for tomorrow evening, a quiet little affair with a few friends." She smiled with the most amiable expression she could put on, and added, "Poor Carola is simply dying to see you, you wicked man!" Which added greatly to Silvano's discomfort.

Meanwhile they had arrived at Ca' d'Orso, and Donna Teresa uttered an imperious grunt which instantly brought the horse to a stop. She got down from the carriage, stubbed out her cigarette against a shaft, and tied the horse's bridle to a ring fixed in the wall—all with an air of great firmness. Then, in the same resolute manner, she planted herself under a window, and called out, "Barbara, my dear, are you there, Barbara?" Silvano's heart thudded madly. Barbara appeared.

"Oh," she said, "whoever's here?"

And now they were together. Much to the disappointment of Donna Teresa Conelli, who did not hide her chagrin, they had been left alone in the little drawing room, where they sat plunged in silence and half-darkness. Silvano's heart was thumping in his chest. What will she say, what will she say, what will she say? It was like a distant refrain. He was scaling the ramparts and bringing light into the dark tower. Barbara's beside me. . . .

He was seated on a great couch of red velvet and she was in an armchair in front of him. A wavering shaft of light was coming in through the half-closed window, across a gap in the curtains, and he watched it striking the edge of the red velvet on its way to the floor, where it faded out. What will Barbara say, what will she say?

She smiled. "You look well, Silvano. You're quite bronzed."

"I'm glad to be here, Barbara, beside you."

She sat opposite him, reserved and unsmiling, holding herself very erect from the waist up, as women do in the Little Valley of God.

Silvano lowered his eyes, made a great effort, and said, "Tell me, Barbara, do you love me?"

She did not reply immediately. Her eyes were upon him, but it would be untrue to say that she was looking at him. There was a strange fixity in her gaze and again he was put in mind of a slow-flowing muddy river; the cloudiness of her eyes, it seemed to him, was a reflection of turbid waters. She had a mysterious air of suspended animation, as if she were waiting for something to happen. In a low voice (perhaps it was all quite simple, perhaps a barrier had fallen, perhaps he was free of it), Silvano repeated his question.

"Barbara, do you love me?"

She made a movement of withdrawal, and even in her eyes there was some flicker of expression. (The river was coming up against an obstacle in its path.) She said, "Why do you ask me?"

"Because I want to know," he said doggedly.

She appeared to reflect.

"It's hard to say," she confessed. Then she added, as if revealing a truth she had been brooding over for a long time, "We're not meant for one another, Silvano." (The river had overcome the obstacle in its path and resumed its gentle flow.)

Silvano felt the blood drain from his face. Another blank wall was rising before him.

"Why not?"

The girl did not answer.

"Why not?" he asked again. But it was a pointless question now. How would he free himself from the blank wall that surrounded him? or deliver her from the waters that flowed irresistibly within her? He felt something strike his chest, like a weight falling from a great height, and bowing his head he murmured, "You're in love with Gustavino?"

She too bowed her head, but for the first time there was a smile on her face which she did not try to conceal.

"What can I do, Silvano?" And with a sort of helplessness in her voice she added, "Believe me, we're not meant for one another!"

There was a fairly long pause while Silvano struggled for words. At last he managed to repeat, in a tone that sounded almost natural, "Why not?"

It was a difficult question. Barbara frowned and seemed to be considering what answer she could give him.

(17)

In Which We See That Flowers May
Grow Even on Dunghills

IN the Little Valley of God the people enjoy work after their
fashion but naturally they are fonder still of play and they like
jolly entertainments. And so, as this summer drew to its end,
the parties followed one another in quick succession and there
wasn't a family of any consequence that did not think of giving
its own. Having decided to hold a reception the head of the
house then had to use all his ingenuity and find a suitable pretext to justify it. For Signor Aquilante this wasn't difficult; he
had just been honored with the title of Chevalier, a coveted
distinction.

It created quite a stir in the neighborhood. Aquilante was
known for his gaiety, his love of pleasure, and his conversational
gallantries. And so numerous friends and relations hastened to
send him letters and telegrams of congratulation. Aquilante replied by despatching invitations to all and sundry for the following Saturday. He said he was having just a few close friends and
that it would be a strictly private affair. But at the same time he
ordered stacks and stacks of cakes, fancy biscuits and macaroons,
prepared the finest wines, and held weighty conferences with
the best musicians in the valley.

The party began at eight o'clock in the evening; by eleven
most of the guests were more or less intoxicated and the atmosphere, which you could have cut with a knife, was heavy
with the acrid odor of cigarette smoke and perspiration. A sort

of platform had been rigged up by joining two tables together. Chairs had been set upon it, and here the musicians were playing and sweating away without giving themselves a moment's rest. Waitresses went round with brimming glasses of red, white, and rosé wine; they offered bowls and dishes piled high with sandwiches, sweet biscuits, and bunches of grapes. Men and women were dancing and carrying on amid a hubbub of laughter and raised voices; everyone agreed that Signor Aquilante was doing them proud. What fun! What a delightful evening! Meanwhile Signor Aquilante went from one to the other, his Chevalier's cross conspicuous on his chest. He was a tall thin man with tufts of pure white hair, and he was wearing an elegant gray uniform. Like all the youths of the Little Valley of God, the young men who were dancing had big dark-skinned hands, muscular shoulders, and lustrous curly hair. Signor Aquilante looked at them long and closely, with a curiosity in which there was a great deal of affectionate interest. For he was a man of refined feeling.

When, toward midnight, the musicians took a brief rest from their labors, the frenzied dancers made a dash for the cabinet gramophone, demanded a record entitled "I'm Goin' Alone to the Town," and cavorted in boogie-woogie rhythm. The old house that Signor Aquilante's grandfather had built so solidly from the rock of the mountains was shaken to its foundations. But it was such fun! Everyone was agreed on that. All except two old men who exclaimed with one voice, "It's not up to the rigadoon, is it?" and found that they shared each other's opinion.

They were two old men, Fiorello and Lio by name, who always went about together.

Toward one o'clock Silvano was seized by a feeling of utter exhaustion, and he let his glass slip from his fingers. This din was altogether too much for him. He grumbled to himself that he had come here to see and speak to Barbara, but that little flirt was making it quite plain that she wanted to avoid him at all costs. She had been sharing dance after dance with Gustavino; she hadn't missed one. Oh Lord, groaned Silvano. Then he took a momentous decision and walked over to Dr. Recoaro, who was lying in a great armchair with his eyes partly closed.

"Lend me your car, Martino."

The doctor opened his eyes; his face was covered with red blotches. He hiccuped, "What for?"

"I want your car," said Silvano.

"You've told me that already. All the same, I'd like to know . . ."

Silvano interrupted him with a certain irritation. "I need your car, Martino. Don't make such a song and dance about lending it, for God's sake!"

"This is what happens nowadays," said the doctor. "This is what the world's come to. You want my car; I must be quite ready to let you have it and I can't even ask you what you want it for. Woe betide me if I ask you what you want it for. You fly in a rage, you abuse me." He flung himself back in his arm-chair, with his legs wide apart and his eyes closed. He's flat out, thought Silvano, and felt rather disgusted. The doctor continued, "It's just another of the things that can happen in this damned country." He hiccuped again, more violently, and a thin stream of saliva trickled from his lips. "Listen, I've had more of this country than I can stand. I want to get out—to the Argentine, to Rhodesia, to hell. I don't care where I go, so long as it's far away from here. Listen, haven't you had enough of this govern-ment? We call it democratic, we say it's an expression of—what's the phrase?—the will of the people. The will of the people. Have you tried saying that two or three times over? The will of the people, the will of the people, the will of the people. Grand, eh? Why don't you try it? But all the same I've had enough, I've had enough, I tell you, I can't go on. When I've had enough I've had enough! Democratic government. It's a mighty queer kind of democracy, little brother, truly it is. Pretty strange, I'd call it—"

Silvano interrupted him.

"Give me the key, Martino. At once."

"But what key?"

"The key of your car. I'm in no mood for joking, Martino. You're drunk, and I'm not feeling myself. I've got to have that key. Listen . . ."

"Now just wait a moment. I . . ."

(113)

"Either you give me that key, or I knock your head off."

"Ah, now you're talking," hiccuped the doctor. "I like strong men. Signor Aquilante, for instance. Here, there's the key; you can take the car. By the way, you know Aquilante's latest girl? A little while ago I saw the carpenter's son, a boy of eighteen, with hair as blond as . . ."

"Oh go to the devil!" said Silvano.

Not without some difficulty he succeeded in extricating the doctor's yellow Fiat from the jam of cars and carriages. Soon afterward he was speeding along the straight dusty road that cuts the Little Valley of God in two.

Now he was racing across the countryside, his hair ruffled by a light wind. It was a clear night; there was no moon, but thousands of distant stars—dear familiar stars—glittered tranquilly in the August sky. A sweet heavy perfume hung in the darkness and smote the onward-rushing car like the folds of a curtain. Above the hum of the engine could be heard the vast chorus of the cicadas, mingling high notes and low in a concert that went on interminably and without interruption. From time to time a shooting star streaked across the wide arch of the sky. Silvano breathed long and deeply; he was feeling much better, and as the night wind drove the fumes of alcohol from his brain he was aware of a growing lightness and clearheadedness. They can all go to the devil! he thought. Little by little his anguish melted away and almost before he had realized what was happening it had gone altogether. He was left weak and exhausted, but free and at peace with the world. Barbara can go to the devil! he said to himself. If it's Gustavino she wants, she can keep him! The headlamps of the car were picking up the dusty hedges that bordered the road and turning them the color of driven snow. From time to time a hare dazzled by the lights would make a timorous bolt across the road and to avoid running it down Silvano would hurriedly ram on his brakes. This braking and slowing down gave him a chance to steady his nerves which he rather welcomed; but at one point there were so many hares on the road that he had to reduce speed and switch off his headlamps; it would have been terrible to drive over these soft warm bodies. (Thinking of it gave him a queer sensation.)

(114)

He went on driving across the countryside in this fashion for an indefinite length of time, until suddenly he saw a dark shape move out from the edge of the road and hurl itself at the car. He braked, but he was too late; for he heard a kind of yelp, an anguished moan that cut across the stillness of the night. He switched off his engine and, overcome by a vague feeling of horror that made his legs tremble, he got out to see what had happened.

He saw nothing but a dim shape lying spread out on the white dust. Still trembling, he knelt down to get a better view; then at his feet he saw a big curly-haired dog. It was lying on its side and moaning feebly.

With nervous haste Silvano got up and again switched on the headlamps. The two cones of light drove a tunnel into the darkness and he backed the car until they were striking full upon the injured dog. Then he knelt down again to see how badly it was hurt. He heard his heart hammering against his ribs in time to the chorus of the grasshoppers, which went on as before, high and low, high and low, eternally and without respite, all over the countryside.

It was quite plain that both the dog's forepaws were out of action. I must have run over them, he said to himself. As gently as he could he tried to move the animal off the road, and it made no protest; the low moaning sounds that came from it seemed to him to express pain rather than anger. Though he could not see its eyes, he guessed that they were large and dark, full of inarticulate anguish and despair. It's a mongrel, he thought, perhaps a sheep dog. He murmured, "How are you, boy?" and he felt deeply moved. He got up again, went back to the car, and looked for a rug, a cushion of some sort. He was lucky enough to find a blanket. He carried it out and unfolded it beside the dog. Then with extreme gentleness he took the animal in his arms and put it down on the blanket (it went on moaning); by making a sort of litter he managed to get it into the car, where he laid it on the back seat. Then he lit a cigarette and said to himself: I must find a house. He felt curiously touched and distressed by the animal's persistent moaning.

He looked round. The countryside appeared to be deserted and nowhere in the neighborhood was there a sign of a house or a glimmer of a light. By the glow of his cigarette he examined his watch. Twenty to three, but perhaps it was a little slow. It must be three o'clock or nearly. Three o'clock.

Making a rapid calculation of the distance he had traveled, Silvano reckoned that he must be on the Galleux Alps, at the other end of the valley. He saw that the road ran between bare empty fields; here and there could be seen small patches of shadow that must be juniper bushes and the outline of great white boulders lying close to the ground. I must be on the summit, Silvano said to himself. Damnation! This had to happen here of all places! It was rather chilly; suddenly the moon came up, a reddish smudge in the sky, a carnival lantern hanging empty in the great vault of the heavens. Silvano gazed at it for a second and then turned toward the car, thinking of the dog.

At that moment he became aware of a sort of rustling a few paces away from him and heard a muffled whisper of voices. Startled, he swung round and called out, "Is there anyone there?" At first there was no reply; then a calm voice broke the stillness, "Don't move or we fire."

Three shadowy figures rose up from the side of the road, followed by two more; and all five came toward Silvano.

He felt strangely exhilarated. These must be bandits, he thought with a secret satisfaction. Well I never—the famous bandits of the Galleux! Without moving he let the five men surround him. One of them hissed in his ear, "If you have any weapons on you, out with them and be quick about it—no arguing."

"I haven't any weapons," said Silvano. "I've a pocket-knife. . . ."

A hand was held out. "Here."

"There you are, I've no other weapons."

"Now, hand over everything you've got," ordered the same voice. "Wallet, watch, rings, gold fountain pen if you have one. And throw away that cigarette." It was a youthful voice, the voice of a man who meant business and had no time for trivial conversation. Silvano tried to see his face, but it was masked by a dark scarf. The bandits had their Tommy-guns trained on him; the barrels gleamed in the light of the headlamps.

Silvano began to unfasten his wrist watch.

"Where shall I put it?" he asked.

The bandit who was conducting the proceedings—evidently the leader—showed some surprise. "Put what?"

"My wrist watch."

"I want everything, I tell you." He spoke with a certain uncouthness. "Don't you try to be funny."

Silvano gave him his watch and then his wallet. He noticed that two of the men had separated from the little group and were doing something or other around the car. Without thinking he asked the bandit chief, "Are these your comrades?" He was immediately sorry he had spoken; it was an idiotic question.

"Mind your own business," said the bandit. "You'll get a bullet in your stomach if you're not careful."

"I don't fancy that at all," Silvano replied. He was beginning to enjoy himself. What wouldn't certain journalist friends of his have given to be in his present predicament? "I hope you won't mind if I ask you a few questions. I'm a writer; I'm not sorry to have met you. Will you believe me when I say that I'm really rather pleased about it?"

The bandit chief said nothing; neither did his companions. But one of the men who were moving around the car asked in a harsh voice, "You're one of those people who write books?"

"Yes," said Silvano.

"And you write for the newspapers as well?"

"Yes."

"Well, try telling the truth for a change. D'you understand?"

Silvano felt more and more amused.

"Would you like to give me a subject?"

"Subject? A subject for what?" asked the bandit leader.

"Tell me what you'd like me to write about."

"Why should I?" retorted the bandit leader, who seemed to have taken command of the conversation. "What does it matter to me?"

"I intend to write something about you fellows," said Silvano. "Your friend here has asked me to tell the truth. What truth?"

"Is there more than one sort?"

It was Silvano's turn to ask, "What are you talking about?"

"The truth."

"I don't know if there are various kinds of truth or just one. All I know is that I've a great deal of sympathy with you. I'll write an article about you. But why not give me some indication of what I ought to say?"

One of the men guarding the car stepped forward.

"Say that we work for our living. Say that we're a good deal more honest than the people who make money on the black market and rob the starving poor. At least we risk our lives. And if we do rob, we only rob men like you, men with cars and gold watches and gold-nibbed fountain pens; never a poor woman who hasn't enough bread to feed her family." The man said all this in a tone of indifference, as if it was not a matter that concerned him. Then he pointed to the car and asked, "What's wrong with this bit of junk? Won't it go?"

Silvano had almost forgotten the dog; his mind reverted to it and this made the situation appear less comical. He replied, "No, it goes all right, but there's a maimed dog inside it. You'd better be careful."

The bandit chief showed signs of bewilderment. Silvano thought he must be very young.

"A maimed dog?"

"I ran over a dog," Silvano explained. "Poor brute! I'm afraid I've broken its front paws."

"Here it is!" exclaimed one of the bandits. "It's moaning, that means it's in pain." And he went on angrily, "You and your damned motorcars. You drive like lunatics."

"No," said Silvano, "this mishap occurred because I was driving without lights. I didn't want to catch the hares in my headlamps. There seem to be swarms of them about here."

The men crowded round the car, all except the leader, who kept his Tommy-gun trained on Silvano's stomach.

"D'you know whose it is?" the bandit asked. Silvano failed to grasp his meaning at first.

"I beg your pardon?"

"The dog. Whose is it?"

"I've no idea."

The bandits conferred round the car. One of them investigated rapidly with his pocket torch.

"And what would you have done?" asked the chief.

"Well," said Silvano, "I should have tried to take it home with me; there isn't a living soul around here."

"Except us bandits."

"Quite so. Except you bandits."

The man sighed. "It's a wretched country, a hell of a place."

"Do you want my coat?" asked Silvano.

"No, keep it. It's of no consequence."

"Thanks. You'd never think this was summer, would you? It's quite cold at night. But after all, what else can one expect? It will soon be the end of August."

One of the bandits came forward.

"Yes, both the dog's front paws are broken." He seemed upset. "Poor brute! It's a beautiful sheep dog."

"Stay here a moment," said the chief. "I want to see for myself."

Silvano had not been joking when he spoke of the chilliness of the night. It was getting really cold; a light but persistent wind had sprung up. But what of it? All this would have been rather fun if it hadn't been for that poor dog. And Silvano's heart contracted. Poor brute. Then he thought of Dr. Recoaro and came near to smiling. What's the doctor going to say about this? A fine state he'll be in! Hell, it will take me three years to pay him back a fraction of what this car cost. And I won't do it by writing articles either. Never mind, it will be a good reason for getting down to work in earnest.

Meanwhile the five men had closed up and re-formed into a silent group. Once again Silvano thought of the state the doctor would be in and he began to laugh.

"What are you laughing at?" said one of the bandits. "There's nothing to laugh about."

"I was thinking what the owner of the car will have to say when he hears about this," said Silvano. "He's one of my friends —the doctor of this Little Valley of God."

The bandit chief let out an oath.

"To hell with you," he shouted, "you and your damn car!"

"But . . ." began Silvano.

"Go on, get cracking. Beat it! Take the car and get out!"

"But why?" Silvano asked again. There was something here

that he did not understand and he had no intention of moving a step until he had been given an explanation. With as much composure as he could summon up he repeated for the third time, almost in a whisper, "But why, for heaven's sake?"

Then the bandit chief came forward. "Listen to me," he said in a frigid voice. "Don't ask any questions—clear out. It's the dog we're thinking of—can't you see that? You've got to take it to the vet straightaway. That's what my friends and I have decided. And mind, it's up to you; that dog's got to get well again."

Silvano jumped into the car. "Thank you, my friends," he said, and he held out his hand.

"Ouch!" said one of the bandits.

Silvano let go and switched on the engine.

The dog kept up its gentle moaning. Silvano reckoned that he would be at the vet's in less than an hour. An hour at most, he said to himself. The dog's paws would be put in splints and the poor brute would soon be all right again. The stars were paling, the reddish moon rode high in the heavens, he sensed that the dawn was near. It was now really cold. When he had driven a few miles Silvano felt that his eyes were full of tears. It must be the wind that's making them water, he thought. Oh Lord, he said to himself. And he remembered an old saying he had heard in the Little Valley of God: Flowers may grow even on dunghills.

Dedicated to these bandits, in fulfillment of my promise.

(18)

The Bishop and the Demon

AN evil spell hung over the manor of Dolciacqua. There was no one in the Little Valley of God who did not cross himself devoutly when its name was spoken.

The trouble seemed to have started about twenty years earlier. At that time the Count Bishop Domenico Domenici was living in the ancient family home to which he had retired at an advanced age after journeying about the world for fifty years in the service of the Lord. He thought one day that he had earned the right to take life more easily and he moved into Dolciacqua with a young priest as his secretary. The servants threw open the old windows that had been closed ten years before, on the death of the Marchesa Clotilde, cousin of the Bishop. And he lived there more than fifteen years, until the day of his death.

What happened at Dolciacqua during those fifteen years can be learned easily enough from the gossip of the valley folk but more particularly from the journal of Don Claudio, who was in the habit of noting down each evening what had happened during the day. A journal covering more than fifteen years constitutes an interesting but rather lengthy document; however, we have only to skim through a few of the notebooks in order to learn the story of the Bishop and the Demon:

October 15th, 1928
Sancta Maria Magdalena, ora pro nobis. Last night I heard

it again. I was sleeping quietly in my room when a sudden tempest roused me. A violent gust of wind blew in through the casement, which had been flung wide open; the black sky was seamed with arrows of fire; the thunder rolled continuously. I closed the window and offered up a short prayer to Mary, Helper of Christians; then I went back to bed, pulling the blankets over my shoulders and entrusting myself to their protective warmth. However, I did not go to sleep again; something kept me awake, a strange commotion that made me shake and tremble as if I had been stricken with fever. I thought suddenly that Monsignor might have need of me, and I got up again.

Along the dim corridors I made my way to his room. As all the lamps were out my only guide was the glare of the lightning, which flickered without ceasing and with each flash rent the sky asunder, opening up new chasms in the tormented darkness. I must confess that for a moment I felt a chill of mysterious terror, and it reached such a pitch that I nearly woke Giovanni, the valet de chambre, to ask if he would go with me. But I reflected that he was very old, and with the aid of a short orison I succeeded in banishing this cowardly temptation; after I had pronounced these few words, kneeling on the icy tiled floor of the corridor, by the grace of God I felt a new strength mounting up from the depths of my being and penetrating my soul. And thus I arrived outside my master's room.

He seemed to be awake, for a thin pencil of light was showing underneath his door. I drew near in silence, almost holding my breath. Perhaps he's unwell, I thought. The storm was still raging. At that moment I heard the voice.

January 24th, 1929

Sancti Fabiane et Sebastiane, ora pro nobis. For the past week I have been anxiously turning to the spiritual forces that surround me, within and without, in search of some counsel or directive. My life has become a hell; peace is denied me even in the brief moments when I am asleep. And the worst of it is that I don't know whether I ought to unbosom myself to my master and reveal my secret fears. Sometimes it seems to me that I am guilty of disingenuousness and mistrust; but whenever I prepare to have a talk with the venerable old man my tongue seems to cleave to the roof of my mouth. Even during Holy Confession, I have not succeeded in speaking to him. I am beginning to think that there may be the hand of the Devil in this inhibition of mine.

In the few moments of calm that are vouchsafed me I ask myself if this persistent and overpowering desire to be present at these supernatural interviews ought or ought not to be regarded as a sin. And I should have no hesitation in saying yes to that if I didn't tell myself that really I am acting as I do so that I can be of service to my Bishop. Unworthy though I am, I wear the cloth; and God alone knows whether one of these days I may not have to intervene, with the authority that comes to me from the Holy Spirit, and defend him against the mysterious assaults of this Demon.

March 3rd, 1929

Sancta Catharina, ora pro nobis. Last night the struggle between the forces of Good, personified by my Bishop, and the diabolic cunning of Satan reached an intensity that went far beyond anything I have witnessed up to now. As I write these words I still feel terror stricken in mind and spirit. I have sought reassurance in a fervent prayer to Mary, Refuge of Sinners. Ne nobis inducas in tentationem, Domine; Domine, exaudi clamorem meum.

Monsignor was evidently seated in his great armchair, beside the hearth. The spring is upon us, but the nights are often chilly; and my Bishop is an old man, a very old man indeed. When the duologue began I heard my master expressing himself with his customary gentleness and serenity, scarcely overlaid by that sternness which it behooves one to display when one is addressing a creature from the nether regions. As I approached the door, His Excellency was speaking of his past life in a calm, mellow voice. "Eighty years is a long time," he was saying, "even for one who has been protected by the garment of the Lord; and very few men without stain are to be found on this earth. But it is not for thee, Satan, to tell me so!" Then, as

I knelt there on the icy flagstones, I heard the well-known voice break into sarcastic laughter. "Oh, you needn't play the hypocrite, not with me anyway! I know everything, my friend; do you think you can deceive me? Old age has dulled your memory. Bishop, cast your mind back. Do you remember that lady of Lima?"

(Here I ask myself agonizedly if I have the right to transcribe such impieties in this journal. I pray God will forgive me. He knows everything, He sees both the good and the evil in our hearts.)

Monsignor was silent for a moment. Probably he was busy with his thoughts, drowned in a sea of memories. And sure enough when he did find his voice he said faintly, in half-sorrowful tones, "I don't remember, I don't remember. I went to Lima so many times in my life. And always to serve God, always."

The devilish creature laughed more heartily than ever. "None of your fine speeches!" it cried. "It's the young Spaniard I'm talking about! Don't you remember her? Her name was Dolores Vasquez; she told you that herself when you besought her to reveal who she was. What is your name? you asked. May I have the honor of knowing it? Dolores Vasquez, Excellency, at your service, she replied. And in a friendly tone you answered, Thank you, thank you, Señorita Vasquez. You were alone in the coach; the place was a barren and waterless desert; it was the month of June. She was wearing great earrings, a pearl-colored silk dress, and a black mantilla. Now do you remember?"

Holy Mary, how feeble grew the voice of my master! And what a depth of loathing I felt for this creature from nether darkness! The Bishop answered, "Yes."

The infernal being hooted with laughter. I was still on my knees and I felt the blood rush to my temples. The fury boiling within me was such that I wanted to put on my sacred vestments and burst into the room to confront the Demon and drive him back to his natural abode—the pit of Hell. I restrained this burning but senseless desire—not from fear, as God is my witness, but because it seemed to me that such an impulse reflected on the authority of the Bishop, so much higher than mine. I said a hurried prayer to the Consoler of the Afflicted and I went on listening, shaken with rage and hatred.

The Demon, as I have said, roared with laughter. "And didn't that woman have a splendid cross on her breast?" he asked presently.

I heard the Bishop gasp. "You must answer me," the Demon insisted furiously. "I must have an answer. Was she wearing a cross round her white neck—yes or no?"

The Bishop replied, "Yes."

Then the Demon jeered in a hoarse, mocking voice, "And tell me this, holy man. After weighing the matter in your mind again and again, after wrestling and hesitating and vainly seeking salvation in a prayer you could no longer utter—tell me, didn't you ask this lady if she would allow you to examine the jewel more closely? And tell me," continued this obscene visitant from nether darkness, its voice rising in a hateful crescendo, "didn't you go on to ask if you could stroke her milky white, virginal neck—stroke it with your holy fingers, with that hand you raise to pronounce benediction, the right hand of a consecrated priest?"

But at that point I heard the Bishop's chair crash backwards. I almost stopped breathing; I waited. And then to my ears came the dear voice I knew. The saintly old man had risen, doubtless after calling upon the Lord to put forth His infinite power and come to his aid; he had risen to drive the Demon back into the place of everlasting torment created for the enemy of mankind.

"Get thee behind me, Satan!" he cried with extraordinary vigor. "Thou infernal being, what right hast thou to reproach me with my errors? Under God's guidance and with His help I have expiated the manifold desires of the flesh. To Him alone must I render account of my sins and not to thee, thou misbegotten creature! And that is why, with the full and supreme authority of my holy office, I bid thee begone. Get thee from me, Satan!" And suddenly, in the same loud voice, to which his new-found energy had lent remarkable strength and sternness, the Bishop pronounced the holy words of exorcism according to the Roman ritual: "Imperat tibi Deus. Imperat tibi

(125)

Majestas Christi. Imperat tibi Deus Pater, imperat tibi Deus Filius, imperat tibi Deus Spiritus Sanctus. . . ." Meanwhile he was doubtless making repeated signs of the cross upon the Demon, which began to howl like a dog that has been mortally wounded and finally, with a gnashing of teeth, withdrew from the room. A sharp smell of sulphur came to my nostrils; and, to crown the wonder and glory of this night, I heard my Bishop's voice intoning the canticle of the blessed Virgin Mary: "My soul doth magnify the Lord, and my spirit doth rejoice in God my Saviour."

Then suddenly an unexpected strength flowed into me from a mysterious source. Without thinking of the consequences of my action I rose up, pushed open the door and burst into the room. I was weeping; I flung myself at the Bishop's feet; I seized his hand, I bathed his sacred ring with my tears. And he seemed in no way surprised; he stood before me, affectionately clapping me on the shoulder by way of fatherly reassurance, and not uttering a word. I perceived, as in a dream, that he was very pale.

How long I remained kneeling before him, still in tears, I would not like to say; but I think it was a very long time.

After the Count Bishop Domenico Domenici had peacefully breathed his last, at a very great age, Don Claudio stayed on for a few days and then departed for an unknown destination. A peasant took him in a cart as far as the Shop, which is the usual stopping-place for the bus that serves the Valley. Don Claudio had with him a black leather trunk into which he had crammed all his belongings. After twenty years of honorable and faithful service under the same master he had no worldly possessions apart from this black leather trunk and the few things it contained. But we must not forget that Don Claudio had what the majority of mankind have not and would like to have—earthly happiness and a tranquil mind. And so this priest slipped away from the Little Valley of God as quietly and unobtrusively as he had come into it.

The old manor stood empty for several years; then one day the new owners arrived. They were the heirs of the dead Bishop, a young man and a girl, brother and sister. It was the girl who drove the car along the dusty roads of the Valley. Crimson were her lips and crimson the silk scarf she wore over her corn-colored hair.

Their names were Peter and Lea Domenici, and lightheartedly they took possession of the old house. For three or four days the people of the neighborhood talked about them; then they were forgotten or, to be precise, from then on they became part of the familiar landscape of the Little Valley of God.

(19)

Polite Conversation and a Hapless Young Girl

WHEN a lovesick man knows that his love is requited he has a good opinion of his fellows, seeks their company, and enjoys being with them. He delights to acquaint them with his earthly felicity, through veiled hints and oblique allusions. But when he is not loved in return, when he feels lonely and unwanted, then the presence of other people, aware of his feelings and laying sacrilegious hands upon them, becomes a torture which is more than he can bear. Hence the reason why Silvano, fore-seeing what would happen, cursed Donna Teresa Conelli's dinner invitation—cursed it a thousand times over.

They sat down to dinner in one of those dining rooms, found only in the country, which are so characteristic of rich landed families. Against the walls were pieces of heavy furniture, made from good solid wood and now black with age, upon which gleamed decanters and crystal bowls of fruit. The serving maids went back and forth, carrying plates and bottles; all their move-ments were in harmony with the civilized comfort of their sur-roundings; they spoke in low voices and when they leaned for-ward to serve the table there was an old-fashioned and charming grace about the way in which they handed the dishes; they were in love with their work and the pleasure they took in waiting on the company was expressed in their gestures. Over the windows hung thick yellow curtains; the dying sunlight came through them and fell spent—like an exhausted athlete—on the old stone flags of the tiled floor. The plates on which the exquisite food was served were of white porcelain, the covers were of old silver, burnished with age; everything was heavily hallmarked with the calm self-confidence of people who took their social position for granted and gave no thought to the morrow. Perhaps there was happiness of a sort to be found underneath all this, but Silvano was not sure that he could discover it or enjoy it. In his present state of distress every word and every action increased the torment that racked his soul. Everywhere, in the dark corners of the room, in the sunlight fading upon the tiled floor, in the reflection of the wine brimming his glass, he summoned up the image of Barbara, and it was Barbara's voice that echoed in the discreet murmur of the tablemaids as they moved about. My darling, he thought, can you belong to anyone but me?

In the peaceful old room Donna Teresa Conelli had been talking for more than an hour with indomitable tenacity. She discovered a thousand subjects of conversation and on all of them she had a thousand things to say. The thermometer, literary trends, the best method of preparing eggs, the Valley girls. Chastity, modesty, the speech of the president of the Council. All was fair game for her and there seemed to be nothing on God's earth that could not inspire some remark.

Next to her young Carola sat pale and mute, heaving gentle sighs and waving away course after course. She had greeted Silvano with forced cheerfulness and then withdrawn into silence. From time to time Silvano lifted his eyes from his plate and tried to meet hers. He knew that they were gray and soft and had a look of indefinable suffering that was pitiful to behold.

On the other side of the table sat the Marquis Don Defendente, his shock of curly white hair illuminating the half-darkness of the room. He said nothing, but not because he had no wish to take part in the conversation; he would have liked to join in and he hated his wife for monopolizing it. His hatred of her was of such long standing that he was no longer conscious of it; he had got used to his state of subjection. But how he wanted to talk! He knew he was a man of culture; he would have liked to demonstrate it, to shine in intellectual discussion. And his wife prevented him from getting a word in edgeways;

(129)

it was always she who did the talking, she was never quiet for a moment.

Tonight the Marquis was feeling even more demoralized than usual. Before dinner he had tried to come out of his shell, while Donna Teresa was occupied with the final preparations. Taking advantage of these precious seconds he had said everything that he had to say. No, not everything; gracious heaven, there was so much else that he could have said! He had sat with his guest in one of the drawing rooms of the castle; shafts of sunlight had rested on the tapestries, on the damask curtains, on the great paintings, black with age, that hung against the walls. "I don't know what the world's coming to," Don Defendente had wound up. "Even in the Valley we hear rumors of what's happening. Admittedly they're faint by the time they reach us, but all the same they're disquieting. I believe it's a fact that in our country we are seeing the twilight of civilization—of a civilization, if you prefer to put it that way. Look at the towns, look at the countryside. Those strange dances, for instance. Our young people have no use nowadays for anything except what comes from abroad. If you want a fine fabric it must be English; only America produces good dance music; Swiss cigarettes are a thousand times superior to those manufactured at home. Everyone despises his origins. Let's suppose you have been a worker on the land for years and have a son to follow after you: one fine day you discover that your son has taken a dislike to the land. At fifteen the girls insist on going their own way. You've no sooner finished dinner than you hear a whistle under your windows, and up jumps your daughter and says, 'It's all right, it's nothing; that's a boy who's come for me!' As for the youths, they're just like girls; they don't even know how to march now, they can't even fight each other. They wear clothes of every color under the sun, like the clothes you see on women; they strike effeminate attitudes and they speak foreign languages. They scorn women or ignore them, preferring their own sex. That's what's happening here and no doubt it's happening to a still greater extent in the towns. We're losing the faith of our fathers, alas; people go to church to show themselves off. And where politics are concerned no one understands what he's talking about. . . ."

Don Defendente had said all this and much else in his few moments of freedom from the tyranny of his wife; but now she was again overshadowing him and he sat in passive silence, contenting himself with an occasional gesture of protest which served no purpose whatsoever, for he knew that it was useless to offer any opposition; nothing could arrest his wife's flow of words. He would have to adopt other methods, take advantage of unexpected opportunities, and, in short, have recourse to the time-honored strategy of prolonged patience.

Donna Teresa was developing the thread of her discourse. She now put forward the proposition that men are all idiots, and it was obvious what she had in mind. "They have lost all regard for modesty, restraint, and other such virtues. Aren't you of that opinion, Professor?"

Silvano raised his eyes from his plate. A reply was expected of him, but what could he say? "That depends," he declared. Becoming more explicit, he said that if an answer in the affirmative could be taken to mean that he was with those who despised such virtues, well then, the answer was no, since for his part he esteemed them very highly. But if on the other hand an answer in the affirmative meant that he agreed with her, then it would be proper to point out . . . He was a little weary, and that was why he expressed himself in this fashion. The sole reason for it was fatigue; normally these fine-drawn distinctions would never have occurred to him.

The Marchesa had again taken command of the conversation. "Anyway, one doesn't often find them." (She was evidently still alluding to the virtues she had been talking about.) "I know girls in this Valley—girls from very good families—who are as little acquainted with them at eighteen as my coachman is at sixty. My coachman," she added, by way of fuller explanation, "served in the army for eight years and was an innkeeper for fifteen."

Silvano despised himself for saying it, but he could not help remarking that this must be a man who had learned a lot about life. She would understand that he was speaking of her coachman.

"Naturally!" exclaimed the Marchesa. "And yet I assure you,

my friend, there are little girls who know more of life than he does. Girls of this neighborhood, I mean."

This time Don Defendente showed that he had his wits about him. He saw that his wife was pouring herself out a glass of wine and he thought to himself: It's obvious that she's going to drink it and it's equally obvious that while she's drinking she won't be able to talk. And so he got ready to steal a march on her. His patience was rewarded at last and he managed to say quickly, "The freedom of the sexes. On my travels in Denmark I saw with these very eyes how far things can go in that direction. I recollect that once in Copenhagen, a city which I should say is comparable in certain respects to Venice . . ."

But Donna Teresa had put down her glass.

"My dear," she broke in firmly, "I have an idea that the Professor would like to tell us something. Isn't that so, Professor?"

A clever move. But Silvano smiled and waved his hand.

"Not at all, Don Defendente. Please go on."

"As I was saying, I recollect . . ."

But at that moment the Marchesa announced that it would be best if they now went into the drawing room for coffee.

Seizing a moment when young Carola had made herself scarce, Donna Teresa leaned her enormous bosom toward Silvano. Her voice grew warmly confidential and even motherly. She murmured, "How do you find my daughter, dear friend? What I mean is," she went on to explain, giving him a playful tap on the chest with her half-open fan, "do you find her changed?"

Silvano felt more and more exhausted; the name and the image of Barbara continued to haunt him and a leaden weight numbed his limbs. Nevertheless he made an effort and said that no, he had really not noticed anything, he had not found any change in her. But why ask him such a question? Had she changed? Donna Teresa heaved her bosom still closer to his face; he could clearly see the little black curly hairs on her oily skin. She murmured with an air of mystery, "Carola is writing poetry!"

She had discovered this by chance, she confided. Searching for something or other in her daughter's room, she had noticed

(132)

one of those boxes in which women arrange the little things they put in their hair—curling pins, to give them their proper name. She had found there a bundle of papers and she had glanced through them. "Works that I make bold to say are quite wonderful, Professor. She's a great poetess! Such a curious feeling came over me when I realized that I was the mother of a great poetess!"

This gave Don Defendente an opportunity to get a word in.

"I was in Denmark at the time," he said quickly but despairingly, "and purely by accident I got to know a group of poets. I must confess that one day . . ."

"You'd better put out that awful cigar," said Donna Teresa, giving him no encouragement. "Don't you see that our friend can't bear the smell of it?"

Silvano said that a gift for poetry was indeed a wonderful thing. As for the cigar—no, really, it wasn't bothering him at all. "Please don't disturb yourself on my account . . ." But the Marchesa cut him short.

"That's enough, Defendente; the smoke's getting in my throat, and it stops me from talking. Put it out."

"By all means, my dear," the nobleman just managed to say. And he stubbed out the cigar.

Donna Teresa then addressed herself to her daughter, who had now come back. "My little pet, I have been talking to the Professor about your poems. Suppose you were to read some of them aloud? He would be so grateful if you would."

The young girl turned pale, then flushed a deep crimson. Silvano averted his eyes and said, "These poems must be very fine, signorina. But perhaps you would rather . . ."

"She is very shy," interrupted her mother briskly. "I'd go so far as to say that she's too shy and always has been. The least little thing makes her blush. I was just the same, so they tell me, when I was a girl. You see how she blushes at the very idea of reading her poems. That kind of modesty has quite gone out nowadays; it isn't the fashion any more, dear me no! But in my time it was, Professor. As I was saying, when I was a child the least little thing used to make me blush. Defendente could tell you something about that. . . ."

Don Defendente indicated that he did indeed want to say something. "And even in Denmark," he put in, "if I may go on from where I left off . . ."

"But all the same Carola will read her poems," Donna Teresa caught him up. "You will read them to us, Carola, won't you?"

She looked fixedly at her daughter, who lowered her eyes.

"Yes, Mama. I'll go and get them."

But it was clear that she was desperately unhappy.

(20)

Friendly Advice and Love Spells

ONE Sunday during High Mass Professor Silvano suddenly dissolved into tears. It was just an attack of nerves; he had let his feelings get the better of him—that was all. But there was not a soul in the church who did not turn and stare at him. And Don Marcello himself, who was in the middle of his sermon, stopped speaking for a moment. Silvano left the church with his face buried in his hands; no one uttered a word and silent glances followed him as he went out. Don Marcello had just been expatiating eloquently on the miseries of this sad vale of tears. He sighed and continued: "And it is not only the disinherited that weep but the rich also; not only the ignorant and illiterate, those who have never studied the arts and sciences, but also the wise ones of the earth, those who have plumbed the mysteries of the universe and can recognize truth in the things that have come down from antiquity." He was genuinely unaware of any feeling of self-satisfaction as he said this.

The mass came to an end and the faithful dispersed in small groups over the grass-grown square in front of the church. Silvano's friends decided to hold a conference, and they chose Maddalena's house as the seat of their deliberations. Those present included Otello, young Toni, Signor Benetto Peri and also Piero the Vagabond, as he was called in the Little Valley of God. They disposed themselves either on chairs or on their hostess's bed; she went from one to the other, dignified and smiling; from an oak kneading-trough she took some fritters which she had cooked the night before, and handed them round. Peri, letting it be understood that he could not think without liquid refreshment, asked for wine and got it.

It was he who plunged straight into the subject they had come to discuss.

"I'm proposing to knock that scoundrel's head off," he said. He was thinking of Gustavino, and he was a man of great determination. Moreover, he had just been drinking.

"That would give me a great deal of pleasure, I must admit," Piero declared. "I too have an old account to settle with that fellow. Upon my word, he's one of the most unlikable characters . . ."

"What has he done to you?" interrupted Benedetto Peri, who was interested.

". . . I've ever met. One of these days you'll see."

"We're here to talk about Silvano," Otello intervened. "Don't let's get sidetracked, my friends."

"You'll see; I'll show him the sort of man he has to deal with," Piero concluded.

"All right, all right," said Otello. "That's enough about you and your private feuds. Let's talk about our friend. What on earth took him this morning?"

"He saw what was happening under his very eyes—that's what set him off," exclaimed young Toni. The lad was rather proud of having been admitted to this gathering of grown men. "Did you notice how the pair of them were carrying on during mass? I felt so furious I nearly wept with rage myself."

"Let's keep a sense of proportion," said Otello. "If you'd started blubbing as well that would have been the last straw. Would you like to give us another demonstration that Don Marcello is right when he talks about this sad vale of tears?"

Maddalena was busy serving drinks.

"What's that?" she asked Toni. "I was at the back of the church, and believe it or not I didn't see anything wrong."

"Nothing wrong?" said Benedetto Peri. "Didn't you hear the Professor weeping?"

"I'm talking of what happened between Barbara and Gusta-

(136)

vino," Maddalena explained. "Of course I heard him weeping. D'you think I'm deaf?"

"You would have heard him even if you had been," sighed the Vagabond. "He was weeping like a crocodile, poor boy!"

"They were winking at each other all the time," Toni exclaimed heatedly. "She was looking at him and he at her, and their eyes blazed with an insatiable desire for each other." Toni had got this expression out of a novelette and he was very pleased with the effect it produced on the company. In fact, everyone turned and looked at him.

"What desire?" asked Signor Peri at last, in a tone of suspicion.

"Well," said Toni, stammering a little, "I mean they wanted one another. It was just as if they were kissing with their eyes."

"The little flirt!" Signor Peri exclaimed. Then he spat out of the window and poured himself another glass of wine.

They were silent for a moment, each following his own train of thought. At last Otello corrected the statement that had just been made.

"It's not quite true to say that she's a flirt. In actual fact Barbara isn't a flirt at all. In my opinion the blame doesn't rest with her."

"Whose fault is it, then?" Toni demanded belligerently.

Otello was unruffled. He was convinced that what he was now saying was the truth.

"It's his fault. His—Silvano's. He hasn't known the right way to go about this business, and that's the cause of all his misery. Little girls don't behave like that. And after all, between ourselves, Barbara is only a little girl. So much the worse for him. In certain respects he's a poor fool!"

Toni got up, red with anger.

"I won't allow anyone to talk like that about Silvano. He's a damned nice fellow, well educated and distinguished. There's no one in this Valley who's fit to lace his boots. And I won't——"

"Shut up," cried Otello. "D'you think you're telling us something we don't know? I know it as well as you do. But it's no good denying that he hasn't been able to make her fall in love with him."

(137)

"Perhaps because he loves her too much," suggested Maddalena.

"I'd be willing to bet anything you like that he's never kissed her," exclaimed Signor Peri. "He's reserved, he talks well, he dresses well, he seldom gets drunk. And he never swears—oh no. He's rich. He writes very fine things. I read a story of his— what was it called?—and it nearly made me cry, silly old dolt that I am. I tell you it was something quite extraordinary. It was about a shepherd who talked to his dog, and the dog sat there like a Christian, taking everything in and not missing a word, and at one point he said, I mean the shepherd said, 'My friend . . .'"

Otello passed him the bottle, which was now almost empty.

"That's enough about your shepherd, Benedetto. So far as I'm concerned the only shepherds who matter are those who won't hand over the share of wool that's due to me. Let's consider what we're going to do, shall we? Once and for all: either Silvano must give Barbara up, or she must fall in love with him. There are no other alternatives that I can see. What say the rest of you?"

"I should rule out the first straightaway," said Maddalena.

"You think he'll never be able to forget her?"

"I'm absolutely sure of it," said Maddalena warmly. As she seemed to know what she was talking about the others quickly allowed themselves to be convinced.

"Well, what's to be done?" resumed Otello. Then once more he stopped talking so that he could ponder the problem more intently. The clear morning sunshine was lighting up the room and the hens could be heard clucking in the courtyard.

"What about burning a few candles to St. Barbara?" suggested Maddalena. "Ten, let's say, and we'd promise to light others when our petitions had been granted. I don't know a great deal about St. Barbara," she added, seeing that the men were looking at her with a dubious air, "but I think she must be a very important personage in heaven."

"A sort of representative up there?" said the Vagabond, and he was not smiling.

"Suppose we resort to witchcraft?" suggested Benedetto Peri.

(138)

At that moment Maddalena got up and closed the window. The sky had suddenly darkened and a light wind had blown into the room.

The task of approaching Silvano fell to young Piero Zei, not only because he had virtually nothing to do but also because his natural amiability seemed likely to win the Professor's confidence. He was a tall, fair young man with an ungainly walk and laughing eyes. In certain matters he was astonishingly efficient. He met Silvano the same evening.

"What fair wind brings you hither?" he exclaimed in the pleasant way he had. "How goes it? It's so long since we saw each other." He clasped Silvano's hand warmly and then began to consider him with affectionate interest. Finally he shook his head. "Something's wrong, something's wrong. You're not well, Silvano. Tell me the truth: you're not well, are you?"

Silvano had to admit that he was in fact a bit under the weather. Then Piero put on a long face and asked, "What's the trouble?"

And as Silvano did not answer he caught him by the arm and took him home with him. First of all he made him sit down and offered him a glass of wine; then in a warmly sympathetic tone he urged him to speak frankly.

"You needn't hide anything from me, Silvano; I'm your friend. You know I'd like to help you, don't you? What on earth is the matter?"

Silvano was still silent. Then Piero asked in the tone of a man deliberately refusing to strike an attitude suited to the occasion, "A woman?"

Silvano nodded his head. "Yes."

Piero seemed to reflect for a moment; then he got up.

"I have a cure," he declared. "A miraculous cure. If you're willing to follow my instructions I'll arrange everything."

"But you don't even know who she is!" Silvano protested, gloomily.

"Who?"

"The girl. You've never asked me who she is. And I've never told you."

Piero shrugged his shoulders.

"There's absolutely no need for me to know."

"Isn't there?"

"None whatever. My cure takes no account of persons. It works with all women."

"What's it supposed to do?" asked Silvano. "Make me fall out of love?" He spoke in such an aggressive tone that Piero was offended.

"Here, what do you take me for?" he exclaimed. "I'll make her fall in love with you!"

"Prove it," said Silvano.

They went to see old Marion—aunt of the milkmaid who had presented Gio, the blind basket-maker, with a stillborn child. When they arrived at her house they found her spinning wool. Piero went into the kitchen and said, "Good evening, Marion." Then he added in a playful tone, "How goes it, Marion, old girl?"

The old woman was tall and strong, and white ringlets framed her dusky face. She did not raise her eyes from the spinning wheel and without interrupting what she was doing she murmured, "Evening, Piero."

"We need your help," said the young man.

Marion made no movement and observed indifferently, "I'm very poor. And the Lord has cursed me with a niece who goes roaming about the countryside and getting herself into trouble."

Piero thrust his hand into his pocket and brought it out again with something in it.

"I thought of giving you a little present, Marion, my dear."

The old woman took a quick look at the pile of silver on the table and calculated how much it was worth.

"Once upon a time I would have been ashamed to take it," she said. "But all the same I've got to live. When my pride wouldn't let me accept presents it was because I was rich. Now I'm a poor old woman and I've no pride left. There, sit down, young people, and tell me what's brought you here."

Piero wasted no words.

"My friend," he explained, "is in love with a girl, and she won't have anything to do with him."

"And he wants to catch this girl?" asked the old woman.

Piero looked doubtfully at Silvano and then put the question, "You want to get her, don't you?"

"What?" said Silvano. It seemed to him that he was living in a dream and the sound of his own voice surprised him.

"She's asking if you want to catch this girl," Piero explained, feeling rather embarrassed.

A light shone for a moment in Silvano's eyes and immediately faded out. "I would like her to love me," he said at last, with sadness in his voice. "You know that very well."

The old woman shook her head and the little white ringlets formed themselves into a crown.

"It's exactly the same thing," she declared, with the wisdom of long experience. Then she thought for a little and said, "Pretend that you want to cast her horoscope, my son. It can be done in various ways. You take her to a lonely spot and you say: Look me in the eyes. Or rather don't say it, if you'd rather not. The important thing is to make sure your eyes meet. Then when you feel her eyes resting on yours, concentrate all your thoughts on her, don't think of anything else, and say these words: Kafe, Kasita, non Kafeta et publica filii omnibus suis—like that. It's Latin, very nearly."

"I doubt it," Piero said. "We once learned Latin ourselves, you know. But Marion, this is ridiculous."

The old woman picked up the money that had been left on the table.

"No," she said, "it isn't ridiculous. Words a thousand years old aren't ridiculous. This spell may produce results or it may not. If it doesn't, come back. There are other things you can try. Good evening, young gentlemen."

Silvano said nothing. Piero bade her good evening.

A few minutes later, as the two friends were walking along the stony path, the Vagabond asked, "Do you remember the formula, Silvano?"

"Oh yes," he replied, "perfectly."

Shortly afterwards Piero said, "It's chilly tonight. The wind has got up and the air feels much cooler, don't you think?"

"Yes," said Silvano.

(21)

In Which the Reader Will Perforce Suffer a Disappointment

IT can hardly be said that the men and women of the Little Valley of God had an excessive regard for the arts and sciences; nevertheless, it is a fact that as soon as their children reached the age of six they sent them willingly enough to the only school in the valley, duly equipped with provisions, spelling books, and sound advice. Behave nicely, don't fight, obey the mistress —no grunting, Pallino—and above all don't dirty your aprons. The classes were held at the oddest hours, for the distances were great and as far as possible the lessons had to be fitted in to suit the convenience of all the families. It should be added that while the children were at home they did little jobs for their parents. For instance, they would be sent to pick up acorns for the pigs. Thus it came about that in the Little Valley of God pigs were considered the most inveterate enemies of knowledge.

Since there were schoolchildren in the Little Valley of God it followed that there had to be a schoolmistress. She was now busy correcting her pupils' exercise books and she had just read what a little girl of seven had written:

"Today is a lovely sunny day the lizards are coming out of their holes."

Mirella smiled. Mirella Pinucci—to give her her full name— had been sent to the district by the education authorities to conduct a summer course. She was a young girl with delicate features, a very white skin covered with freckles, and fair hair which she wore piled up on top of her head. She had green eyes and everything about her conveyed an impression of ingenuousness; she seemed in a state of perpetual bewilderment. Today she was wearing a cheap cotton blouse with a pattern of squares and she had sandals on her feet, a little down-at-heel.

She picked up another exercise book and read:

"This morning the sun broke through the clouds. It's fun to watch the sun come out. When the water is clear the sun makes it glitter."

The child who had thus expressed his feelings was a nine-year-old called Rino. Such a naïve way of putting things would probably have made an older mistress laugh or groan with despair; but Mirella was nineteen and she was really fond of children, so she merely smiled. Then she got up, leaned her elbows on the windowsill, and gazed, wrapped in thought, at the valley below her. It was Sunday, her free day. The school had been housed in an old stone building and there was only one room with a dozen benches and twice as many stools; but from the window one could see the whole sweep of the Little Valley of God, with the white road that cut it in two, the bed of the river with its shining pebbles, the cultivated slopes, the solid ramparts of the mountains. The sky was rather overcast; perhaps it's going to rain, she thought. But no; when she looked hard at the clouds she saw that the sun was hiding behind them; from time to time the wrack parted, and a ray of light poured down upon the earth; at such moments a luminous column seemed to stretch between heaven and earth, a mysterious ladder of sunlight. Then at the bottom of the valley, in the foreground, a long trail of blue mist could be seen stretching across the plain like a protective covering, almost as if a mother were shielding her child. That's the Town down there—and our house, Mirella said to herself. She thought of her widowed mother and her two little brothers; perhaps Mama is mending one of those stockings that always seem to be in holes. Those kids! you'd think they tear them deliberately. Or perhaps, for all I know, she's preparing the midday meal. . . . Eleven o'clock; the people of the Town are coming out into the streets, the boys in their Sunday clothes are courting the girls, the bells of the cathedral are ringing, what a pleasant holiday feeling there is in the air! And the streets of the Town are old and narrow, scarlet poppies blaze on the balconies of the houses, pigeons alight on the paving-stones of the old square with a gentle fluttering noise; and the fountain, how the fountain sings.

Here Mirella sighed; she was a plucky girl, she was not afraid of life, and its difficulties held no terrors for her; but poverty and hunger and all the hardships of these last few years had been too much for her, almost beyond endurance. My little brothers are always hungry; who will give them enough bread to fill their stomachs? Mama is worn out, her clothes are in rags, her hands are coarsened with toil; who will give me money to make life easier for her? All Mirella's hopes were pinned on this schoolteaching job; if the authorities kept her on, it would mean that she and her family could at least be sure of their daily bread. How wonderful it would be not to feel hungry any more, not to have to keep asking yourself: Who'll lend me two hundred lire? Not to feel hungry any more. . . . O God, the awful gnawing of hunger! Going to bed hungry and saying to the others: I'm full, I've had enough, you eat what's left. Feeling hunger within you like a raging river, devouring you like a river tearing at its banks! Lord, let me be kept on in this job. Bring it to pass, O Lord. Why shouldst Thou not, Thou who canst do all things? Since the inspector must come let him come, let him inspect as much as he likes; but let him be pleased with what he finds and go away pleased, so that I can be kept on in this job. O God, hear me!

Mirella left the window and went to the desk she used when she was teaching. The San Sebastiano church bell had begun to ring: one, two, three . . . eight, nine. . . . The woods and the blue sky sent its peal echoing back and forth in a kind of game, as children bounce a ball to one another. Its note was deep and harsh; that of the Town bells was gentler—gentler and at the same time more solemn, more majestic; they had been sounding

(144)

like that for years, for centuries. . . . Mirella wanted to forget
her troubles. What was the good of worrying? After all, it was
enough that for the present they had bread to eat. Lord, Thou
canst so easily grant what I ask! she sighed. Then she went on
with her correcting. One of her little pupils had written:

"Yesterday we went for a walk with the lady. I fell and
bumped my head and I didn't go any farther. We gathered little
flowers. The lady told us stories, and we sang songs on the
mountain."

The following day the inspector came up with the post-bus.
It was almost noon, and he had some difficulty in making his
way to the school, for the heat was overpowering and as he
walked along in the blazing sun he felt the stones burning
through the soles of his feet. Damn this summer school, the inspector said to himself. What's the use of teaching these snotty-
nosed ragamuffins to read and write? I can't see the point of it.
What good does it do them? And here the inspector took off
his Panama hat and began to fan himself. Where is it, this confounded school?

The cicadas were in full chorus, deafening the countryside;
there was a smell of parched earth and dust, and the stones
glittered in the sun.

With a bitter sense of grievance against the human race in
general the inspector thought of the shameful way in which he
was being treated. That schoolteacher! She hadn't even con-
descended to come and meet the bus, and yet she must have
been told about his visit; she must have had warning—but perhaps she hadn't been told after all. It was forbidden to give
advance notice of school inspections; that was down in the
regulations. And you could understand why. You could always
tell when a schoolteacher had got to know that you were coming. Here, sir; there, sir! can I show you this, can I show you
that? And she would have seen to it that every child had its
nose blown; she would have made the class learn by heart that
three times three is nine. Did they think an inspector couldn't
see through their little tricks? What a hope! As if we hadn't

all done the same in our time! Oh, damn these inspections. At that moment the inspector perceived that he was passing in front of a group of old houses, and so he put his hat on again—for he set great store by the outward marks of the dignity proper to his calling. He was a very tall man and already running to fat, though he was still young.

A clamor of childish voices, coming through an open window, informed him that he had reached the school. The door had not been closed and he went in without knocking.

Children were laughing and singing in the disordered classroom; and a young girl was laughing and singing with them. The inspector stopped on the threshold and silently contemplated the scene. He was suddenly struck by the whiteness of the young teacher's neck; it seemed wrong and almost unfair that a schoolmistress should have a throat like that, and the sight of it roused in him a feeling akin to irritation. The shrieks of laughter grew ever louder and louder, and for all the notice that was taken of him they might have been utterly oblivious of his presence. At last he was reduced to shouting, "Where's the schoolmistress?"

A hush fell on the children; the young girl turned round. Her green eyes were dilated with fear, like the eyes of someone who doesn't understand what is about to happen but guesses that it must be something very serious. Her well-shaped mouth hung open and all the blood had drained from her lips. The inspector stared at her with a smile that was half a sneer.

"All right, miss, all right. I'm the school inspector. I've come to look round."

The petrified children were now silent; the little girls in particular seemed terrified. And it was a little girl that the inspector tried to bring to the blackboard. "Come here, you!" he said to her. It was the little girl next her who came forward. "No, the other one. Not you with the braids. It's the other one I want." At last the girl he was pointing to got up, with terror in her clear eyes. "What's your name?" asked the inspector. He was sitting on the platform and beside him, pale and rigid, stood the schoolmistress. The little girl did not reply; she had long hair tied with a faded ribbon. "You won't tell me your name?"

(146)

persisted the inspector. "Haven't you got a name?" The little girl opened her mouth several times and then said in one breath, "Mariagraziacecconi." And she kept gazing at the inspector with her big helpless eyes until in the end he looked away.

"What year is she in?" he asked the schoolmistress.

"She's in the third year, but she's very shy, and your presence . . ."

The man made an impatient gesture. "My dear young lady, I don't bite. Listen to me, little girl," he resumed. "If I have a tart and I divide it into eight slices, what would you call each slice?"

The child did not answer.

"You don't know?" asked the inspector after a moment's pause.

The class was so quiet that one could have heard a pin drop in the schoolroom; the mistress herself did not utter a sound.

"Come, come, isn't there anybody here who can tell me what we call each of these slices?" Silence. "Each slice of the tart?" No reply.

This time the inspector questioned the mistress. "You don't teach fractions in the third year, I see? How's that?"

"They haven't got as far as that yet," Mirella replied.

"No? May I ask why?"

"They were very behind when I came here. They knew practically nothing."

"Really?"

"Yes, really." How difficult it was to explain! "I had a lot of trouble teaching them the rudiments of reading and writing. With some I had to begin by showing them how to make strokes. I . . ."

"And now they can read and write?"

"I think so. I . . ."

"You only think so?"

She did not reply. She stared at him with her green eyes, and she had the same helpless look as the little girl who was standing rigid by the blackboard.

"How old are you, young lady?"

"Nineteen, sir."

(147)

"Kindly show me the copybooks."

She handed him a pile of exercises, and he began to look through them.

"When it rains I stay in my room and play at being a plumber; I stay in the house and draw; I stay in the hayloft and snore."

"A fine way of spending the time," observed the inspector.

As the bus did not go past before seven in the evening the inspector was in no particular hurry to reach the Shop, where the old boneshaker made a daily halt. The blaze of the sun was already less overpowering, and a gentle breeze, as light as a stolen caress, had sprung up to temper the heat. The inspector thought of the report he had to write and wondered who would be sent to replace Mirella Pinucci as schoolmistress of the Little Valley of God. "Mirella," he said aloud. "What odd names people invent sometimes!"

The path was rather steep and the inspector had to look where he was going. All of a sudden, when he had almost reached the highroad, he heard the sound of footsteps behind him; then a man went past, stopped near him, and asked politely, "Could you please give me a light?"

"Why yes, of course."

The passer-by, a man still young, shielded the cigarette he was holding in his mouth, and lit it. He had a thin narrow face and very white hands; the inspector was much struck by their whiteness. Doubtless the young man was a laborer, but it could not be said that he had altogether the appearance of one. The inspector thought for a moment. Where have I seen this face before? he wondered.

They walked side by side in silence for a little while; then the unknown asked, "I suppose you're going to wait for the bus?"

"Yes. Are you going to wait for it too?"

The man smiled vaguely. "Me? Oh no, I live hereabouts."

The inspector observed, "From your accent I wouldn't have put you down as a native of this district." And he looked at the young man's hands with lively curiosity.

(148)

"You're right, I don't belong to this part of the world."

The stranger's handsome face and refined features continued to jog the inspector's memory. Surely he must have seen this man before? But where, and who was he? The inspector kept asking himself these questions and was annoyed that he could not answer them. Then, for something to say, he went on, "Do you like being here?"

"Very much," the young man replied. "As a matter of fact I'm quite happy wherever I am. It's very pretty around here and the people are easy to get on with."

He had a most pleasant way of speaking, and that was probably why the inspector was moved to confide in him.

"I've just been inspecting a school. Queer sort of youngsters you have in this part of the country."

"What makes you say that?" inquired the young man.

"Well, because, good heavens . . ." The inspector did not know how to put it, now that he was being asked to explain what he meant. "I had a look at the children's exercise books. Sheer balderdash, upon my word. But perhaps it's not altogether their fault; it's largely the fault of the teacher. Complete and utter nonsense, I tell you."

The sun had set and a light breeze was blowing across the countryside. After the scorching noonday heat it was a rare and unexpected pleasure to feel its cool caress on brow and cheeks. The horizon was blood-red; a purple mist stretched toward the plain, in the direction of the Town. The inspector drew a deep breath; he felt happy. In a little while, he thought, I shall be home, and I shan't be sorry to get back. This summer inspection —I won't forget it in a hurry!

"What's so nonsensical about them?" asked the young man.

This question surprised the inspector; it took him off his guard. He could not have said why, but he felt that something was wrong.

"I beg your pardon?" he said at last.

"Complete nonsense, you said. Why? What was complete nonsense?"

"Listen," said the inspector. He pulled a notebook from his pocket, and skimmed through it until he found what he was

(149)

looking for. "Listen to this, I copied it word for word from a little girl's exercise book. This is what she had written." He read aloud:

"The little daisies are in flower and they are beautiful and they smell very nice and people carry them to the cemetery and put them on our dead and on Sundays they take the little daisies and they wear them on their hearts."

When the inspector had finished, the young man turned to him with a dreamy, meditative look on his face. "How beautiful that is!" he murmured.

"Stuff and nonsense!" snorted the inspector. "The teacher will have to go."

How pleasant it would be if I could say now that the heavens opened, that the flight of time was halted, that a miraculous happening made the inspector understand that blessed are the poor in spirit, children, dogs, flowers of the field, illiterates, women who murmur Ave Marias in the churches and do not even know what they are saying, the eyes of a rabbit, of a kid awaiting the butcher's knife—all this hymn of praise to the glory of God's holy name! It would be pleasant to say that Emanuele miraculously melted the thick ice that imprisoned the inspector's heart and made the scales fall from his eyes; oh, how I wish I could say it! But alas, I cannot: for if men were not free to do harm without intending it, life would lose all value and all meaning. The young workman has already intervened to soothe the pain of a boy who had killed his dog; he has already quenched the flame of anger that was smoldering in the peasants' souls and he has cured the landowners of the greed that was poisoning their hearts; he has rescued an innocent sinner from a crowd of sinners intent on doing her to death; and through him a fallen woman has heard the gentle rustling of love's wings. He will work many other miracles in this Little Valley of God that he has rejoiced with the light of his countenance and through the radiance that shines from him he will banish the satanic shadow of Evil. But here he must be silent, that God's plan for this world may be accomplished. He must let the inspector climb

(150)

into the bus with his dreadful purpose in his heart; he must let Mirella go back to live with her widowed mother, to hear her little brothers asking for bread, to see her mother dying slowly, day after day, from the remorseless cruelty of want. He came not to send peace but a sword; for pain is the sign-manual of life.

I would at least wish to shed tears for thee, Mirella, thou who art the sign and symbol of all the pain in the world. But no! it cannot be; my destiny is only to write, to write. . . . Be still, I must say to my heart; O heart, cease thy lamentation or thy laughter; for I must leave them alone, these characters I have created, who are my children. And if any man wants to weep in my place, he can weep; and if he wants to be silent, he can be silent; for all things must be possible. Like pain, which is the sign-manual of life.

(22)

In Which an Old Priest Receives
an Important Visitor

IT was naturally impossible for Maddalena to follow Emanuele about and keep a check on what he did. And so she got into the habit of asking all her visitors for news of him. She would have liked to know the most trivial details of his existence. What is he doing? Where is he going? What does he eat?—these were the subjects of the conversations she had with her friends. Sometimes she would get up in the middle of the night; she would gaze at the starry vault and the white moon swimming in the heavens, she would listen to the shrilling of the cicadas; and she would meditate for a long time on what her visitors had told her. But there was one inquiry Maddalena never made: how Emanuele behaved to other women. Indeed she just could not imagine him associating with a woman and she absolutely refused to ask herself the age-old question that torments people in love the world over.

Her visitors replied indefatigably to her endless questions. In the whole of the Little Valley of God there was no one who did not consider himself under an obligation to be nice to young Maddalena; so they gladly put up with the monotonous repetition of her inquiries, and without ever seeking to know the why and wherefore of such requests for information they all answered her as best they could. They told her that Emanuele was a laborer—poor but honest and upright—who lived by himself in a deserted cabin; that he had no friends except, it was said, the blind man Gio, whom he often visited. "That's odd," Maddalena would say. "Isn't Gio out of his mind?" Her informants smiled. "Not when he's with Emanuele," they declared. It was really very difficult to explain, but Emanuele was—well, how could one put it? Then Maddalena would become more insistent. What was Emanuele like? Was he like other men—like so many others? Here her visitors shook their heads. No, no, he was not like other men. Well then, what was different about him? Ah, they just didn't know. He was different from other men; that was all they could say.

At this point they usually tried to change the subject. Not because they had had enough of it, but because, with the best will in the world, they found it very difficult to speak for any length of time about something that inevitably eluded them.

Indeed in some respects young Emanuele was a mystery to everyone; through his strange ways he had ended by arousing the fascinated interest of all the valley people, both men and women. It was not a question of inordinate curiosity, of course, but no one could deny that there was something singular about the young laborer's countenance, to say the least. It was said that with a smile or a gesture he could still the most furious arguments and pacify the most rebellious spirits; it had to be admitted that children, lunatics and animals behaved strangely in his presence; and everyone noted certain significant facts about his speech and behavior. For instance, it was undoubtedly the case that this youth never went near a woman, never blasphemed, never got drunk. And no one could have said how he spent his leisure hours. Moreover, no one had ever seen him in church.

That was precisely what was troubling Don Marcello's mind at this moment. He was seated at his table in his own little room, his favorite books within reach of his hand. The dusk was full of tenderness and the sun was still shedding a golden light upon the earth; but it had already left the wooded crags of the high western mountains, and they stood out in masses of dark shadow against the furnace-glow of the sky. It was the hour when the priest was accustomed to take refuge in study and meditation; nevertheless, from time to time he would tear himself away from these preoccupations and with a shade of sadness let his mind rove back over the years of his ministry, which had already lasted so long. The past that lay behind him was frighteningly smooth and untroubled; he contemplated it with such loving and meticulous attention that at times he came to feel a sense of guilt, seeing this affectionate regard for it as something that was worldly and deserving of condemnation. Then in the privacy of his room he would blush with shame and his eyes would fill with tears. I am a bad priest, he would say to himself in despair. I am a silly old man infatuated with his own devices; I am swollen with pride. And he wondered, trembling, whether he deserved the peace and quiet that the Lord was granting him in his declining years.

Whatever is the matter with me this evening? he asked himself presently. Perhaps his uneasiness was due to the fact that someone had drawn his attention that very day to certain things that were not as they should be, certain things he ought to have put right without hints from other people. This question of Emanuele, for instance. I've neglected him, I've never given him a single hour of my time, I've never bothered about him. I've never interested myself in him.

It must be for some such reason that he felt so agitated. He left his table and began to walk to and fro, without any definite object, driven by this vague uneasiness that would not let him rest. The sky was dark blue and peaceful; from outside rose a confused noise: a woman was calling to her hens, tuck, tuck, tuck, tuck, tuck, tuck. This Emanuele must be at the bottom of it, the old man repeated. And he asked himself: what do I know about him? what have I done for him? how have I looked after his spiritual welfare? have I ever inquired how he lives, whether he's in want, whether he's happy, whether he has need of me? People had told him that the young man never put a foot inside the church. But is the fault entirely his? the priest now asked himself. Yes, this must be the reason why I feel so upset. The old stirrings of conscience. . . . And again he wondered: Who can this Emanuele be?

(154)

Having come to this point in his reflections, Don Marcello felt suddenly weary. That's enough for today, he said. That will do for now. Alas, he had uttered those words only too often in the course of his life. When he was tired of anything, when anything was making him unhappy, he would say: That will do for now, enough of that for the present. Tomorrow, he told himself, I'll see about Emanuele, I'll devote the whole of my day to him, I'll seek him out, I'll learn who he is, I'll help him. Tomorrow I'll be a good priest. Tomorrow . . . today I'm so tired. I'm old and tired. That's enough for tonight.

He went back to his desk and tried to concentrate on the papers in front of him. After something of an effort he became completely absorbed and quite forgot himself, Emanuele, his own weariness, and all the things of this sad world.

He took up the work on which he had been engaged for so many years: a detailed study of the antiquities of the Little Valley of God. He had no illusions and knew that the minor works he had published so far would not suffice to immortalize his name. And that was his ambition: to leave something behind, a name or a memorial, that would cause him to be remembered, as children perpetuate the memory of their father. Before he died he would have liked to complete his basic work on the origins of the churches of San Sebastiano, San Donat, and San Rocco in the Little Valley of God. One living church and two that were dead. . . . But the memory of those two dead churches lingered on in the hearts of men, for what has once been touched by the spirit is not easily blotted out. These works are my children, Don Marcello said to himself.

For some years he had been wrestling with a grave problem. He had before him sheafs of documents, dozens and dozens of slips of paper, and very rare books that had taught him all that could be learned in this world. But it was not enough. Something was missing: the vital link, the ray of illumination. Don Marcello had been seeking that illumination for months, indeed for years; and always in vain. A year, a date would have been enough; all the rest would have followed of its own accord. It was the link that was missing, the vital spark. O Lord, grant me that illumination. Let me beget my children before I die. Lord, let the light shine upon me. How often he had prayed thus!

The sun had disappeared and the shadows had spread over the valley. Don Marcello did not notice it immediately; only when he could no longer make out what he was reading did he realize that the darkness had come into his room. Hurriedly he went in search of the lamp, lit it, and placed it on the table; then he closed the window and returned to his desk. He was still absorbed in his thoughts, and from force of habit he rested his eyes on his papers. O Lord, he sighed, I have not long to live, give me the inspiration I lack. Lord, grant it to me. Lend ear unto my prayer; of Thy mercy, hear the words of my mouth! *Verba mea auribus percipe, Domine; intellige clamorem meum.*

At that instant the priest heard a swift footstep on the stairs; he turned round in a flash, a little alarmed, and saw that beside him was the man he had been thinking so much about that evening: Emanuele. He stood on the threshold and he was smiling.

"May I come in?" he asked.

"Yes," answered Don Marcello, as if in a dream. "Yes."

Emanuele came up to the table.

"I don't want to disturb you," he said.

Don Marcello had pulled himself together and he had presence of mind to offer the young man a chair.

"That's quite all right, my son. Do sit down."

The visitor sat down beside the lamp.

The old priest began to look at him. He really did not know what to say. He felt so tired; his head was swimming, the blood was pounding in his temples. Whatever is the matter with me? he wondered. What a strange evening. . . . But suddenly, in a flash of illumination, he understood that *there was something which had to be said;* and that he was required first of all to forget himself, to detach himself from the problems that absorbed him, to think only of him who was sitting there with his hands resting on his knees. Of Thy mercy, Lord, hear the words of my mouth. But whatever was the matter with these hands?

Without getting up the priest searched in the drawer of his desk and brought out a cardboard box. He opened it and offered the young man a cigarette. "Will you smoke?" he asked gently.

(156)

Emanuele took the cigarette and put it between his thin lips. "Why don't you smoke one yourself?" he asked.

"I . . ."

"Yes, do smoke," said the young man.

The priest flushed to the roots of his hair. He had never smoked in public and he thought his secret had been well kept. Nevertheless he did not want to disavow it and he took a cigarette. What an evening, he thought. But *there was something that had to be said.* . . .

They smoked for some time in silence. Then the old priest declared, "It's a pleasure to make your acquaintance, my son. Do you know that I've been taking myself to task this evening?"

"Whatever for?"

"Because I've never come to look for you. I'm a bad priest. I'm so absorbed in my studies that I neglect my parishioners."

So: *the thing that had to be said was said.*

"What are you busy on?" asked the young man. He seemed to be showing a polite interest.

"Historical researches," replied the priest. And without realizing it he was carried away again by his old obsession. "I'm on the point of solving a great problem, a problem that will make my name known. Oh, if you knew how I have worked! I now have all the documents I need. I have ransacked book after book, I have carried out researches in all the libraries, I have burrowed everywhere. What a labor! And now all that's missing is the vital link—the hyphen, so to speak—the flash of inspiration . . ."

His excitement had made him raise his voice. He became aware of this and reddened for the second time. "Forgive me; I'm a bad priest."

"No," said Emanuele.

Perhaps the old man failed to hear him, for his tone changed and he asked confidentially, "Where do you come from, my son?"

The visitor waved his hand vaguely.

"From a village a very long way off. It's called Paintown."

The word raised an echo in Don Marcello's mind—something like a distant recollection of his youth.

"I seem to have heard of it," he said. "But I'm an old man now and my memory isn't as good as it was. What a strange name, isn't it?"

"There are so many strange things in this world."

"You're right, there are, indeed," agreed the priest in a subdued voice.

He wanted to gaze at his companion's features but he could not do it, for Emanuele's face, caught from above and below in the light of the lamp, seemed transfigured. The priest asked him, "Are you alone in the world?"

And the young man replied, "That depends."

Don Marcello laughed softly. "What, you don't know if you're alone in the world?"

"Each one of us may have children," Emanuele replied cryptically.

Don Marcello reddened for the third time. He had learned so much about life in the confessional.

"But it's a sin," he faltered.

"Not for me," said Emanuele. "For me it's glory."

Even then Don Marcello did not understand. He launched into a flood of words—*there was so much else to say.*

"What are you doing now?" he asked. "How are you living? Have you given up your house? I know so little about you, and that's very wrong for a priest, isn't it? What do people say of a shepherd who doesn't know his own flock? They say he's a bad shepherd. . . . Well, I'm a bad priest. I'm a bad priest, I know almost nothing about you, only your name, Emanuele. But perhaps," he went on rather agitatedly, "you're an escaped prisoner of war? Look, my son, if there are any men in this world who deserve to be pitied, surely they're the soldiers of the last war— and we saw so many of them passing through here! So many that if I were a poet instead of a priest I would say that the whole of the Little Valley of God echoed to the sound of their footsteps. There were hundreds of them, I tell you; and if some had dusty packs on their shoulders there were others who had nothing left in the world, nothing but the old torn clothes or the ragged uniforms they wore on their backs. And do you know what they put me in mind of? The Lord Jesus when he was walking the roads of Galilee. Weary like them, and like them stripped of everything. Covered with the dust of the highways like them, hungry and thirsty like them. There goes the Lord of the world, I said to myself. And do you know what I thought one day when I ran across a group of these lads? I'll tell you. I thought that the Lord Jesus might well have come down again upon earth and that he might be among them! I said to myself that the flames of war were still burning in their souls; and he for certain loves fighting battles. I said to myself that they carried sorrow and suffering in their hearts; and he for certain loves sorrow and suffering. And that wasn't all; I said to myself that the Lord Jesus might have an affection for this Little Valley of God that bears the name of his Father. I got to the point of thinking that if I had been the Lord, and had decided to come down to earth again, it would have been this country that I should have chosen, in preference to all others! Because of the name it bears. But that idea was an idle dream, a figment of an old man's imagination, almost a blasphemy. Oh yes, that's the sort of thing that happens when a man gets to my age! All the same I should have liked to put my arms round these lonely starving youths; I should have liked to take them into my house and tell Giuditta (she's my housekeeper) to get a good dinner ready for them; I should have liked to make them sit down at a well-furnished table, and serve them with my own hands, and say to them: Eat, eat, my children, you don't know who may be in your midst. But alas, I did nothing of the sort. I gave them a crust of bread, sometimes a glass of wine—nothing more. And I went back to my studies and took up my old papers once more, saying to myself: This is what will bring me glory and cause my name to be remembered among men, as children perpetuate the name of their father. Then night came and with it repentance; I told myself that I was a bad priest, a selfish old man; and I knew that it would be of no avail, that on the morrow I would be back where I started. And it was always like that, always. I suffered, I still suffer. But I'm incapable of loving my neighbor in the way I would like to love him. Ah, imagine what it is to be incapable of loving one's neighbor as one wants to do! I can see it now, with my life almost over: I've never been capable of love. Do you understand what that means to a priest? My son, could a priest make a more horrible discovery? Not to be capable of love!"

The old man fell silent and his heavy breathing was the only sound in the room. The lamp shone in the stillness and darkness like a ball of light, patterning the walls with shadow. Everything was still; not a voice, not a murmur disturbed the mysterious quiet; nothing but the old man's heavy breathing, which seemed a ghostly echo of the words he had just uttered. And yet it was not a lifeless silence, but rather a silence of anticipation. Something was taking shape in the room—perhaps thoughts, perhaps feelings; in any event something that had life and movement, something that pulsed and throbbed in the stillness. This lasted for several seconds. Presently the old priest continued, in a gentle, almost plaintive voice:

"My son, shall I tell you something? Listen. Sometimes when I awake at night I go over the whole of my past life. And I see it as the bed of a torrent between two high mountain ranges; the summits are lofty and sublime, but the stream runs at their foot through mire and stones, among rotting grass and noisome insects. I have been like that stream—content to run in a bed hollowed out between the mountains. I have never done anything noble or glorious; I have gazed at the summits but I have never scaled them. I put on this priest's habit when I was a youth and had great ambitions; I dreamed then of martyrdom, of a glorious death in China . . . imagine it, a man of my weak character. And I have ended up by failing in this parish—a parish as quiet as a lake between high mountains. I have squandered my days, I have slept in a bed of down, I have given myself up to my studies and my own little concerns. And that has gone on for sixty years. For sixty years the people of the valley have been calling me Father; and during all that time I have been thinking of my body, of my wretched thirst for knowledge, of the garden around my house, and perhaps, now and then, of a remote—and abstract—Deity. That's all. I have never troubled to learn what's so hard to learn. I have never learned to love. I have never known how to love, and that is why I have never taken Jesus into my house, this Jesus whom I sought among the young soldiers and who would have entered into my heart if I'd had the slightest idea how to summon him. I think that one of these days a visitor will call upon me, and his name will be Death. There's something else I must tell you, my son. Mark how I say it, without tears or lamentation, and maybe this is the most tragic part of the business; my manner of saying it, my horrible resignation. Well, this is what I want to tell you, my son. I've lived in vain. It's as if I had never lived. For I've not come to know love, which is the very essence of life. I've not come to know Jesus. . . ."

The priest had spoken in a low voice, with a weary despair. Then it seemed that all of a sudden he was under the dominion of a mysterious force that had taken violent hold of him and was shaking him to the depths of his being. His head sagged forward and he buried his face in his hands.

"What's the matter with me, what's the matter with me, what's the matter with me?" he murmured; and it was not so much a question as a groan of anguish. And he began to weep, gently at first, then more and more convulsively, and the heaving of his shoulders set the table and the lamp swaying, and the shadows widened and shrank on the walls; and he went on weeping like a brokenhearted child, openly, without any attempt at concealment. Emanuele looked at him in silence, looked at him for a long time, with an expression on his transfigured face that was not of this world; then he stood up and raised his hands, white in the lamplight, and with one of them he touched the priest's head, and he spoke his name, "Don Marcello."

The priest raised his eyes, and saw, and cried out, and understood all that there was to understand; and he sank upon his knees. And then into the room, with his soft fierce step, came Love.

(23)

Stroll in the Forest

IN the Little Valley of God everyone is fond of music. Harp and oboe, cymbals and tambourine, the violin and the melancholy flute, even the accordion and the guitar, are high in favor with the young folk. It's wonderful to dance on the threshing floor in summertime by the light of a full moon, say the youths, and if there's a good accordion-player—well, all the better! The old men nod their heads, recalling the days of long ago. We were young once, too! they say. But when they are by themselves they exclaim scornfully: Pah! how silly their dances are! The young people of today know nothing about anything. This generation has lost the feeling for beauty.

And if you had asked these old men what they meant by beauty they would have answered: when someone stands under your open window in the moonlight, serenading you for hours on the viol, or when a very lovely woman plays the harp at sunset, alone with you in a shuttered room—there's beauty for you, that's what we meant by beauty!

But if the sunset hour is the time for music it is also the time for a game of bowls, or a stroll, according to individual taste. The common man, especially in periods of fine weather, prefers bowls; the sensitive soul, on the other hand, loves to roam about with only himself for company. And for those, few in number, who can enjoy being alone, solitude is one of earth's greatest blessings; it is certainly one of the most richly satisfying.

I don't know if you have ever found your way into a wood at dusk. The sky is ruddy, with great trailing wreaths of cloud. And in between the clouds stretch rifts as blue as the sea, as white as milk, as red as a forge. Sometimes the red light is so fiery that it comes down upon the earth and lies there like an undulating curtain, rich and velvety. Suddenly the trunks of the great trees turn to flame; and their leaves, in sharp contrast, are now more black than green, hanging in dark masses against the troubled sky. What could be finer than a walk through the woods at this hour? All is silent. Yes, but just trip over a stone in your path and send it rolling down a slope. As you watch it disappearing between the trees and listen to the heavy thudding noise of its fall, you may well think that you are hearing the throb of a mighty heart.

A little later, when the sun has vanished and the ruddy glow is merging more and more into the shadows of the oncoming night, a deep hush falls upon the voices of the forest, the myriad voices that belong to the daylight: chaffinches, tomtits, sparrows, goldfinches. The big green lizards dare not venture forth on the thick carpet of dead leaves, and even the rustling of the fern and bracken is heard no more. To seek undisturbed repose is now the bounden duty of every living creature, animal or plant. And so the forest is dead to all that has material existence.

Then the spirits come forth. If you have never seen the spirits of the forest, go into a clearing one evening after sundown; you will be sure to see them. Don't mistake them for sylphids, those soft diaphanous beings with fairylike shapes; it's too early for them yet, the moon will awaken them later. No, these are the children of the stillness that follows the sunset, of the gloaming that brings stillness with it; they are the spirits that shun both the light of day and the radiance of the night sky, who will vanish as soon as the moon glides into the forest and silvers the trunks of the oaks and chestnuts. True, their fleeting fantastic life is linked to moments that die upon the hour; but while it lasts, they live this brief twilit life of theirs with feverish intensity. They are born, they feed, grow, chase and love each other, wrestle and play, die and reproduce themselves—all in those few miraculous moments that come between daylight and darkness, between the radiance of the sun and the pale glimmer of the moon. These are the Spirits of Eternal Illusion. During the hours of daylight they live in secret crannies of men's hearts; during the hours of darkness they live in men's dreams, in the play of men's fancies; but when evening comes they forsake their retreats, free themselves from their bondage to mortals, and gather, as they have done for millions of years, in the depth of the silent woods, led by a very old goddess called False Hope.

It was with these spirits that Silvano chose to surround himself now that the month of August was drawing to an end. The lonely enchantment that held him in thrall allowed him to pick up their voices, their hoarse dusky voices. He had at his side the dog he had rescued on that magical night among the mountains. He had called him Aliofante. During the day the dog roamed drunk with happiness across the countryside, amid the sharp and sweet scents that rose from the lush grass. But when evening fell he rejoined Silvano and the two of them roved about in the company of the spirits. Dogs understand much more than we think; they hear many voices to which we are deaf; they see shapes that it is not given to us to see; and they are generous and patient with those who suffer. And so one need not be ashamed to have long talks with them; they possess an ancient wisdom. Silvano and Aliofante talked much together.

Then the moon rose and the Spirits of Eternal Illusion returned to their hiding places. Silvano himself went home, his head sunk on his chest and his hands clasped behind his back. Aliofante stayed behind in the wood; lifting his nose, he barked at the stars.

(24)

In Which We Reopen Maddalena Amato's Diary

THAT faithful mirror of the minor events of the day, Maddalena Amato's diary, included, besides remarks of a personal nature, a chronicle of all the small talk of the Little Valley of God that had become public property. Public in the meaning of the word given to it by the people of the district, for whom (as Don Marcello said one day, right in the middle of a sermon) public meant everything that they took pleasure in relating.

But let us leave these idle reflections and reopen the pages of Maddalena Amato's journal.

Noon, August 25th

I tell myself that in a few days we shall be into September, the saddest and loveliest month of the year. In the evenings when the sun goes down the air is soft and yet there's a sharp nip in it; during the day the sun's heat is less strong. The grapes are almost ready for picking and by God's mercy we shall have a fine harvest this year.

Already it's time to be thinking of winter.

I know nothing of Emanuele, except that he's leading a quiet life and keeping very much to himself. He still does things that make people talk, however, and they have lots to say about him.

Morning, August 26th

Yesterday evening, before I went to bed, I shut myself in my room and I let down my hair. Then I looked at myself for a long time in the mirror of the wardrobe my mother left me. It seemed to me that I had got much thinner.

Before that I'd had a visit from Angolino Dolcecuore and, as always, his coming had stirred deep, calm thoughts in my mind. But I was a little tired, and when he had gone I went to sleep immediately.

Rain fell all last night with a gentle monotonous sound. I began to think of Emanuele, and I couldn't get to sleep again.

Evening, August 27th

When I got up it was such a lovely day and the sky was so clear that I thought: This is spring. You would say that it was a kind of interlude in the march of the seasons, a bridge between the dazzling beauty of the summer days and the cold dreariness of the winter months. Even the hens scratching on the threshing floor seemed happier than usual, my Esther especially.

Toward three o'clock Professor Silvano turned up, but only to talk. As usual he was very kind to me and he even read me one of his beautiful stories, about a blind man driven crazy by love. I asked if poor Gio's adventure had given him the idea; he admitted that it had and he seemed quite upset. I must say I found the story extremely touching.

It's impossible to meet a sadder man than the Professor these days. He told me he had resorted to old Marion's expedients and then he explained what they were. With a good deal of cunning he managed to meet the girl he loves and he tried to cast a spell on her. I think he had to look her in the eyes and pronounce mysterious words. But Signorina Barbara started to laugh, the Professor concluded sadly. I admit that I couldn't find any words to comfort the poor boy.

His sadness is making me forget my own. All the same, I never stop thinking of Emanuele, and I'm not at all sure that it's right for me to do this. I'm proposing to confess it, among other things.

Fiordaliso Teri came as it was getting dark; then, a little later, Max, who brought me a cheese. I gave part of it to poor Fanuel, who lives alone with his daughter; she has been ill for several days.

(166)

Night, August 29th

Otello came and told me a very curious story. Apparently there are strange things going on at Dolciacqua. It seems that a spirit from beyond the grave walks there every evening. The two young people who live in the house, Count Peter and Signorina Lea, are visibly affected by all this.

I was leaning on my elbows at the window, watching the sunset, when Don Marcello the priest went past just below me. He looked up and he gave me a smile! It's the first time such a thing has happened. As a matter of fact, for some days now Don Marcello has seemed a different man; that unexpected smile made me so happy that for the rest of the day I forgot all about my depression.

Fanuel's little daughter has taken a turn for the worse and her illness is causing her poor father a great deal of concern.

I went to see her. She was alone with her father, and so I was able to join them in reciting the prayer for her recovery. The poor darling was so weak that very often she failed to make the responses. Fanuel was rather annoyed, but I begged him to forgive the child, she being so seriously ill.

Later

I don't know why, but I can't sleep. A fixed idea prevents me from closing my eyes and keeps tormenting me. It has to do with Emanuele and the life I've lived up to now. I'm so weighed down with sadness that it seems to me I'm going to die.

Evening, August 30th

The son of the late Simone Lamorte, the peasant farmer, came to see me for the first time. At the sight of this youth standing there in front of me, with a face as red as fire, something came over me—I don't know what—and I asked him politely to go away. He looked at me closely, his face redder than ever; bowed, and went off.

I got rid of Paride Parri likewise, but that wasn't so easy and we parted on a note of unpleasantness. I'm still upset about it.

I wonder sometimes what can be the matter with me. After Paride Parri had gone I sat down and had a good cry.

(167)

Evening, August 31st

They say that Fanuel's daughter is going to die. The doctor who examined her shook his head and looked grave. I went to church and I promised St. Rita two tall wax candles if the child got better.

I spent a very sad day, thinking of the little invalid and of many other things. The weather, though, is mild and springlike. But we haven't got to the end of summer yet and people are saying that the great heat will come back.

September 1st

I'm a harlot, it's true; a cause of embarrassment to other women. They avoid me when they can, and when they speak of me they lower their voices. I know all this quite well; I've known it for a long time. And I can't say that they're wrong. When I think about it, when I put myself in the place of those who judge me, who are not as I am because they lead moral lives, I am ashamed and I despise my own body.

But then I gaze at myself in the mirror and I see that my body is comely, full of life and health; and I say to myself: Truly my sins can't be so terrible in the eyes of the Lord or He wouldn't keep me looking like this. For if He wished He could cover me with sores, and make me ill, and reduce my flesh to such a state that men would shrink from it in horror and disgust!

On the contrary, it seems to me that I'm growing more beautiful; and I believe this strange melancholy that takes possession of me these days is making me more attractive to men. At least that's what all my visitors tell me; and the result is that I quickly recover my spirits and tell myself that I can't be such a great sinner after all!

Later

No, no! These are vain consolations; I am deluding myself, and I ought to beseech the Lord to spare me in His anger!

I am overwhelmed with sadness; I don't know what's to become of me, for truly there is nothing that will cheer me up.

I try to look at the sky, or the hens running around me when

(168)

I bring them their mash, or the transparency of the leaves in the early morning. But all these sights that used to do me good are no longer enough for me.

I feel so alone; I wonder what this sadness and weariness can be.

Night, September 2nd

Otello came to see me and spoke to me again about the incidents at Dolciacqua. He was very kind to me; he must have understood that I was ill at ease and tried to distract me with his conversation. It seems that things have got worse. The young owners of the estate are even thinking of calling in the priest to see whether he can help.

Otello added a curious fact. Apparently the two young people drove over to Emanuele's house and asked him to come with them. And Emanuele refused, no one knows why. The thing seems to me almost unbelievable. But what's the meaning of this story? What is this extraordinary power that Emanuele is said to possess?

Fanuel's little daughter died this evening. She was eleven and her name was Anna Mater Dolorosa Benedetta.

Morning, September 4th

I am still terribly shaken. Yesterday something happened that I'll remember for the rest of my days. Little Anna, whom everyone had given up for dead, is alive! There is no one in the Little Valley of God who doesn't mention her name in the same breath as Emanuele's, for it's thanks to him that a horrible mistake was discovered in time.

Yesterday morning as soon as it was light I went to pay my respects to the little corpse, as our custom is. Although it was still very early Fanuel's humble dwelling was already full of men and women. But the father wasn't there. My questions brought the reply that the poor man had disappeared the night before, as soon as his daughter had drawn her last breath. Now Anna Maria was lying on her little bed, dressed all in white, and women were praying around her. She had been wrapped in the gown she wore at her First Communion, simple and becoming;

and I was immediately struck by the extreme pallor of her face, which seemed to me whiter than the garment itself. This troubled me at the time, whereas now I think it ought rather to have filled me with astonishment. I joined the group of women and I too knelt down by the bed. There was a drifting perfume of flowers and candles in the room, and the murmur of the prayers made me want to cry. I thought of the little corpse; I thought of myself too; and the tears rolled down my cheeks. I told myself that I might have been stretched out on that bed in place of the little Anna Maria; this thought prompted other comparisons and I decided that my life was really very sad, full of loneliness and sin. Oh, what a wretch I am, I moaned and wailed to myself as the tears flowed. I took not the slightest notice of the women beside me nor of their habitual attitude, which is one of scorn and indifference. Though it never fails to hurt me, my sole preoccupation at that moment was with myself and the little girl and the pain of comparing my fate with hers. Wretch that I am, I kept saying in my misery, wretch that I am!

I was plunged in these gloomy reflections—which were not unmixed with a gentle self-pity—when an unaccustomed sound struck my ears and brought me to my feet. Suddenly I was overcome with curiosity; I felt that I must go out, and in fact I did leave the room hurriedly, close behind the other women. And then I beheld a scene that heightened my desolating sense of despair and reawakened my bewilderment. In the midst of the other men stood Emanuele and kneeling before him, sobbing bitterly, was poor Fanuel.

Before I could grasp what was happening or summon up enough strength to ask, I saw Emanuele lean toward the wretched father and touch him on the shoulder. He said something which I didn't catch; a sudden murmur rose from the crowd, and a woman who was beside him cried out: But he's mad, he's mad! Don't build up false hopes, Fanuel. Your little girl's dead, and no one can wake the dead. . . . I still didn't understand; all I knew was that Emanuele didn't appear to have heard the unintentional insult. Or, if he did, he ignored it. He merely remarked to Fanuel: Don't cry, it is as I told you, the child is asleep. And as the man went on looking at him with beseeching eyes, un-

(170)

certain whether to believe him or not, he added: Has the doctor come? Has he certified the death? No, said Fanuel, he hasn't come yet. You see, said Emanuele, it's all a mistake. The child is asleep; why won't you believe me? And he made his way into the house, followed by the father; and a voice said again: He's mad! I felt like hitting whoever had dared to utter such words, but I restrained my anger and contented myself with the reflection: If he says it, it's true; he can't be wrong. For at that moment I was certain—how it came about I don't know—I was as sure as sure can be that he couldn't be wrong. He couldn't be wrong!

When he reached the bed on which the child was lying, Emanuele stopped and looked round him. He looked round him, and then he looked at the little girl and smiled, and then he looked round him a second time, and he never stopped smiling. He looked at the people and at Anna Maria and at me and at Fanuel—at all of us, in fact; and he smiled and smiled. I had never seen anyone with a smile quite like his; it was a slow, fixed smile and it expressed so much. It seemed to me *terribly* full of something; what I mean is that there was a depth of understanding in it, a sort of pain, a kind of agonized conviction that what he hoped for would come to pass. Meanwhile the men and women had stopped on the threshold; only Fanuel had dared to enter the room with me; and he had flung himself on his knees, and he was looking at Emanuele and his daughter and then looking at the floor; and the most terrible part of it all was that there were no tears in his eyes. He didn't utter a sound, nor did we; the people, Fanuel, myself, the little girl—all were silent. What a stillness there was, what an incredible stillness! And at last Emanuele spoke. Arise, my child, he said, and so saying he took the little girl by the hand. And, dear God, she arose!

The people burst into loud shouts, and they rushed from the house, and the women could be heard shrieking and running for their lives. I stood as if rooted to the ground; my heart was a stone in my breast, my hand too was like a stone; all of me had turned to stone; and I stood thus for I don't know how long. Then I saw Emanuele smiling again, but now he had a different sort of smile, merely the smile of someone weary and exhausted, the smile of a man who has accomplished a task. What nonsense, he said. She was only asleep. Then he added: Have you any food in the house, Fanuel? Do you know that the child's hungry? You're hungry, aren't you, Anna Maria? And she said: Yes, I'm hungry. Then I left the room.

I went to get food for the child.

(25)

In Which We End by Believing That
Love Spells Do Work

WHEN Despair enters into a man's soul it robs him of the power of action, makes him rebel in disgust against the ancient laws of the universe which he has hitherto respected and obeyed; and, by destroying his will, puts him at the mercy of the first man who seeks to sway him. This was precisely what happened to Professor Silvano who, after the failure of his resort to magic, fell into the hands of Piero and his friends. However, and let this be said to their credit, they were animated solely by a desire to bring peace to his troubled heart.

Piero had almost to drag him by the hand when he took him to see old Marion for the second time. While they were walking along the stony path that led to the sorceress's dwelling, Piero came out with the remark, "My dear friend, I feel as if I were dragging a coffin."

Silvano said, "Yes."

The truth was that now that Hope had abandoned him he was completely indifferent to everything.

The peasants are carrying a coffin on their shoulders, climbing up the slope where the pebbles roll from under their feet. The graveyard of the Little Valley of God is a small square of turf on the summit of a hill, surrounded by a wall and protected by a row of cypresses. The peasants are dripping with sweat, the cicadas shrill, the bier glitters in the sun, the dead man inside the coffin knocks against its wooden walls, and his flesh is pale as the sky, yellow as the gorse that grows among the stones of the path. His family weep behind the bier. His friends are hooded in white, and their black eyes shine far beyond their white cowls. They carry thick resin torches which blaze and crackle in the sun, spitting forth black smoke.

The priest, swinging the censer, chants the Dies Iræ.

Marion did not seem particularly surprised when she saw the two young people. She was seated at her door and she was spinning.

"I knew you would come back," she said.

"Then why did you make us try that experiment?" Piero said heatedly. "It was just a waste of time, Marion. You seem to be getting old."

She shrugged her shoulders and muttered, "*Ne projicias me in tempore senectutis, cum defecerit virtus mea, ne derelinquas me.*"

"Let me warn you straightaway that I haven't understood a word of that," Piero told her with a gesture of annoyance.

"It's good Latin nevertheless," she said sarcastically as she showed them into her house.

When Piero had something to say he made no bones about saying it. So now he remarked, "Oh yes, no doubt, but we haven't come here to listen to mass."

"Why have you come?" asked Marion.

She addressed herself in Silvano in particular. He answered indifferently, "I've no idea."

Love, in the season of our old age forsake us not; when our bones are become as wax, Love, forsake us not.

What do these people want with me? I'm sleepy.

On All Souls' Day the earth of the burial ground is cut up with the marks of feet. Yesterday at nightfall the dead came out of their graves and danced under the moon and sang a hymn. Today the people have brought them chrysanthemums that shriek

(174)

upon the ground and hundreds of tapers that splutter upon the ground, spitting forth black smoke.

Marion, I don't know why I have come. I'm sleepy, that's all.

The old woman sat down and began to scrutinize the Professor with a vague compassion. "Ah!" she sighed, "what a strange thing love is!"

"It would be more to the point if you told us what we're to do," exclaimed Piero impatiently. "Once upon a time you were well versed in certain matters; it was even said that there was no one to compare with you, in the Valley or anywhere else. Why do you sit there sighing? Come on, Marion, tell us what we're to do."

"Hold your tongue!" cried the old woman with sudden ill humor. "You do nothing but chatter. Keep your mouth shut!"

A little surprised, Piero resumed in a milder tone, "I merely wanted to know why your magic hasn't worked better."

The old woman seemed lost in thought.

"Leave me alone, leave me alone," she murmured.

"You understood my question?" Piero persisted.

"Yes, I understood, I understood."

"Then why don't you answer?"

She shook her head. "There is a reason. There is a reason for everything. Don't you know, Piero the Vagabond, that there's a reason for everything?"

Then she began to mutter between her teeth.

"Do you know what the reason is? Interfering with the natural order of things can be dangerous for those who lend themselves to it. But what's the good of speaking to you in that strain? I know very well that I'm wasting my time. You wouldn't know what I was talking about. Let me think—we'll get on faster if you let me think."

There is a reason for everything: then tell me the reason for Love, Marion, and the reason for Death. We're now letting you think.

Before we put the dead man on the bier, let us summon the old peasant woman that she may wash his exhausted body. Let

us leave the door of the room ajar that his soul may fly out. Let
us put a piece of silver in his mouth that he may have money
for his journey. Let us strew handfuls of rosemary in the coffin
that the body may be scented with it from head to foot.

Tell us, Marion, the reasons for Love and Death. See, we're
letting you think.

They let her think for several minutes. She remained seated
in her wicker armchair, with her curly head bowed on her vast
bosom. Her lips worked in a soundless whisper, as though she
were murmuring some prayer or other. When she had finished
she got up. "It's all right," she said.

Then she went to a rack hanging on the wall, searched for a
moment or two in a clutter of boxes and jars and, with an
abrupt movement, pulled out a green-colored bottle, which she
placed on the table. "Wait a second," she said, and she almost ran
from the kitchen. She was back in a flash, exclaiming, "Dear me,
how hard this wood is—I need a tool." From a drawer of the
table she drew a big black-handled knife and again left the room.
She could be heard humming in the kitchen yard; then she reappeared and threw on the table a piece of dark-colored wood.
"What day of the week is it?" she asked. She spoke in a level
voice; the excitement of a moment before had vanished and they
felt that she was now calmly resolved.

"What day of the week is it?" she asked for the second time.
Piero replied, "Thursday."

"Friday would have been better," she said. "But we can't
change the calendar. We'll go ahead just the same. There's a
new moon and that will help us. Thanks, Piero."

Then, very solemnly, she asked Silvano, "Are you quite sure
you want to try the experiment? Because there's one thing I
must warn you about. It won't be easy for you to escape the consequences of what I'm going to do," she explained. "It will set
terrible forces in motion and the consequences may be serious.
Answer me."

Silvano could hardly bring himself to open his mouth, but he
made an effort and asked, "What consequences, if you please?"

The old woman drew away a little and closed her eyes.

(176)

"It could be the end of everything," she murmured.

"What end?" said Silvano absently. "Death, do you mean?"

"It could be the end, I said."

"You mean—I might die?"

Come Death, for what does it matter to me? Come Death, and the day of wrath, when the world shall be reduced to ashes.

"It could be the end, I said."

"But the experiment may succeed?"

So long as you're in love with me. . . .

"O Lord, I have cried unto Thee and Thou hast heard my prayer," intoned Marion. "Lend ear unto my voice when I turn unto Thee, O Lord."

"Well, I'll be blowed," said Piero.

Silvano's eyelids were heavy and he felt an irresistible longing for sleep. *O God, to let go, to let sleep overtake me.* "Of course I'm ready," he said.

The old woman took his head in her hands. "What name?" she asked.

It was Piero who replied. "Silvano," he said.

"No," smiled Marion. "I want the name of the girl."

"Barbara," said Silvano.

Barbara Barbara Barbara—Barbara.

"Barbara," repeated Marion, as if in a dream. "Barbara. . . ." And from then on the name filled the room. The old woman went over to the table, uncorked the green bottle, poured the contents into a glass bowl, and spread out her hands. In that attitude, with her eyes closed, she chanted in a low voice:

"Lord, I will praise Thee with all my heart
for Thou hast heard the words of my mouth.
I will sing to Thee with the harp in the presence of the
angels

(177)

bow down in Thy holy temple and magnify Thy name,
because of Thy mercy and Thy long-suffering,
because Thou hast glorified Thy holy name above all
else."

At that moment something like a mysterious breath of wind entered into Silvano's soul; or, more exactly, after a long absence something returned to him and gladdened him anew with its presence; and the name of this gentle spirit was Trust, which had forsaken him for so long. He felt it steal into his heart and he rejoiced, filled with a happiness that was half pain; silently he fell on his knees in adoration. Ah, how easily one could let go, how simple it was! He closed his eyes and sank into a chair. One word only came to his lips: Barbara.

Barbara, why don't you love me? Why have you never yet loved me? O my beloved, I would like to raise a song to you in all the tongues of men; to your eyes, your face, your little freckles, your cheeks, your lips, your breasts, your belly, your legs, your feet, to the movements of your body—a song in all the tongues of men. You fill the whole universe, New York, Paris, Rome, Berlin, Japan, myself, the paper and the typewriter in front of me, the dreary winter that I see advancing, the music that comes to my ears, the song of the cicadas on summer nights, and the summer moon, the sea when it sparkles in the dawn, the spring flowers, and the shores of distant islands when a blue haze hangs about them, my dog's eyes when he is suffering, the grasses of the field, the red sunsets, and the poppies scarlet among the golden wheat, the waters of all the rivers of the world, and all the scents of earth and sky. You fill the whole world, O my beloved.

Still holding her arms outstretched, the old woman continued to pray:

"The day when I called upon Thee, Thou didst hear me,
Thou hast restored strength and courage to my soul.
All the things of the earth will praise Thee, Lord,
When they have heard the oracles of Thy mouth."

Then, raising her eyes heavenward, she exclaimed, "Anaele Barbara, Anaele Barbara, Anaele Barbara!"

And after that she was silent; the rite was over, and she sank back heavily into her wicker armchair.

Some minutes passed. The old woman got up painfully; she seemed utterly worn out. With her right hand she took the piece of wood, held it above the glass bowl, and then let it drop. She brought it out dripping with oil, put it on the table, and muttered, "Have you a pencil?" Piero handed her his. With meticulous care the old woman wrote something on the wood; then she said to Silvano, "You tie this piece of cypress to your right arm and you touch the girl's right hand." She brushed his eyelids with her oily fingers and gave him the wood. Finally she said, "Love will now be born in the girl's heart, my child," and she heaved a sigh. Piero had put his hand in his pocket but she shook her head. "No, no, I don't want anything, good night." She accompanied them as far as the door. Piero, who seemed rather frightened, said, "Good night, Marion."

Only a week later Piero happened to run into Silvano. He was hurrying toward Ca' d'Orso, but Piero stopped him and asked, "Well, how goes it?"

On Silvano's face there was a look of ecstasy—and fear.

"A wonderful thing has happened," he whispered.

A few hours later Piero caught sight of Otello at the Shop. "I've seen Silvano," he said. "Something's got hold of that fellow. Angel or demon, I don't know which."

"What?" shouted Otello. Then he tossed off his red wine. "Good luck to him," he murmured.

(26)

"For behold, the Lord of Lords draweth nigh"

IN these last weeks of summer the Little Valley of God seemed to have become the favorite resort of Satan, whose disturbing presence sows terror among men and leads them into great temptation and wrongdoing. Pride, Lust, and Avarice, which usually follow in Satan's train as he journeys about the world, had been let loose upon the Valley, spreading foulness and death. Women sitting together in the evenings took it in turns to tell of the strange happenings that had been reported in the neighborhood; then they crossed themselves and those who had no husbands besought their friends to sleep with them.

One morning Gattino knocked at Professor Silvano's door. The Professor emerged from the hypnotic state that for hours on end had kept him chained to the blank pages of his manuscript.

"What is it, Gattino?"

The boy handed him a note.

"From Signorina Maddalena."

Then he went scampering down the narrow stairs of the old house.

"Dear Professor," ran the note, "I think I ought to let you know that if what everyone is saying is true the Devil has entered into the body of Countess Domenici. The poor woman is out of her mind; she waves her arms about, speaks in unknown languages, rolls the whites of her eyes, and—God preserve us— utters horrible blasphemies. Through Don Marcello her brother,

Count Peter, has sought divine aid. I know that the priest plans to go to Dolciacqua, but I can't tell you exactly when. However, I had to inform you of this, knowing what a great interest you take in strange and unnatural happenings. With kindest regards, yours very sincerely, Maddalena Amato."

Though for some time now Silvano had been like a man bewitched, existing in a state of stupor that set him apart from everyday life, he could not restrain himself from calling on Don Marcello. In reply to his questions the priest said, "I'll go tomorrow about three o'clock. First I have to get permission from the Bishop, and there are so many other things besides that I must attend to." Silvano noticed that the old man was very pale. There were dark rings under his eyes, and in his reedy voice, in his manner of speaking, usually so gentle and dreamy, there was a new dignity, with something rather odd about it. Now, suddenly giving way, he added with a groan, "But I feel so unworthy, oh so unworthy!"

Silvano did not know what to say in reply, so he merely nodded his head.

"May I come with you?" he asked.

The priest looked at him for a moment without any sign of recognition; then he came to himself and seemed to relapse into the same ceremonious stiffness as of old.

"You may come," he said, "but prepare yourself by prayer and meditation."

The next day, about four o'clock in the afternoon, Silvano arrived at Dolciacqua, a great rambling old house surrounded by black cypresses. The sun was beating down on high walls of dazzling whiteness—for the dog days had returned—and a piercing chorus of insects filled the air. Silvano passed through the gateway, all overgrown with climbing plants, and gave a shout. Some men who were at work in a meadow turned round and stared at him. They seemed to be asking themselves: What can this gentleman want?

"Hello, is there anyone about?" Silvano called.

At last an old woman appeared; she was wearing a starched white collar over a black bodice.

"What do you want?"

"Don Marcello is here, I arranged to meet him."

The old woman looked at him with an air of suspicion. "Excuse me, who are you?"

Silvano gave her his name. "Eh?" she said. She must be deaf, he thought. I'll have to shout.

At that moment a voice called, "Hello there, Silvano!"

It was Otello. A young man with fair hair, immaculately turned out, made his appearance simultaneously. Otello introduced him.

"Count Peter Domenici."

The young man bowed and held out his hand. "How d'you do?"

"I'm delighted to make your acquaintance," said Silvano. "I had a word with Don Marcello and I've taken the liberty of coming along. I don't know whether he told you . . ."

"Yes, yes, of course," said the young man. "I've heard about you."

He led the way into the house and conducted Silvano to the first floor. From time to time he turned round and sighed.

"Satan has taken possession of her, my dear sir. What comes out of her mouth when she has these fits doesn't bear thinking of: strange objects, unmentionable words." He spoke with a foreign accent; his expression was gentle and pleasant. "The Demon even foretells the future, and believe me, the accuracy of its predictions is quite extraordinary. I've proved that for myself in cases where the events predicted were about to happen. I've kept a check and found that they happened exactly as it had foretold. One day it said in formal terms that it was Satan and went on to announce that it would manifest itself within twenty-five hours by sending forth a tress of raven-black hair. Well, twenty-four hours went by, and then, sure enough, out of my sister's mouth came a tuft of jet-black hair, with a remarkable gloss on it. Awful things are happening—things no one would credit."

They had now reached a little drawing room, furnished with dark, solid-looking chairs and sofas, hung with pictures, and adorned with a lovely old fireplace. "Sit down," said the Count. "But where has my dear Otello got to? Delightful fellow, don't you agree? Most attractive." Silvano remarked to himself that the Count seemed more interested in Otello than in his sister's terrible plight.

"Have you known Otello long?" he asked.

"Oh no," the young man exclaimed. "Only a few months. But I'm already very fond of him."

Silvano was a little embarrassed. It seemed to him that something was wrong. So he tried to change the subject.

"What do the doctors say?" he asked.

The young man looked at him absently with his large clear blue eyes. "Eh, what's that?"

Silvano repeated the question.

The Count shrugged his shoulders. "Oh, they talk of hysteria. Or, to be exact, they were talking of it. Now they just don't know what to say. It's all so mysterious and wonderful."

"Wonderful?"

"Yes, wonderful. Don't you think so? I mean—it's terrible for my sister, but, if you can look at it objectively, it's an extraordinary thing. Satan is living in this house; have you thought of that?"

Silvano looked at him. "I have thought of it," he said. "Listen to me, sir—do you believe in Satan?"

The young man answered with solemn deliberation. "My friend, there isn't one corner of this Valley where Satan hasn't taken up his abode. I noticed it the moment we came here. He's in every pebble, every tree, every clod of earth."

"And have you ever wondered why?" asked Silvano. He was convinced that what his host had just said was the truth. Why, it was as clear as daylight. But how is it that I've never realized this before? he asked himself. Then a voice spoke within him: No, you haven't only just discovered this. Think what you're saying and tell the truth. You've known this for five or six days. You've known it since that afternoon when Piero took you to see Marion. Yes, you've known it since then. Why deny it? But quickly he stifled the inner voice. No, he wouldn't—he mustn't —listen to it. Barbara . . .

(183)

The Count answered his question. "I think," he said, "that a great Presence has summoned Satan into this neighborhood. I believe that this Presence is watching us. Satan is but the shadow of God, and God will vanquish him. They are fighting for possession of the Temple . . ."

At that moment a servant announced Don Marcello. He came in followed by a choirboy wearing an embroidered surplice. The boy had black hair and a wild look; he was obviously intimidated by his unfamiliar surroundings.

The Count turned to him after greeting the priest. "What's your name?" he asked gently.

The boy gave him a sly look and answered, "Ferruccio."

The Count considered him for some time. "Ferruccio, eh?" he said.

Don Marcello seemed agitated; his face was more drawn than usual, and a strange excitement showed in his eyes. "Why aren't we moving on?" he asked impatiently.

"Follow me, please," said the Count. They passed through great deserted halls and came to the madwoman's room.

Dressed in white, she sat buried in the depths of a huge armchair lined with yellow satin. Beside her, on the watch for the slightest sign of movement, stood two silent maids. Her head was leaning against the back of the chair, her eyes were half-closed, and her hair flowed in a luminous yellow wave over the yellow of the satin. She seemed to be asleep; when the men came in she did not stir. The room was almost in darkness; heavy curtains shut out the fierce glare of the sunlight and prevented it from dispelling the murky sensation of fear that hung about, like the panting of an animal. The maids' aprons were two harsh and startling white spots in the surrounding gloom. Deep within him Silvano felt a dreadful, mounting anxiety; he wanted to dash from the room, to call out, to shout with all his strength so that he could hear the sound of his own voice; but he knew that it could not be and that he must stay where he was, in front of the armchair, in front of the motionless girl. Perhaps she was asleep, perhaps she was dozing; who could tell? He saw that Don Marcello was swiftly putting on a purple stole and his eye took note of the color; he saw the priest motioning everyone to be quiet. Quiet, quiet. And now Don Marcello knelt on the floor and pulled toward him the holy water sprinkler which the choirboy, more and more panic-stricken, was holding out; and, almost as though he were in a hurry to begin, he pronounced a blessing on the spectators. Then the girl stirred, opened her eyes, raised her head a little, sat up in the armchair, and, speaking in a toneless voice that seemed miles away, began to pour out a stream of blasphemies.

She went on like this without even a second's pause, long enough for the bystanders to lose count of time. The priest did not seem to be listening; he was praying in a low voice, with his eyes fixed on the floor, and the spectators could see his lips moving, though they could not hear the words. Presently he raised his voice and Silvano, as if in a dream, recognized the rosaries of the saints. The two maids knelt down and repeated the responses in a flat monotone; the elder had stuffed her fingers in her ears so as not to hear the blasphemies that her young mistress was uttering. There were thus two streams of colorless words flowing uninterruptedly through the heavy silence—one coming from the girl and the other from the spectators who were praying on their knees beside her. Silvano stood a little apart; nevertheless, he could not fail to notice the growing pallor of the madwoman's face and of the hands that hung limp on her knees. It was a frightful, a terrible pallor which had a mysterious and yet a definite significance, precisely the same as that of the blank white silence that surrounded her. The silence was vast and empty, utterly dead, unbroken even by the usual country sounds —the drone of insects, the clucking of hens, the bellowing of cattle; it held nothing but the threadlike and barely perceptible rivers of toneless speech, that went on and on. O God, thought Silvano, when will this end? He knew that he too was a captive, just as much as the blaspheming woman; that he too was in bondage to something that was soft and evil. Oh, how would he ever break free? At that moment he felt a hand touching him; he swung round and saw the Count's delicate face and shining eyes, heard him murmur, "Could you translate what the priest is saying? I don't understand Latin." Silvano made a sign of assent and drawing the young man into a corner of the room he began to translate, still under the domination of a spell. "Oh, how shall I ever break free?"

The priest went on praying, either alone or with the kneeling women. The girl had rested her head on the back of the chair and now she suddenly fell silent. Only her body quivered when Don Marcello, bringing the ritual to an end, made the sign of the cross on her forehead, mouth, and breast. Then the priest's voice rose and became harsh, imperious, almost malign.

"What is he saying?" whispered the Count.

"He's trying to find out who the Demon is," Silvano translated softly.

"But we know," exclaimed the Count. "He knows. I've already told him. It's Satan." He seemed almost irritated and muttered some words that Silvano did not understand.

"There can be more than one Demon," said Silvano, hardly knowing what he said. And suddenly he was astonished by his own words. Did they come from me? he wondered dreamily.

The young man persisted, "It's Satan. Satan and Satan alone is in my sister's body."

Silvano saw his eyes; how they gleamed—like torches in a pitch-black night!

The priest had lowered his voice; he was now reciting something with bowed head. He prayed thus for a long time, as if talking to himself. Finally he stood up; gently and sadly he placed the hem of his stole on the girl's neck and stretched out his right hand over her head. And now there was a new element in the drama; this white outstretched hand. Raising his eyes to the ceiling the priest called upon God to help him. He did so with a trustfulness and familiarity of manner that lacked nothing in respect; there was something magnificent about it—he appeared to be talking to a friend rather than to a master, or at least to a master whose consideration and affection for his servants were known to all. And then suddenly the priest's voice hardened. "I bid thee begone, unclean spirit!" he cried. And as he spoke these words a shudder ran through the girl lying in the armchair; for a moment her body writhed in the throes of incredibly violent convulsions. The two women at her side uttered low moans and held on to her arms to stop her from throwing herself to the floor. Silvano was aware of the Count's pale effeminate face an inch or two from his own; he felt his breath and was conscious of his burning eyes; but he could not avert his gaze from the girl's white quivering neck and the stole wrapped around it. The whole universe was in that neck—yes, and all his life, present and to come. And meanwhile, almost without realizing what he was doing, he went on translating Don Marcello's words. The priest had risen to his full height and was speaking in a harsh, fearless voice: "Hear me and tremble, O Satan, enemy of the Faith, adversary of mankind, bringer of death, despoiler of life, despiser of justice, root of misfortune, sink of iniquity, seducer of men . . ."

And then, above the madwoman's screams, he pronounced the exorcism: "Give way, unholy monster, give way to Christ, in whom thou wilt find none of thy works; who dispossessed thee, destroyed thy kingdom, and reduced thee to bondage . . ."

How long all this lasted—the girl's shrieks and blasphemies, the muttering of the prayers, the long exorcism—it would be impossible to say. There came a moment, however, when all of a sudden the priest's strength seemed to give out; it was as though a weariness against which he had been fighting for a long time had suddenly overpowered him. Without warning his voice failed him; he moved away a few paces, stricken by a humility he had not hitherto shown. And so the girl's neck, no longer covered by the stole, was exposed in all its whiteness and nakedness. And the priest said, "It's no good, he's too strong for me," and he flung himself on his knees by the empty bed and began to sob like a child, discouraged and disgraced. Silvano saw his shoulders heave, saw his stringy neck swell; he had buried his face in his hands, and his whole body had crumpled under the violent onset of this fit of weakness.

At first Silvano looked on as if this scene were part of a fleeting nightmare in which he was only indirectly concerned; then all of a sudden an immense pity caught him unawares, choking him and making him ill; pity for the old man who, clothed in a purple stole and armed only with his faith, had dared to challenge an infernal power; pity for this old man who was crying like a child; a pity that tore at his heart. And this banished the mists that had thickened around him, and he fell through space and found himself alone on the ground, crushed with compassion. What has happened? What has become of me? Where am I? Where have I lived till now? And for a moment, overwhelmed by the self-awareness that he had just rediscovered, Silvano could not speak; the others too were silent. The priest's mournful weeping was the only sound that rose in the stillness; for the girl was no longer moaning. At last, after what seemed an eternity, a voice broke the silence; the urgent, impassioned voice of the Count, who was saying, "Why don't you try again, Don Marcello? Oh why don't you try again?" Then Silvano realized that the words were precisely those he would have wished to utter. Yes, it was I who put them into his mouth, he thought triumphantly, it was I who said them, he only spoke through me and because it was I—I who willed him to speak! And a new vision and understanding came to him, a strength that nothing could resist.

Now at last he could speak. He expressed himself with a gentle sternness, as a father might address a dearly loved son. He was twenty-six and the priest was eighty at least, with the snows of many winters on his head; nevertheless it was Silvano who was the older and wiser of the two. For the priest had abandoned hope, whereas Silvano felt it surging in every vein. The priest was only a defenseless child; time had rolled back and he was no longer an old man burdened with the weight of years, he was now nothing but the wistful, love-starved boy of his seminary days, the boy who had shed secret tears when he could not translate his Latin exercise or work out his algebra. The priest had no hope, whereas Silvano had his love for Barbara —he had the whole world. Love can conquer Satan; O Barbara, is it not so? And it was his love for her that he invoked as he now addressed the priest with disciplined emotion and the calm sternness of a father.

"Why are you losing heart like this?" he said to him. "Do you think you can overcome the Demon so easily? Think; the Demon is a celestial being, although steeped in sin. Try again, Don Marcello, try again; isn't it worth the effort? Isn't the rescue

(188)

of a lost soul an object worth achieving, even at the cost of further suffering and further struggle? Isn't the world full of evil—full, full to overflowing, choked with evil? Might not victory over a single one of its manifestations have a symbolic value? Might it not kindle hope in others, might it not be a sign to all who hope that they need not hope in vain? Oh, Don Marcello, let Love conquer. . . ." And Silvano went on for a long time in this strain, until the priest rose and said, "Yes, my son," in a dull but steady voice. He went over to the girl and resumed the sacred ritual.

The priest's body had taken on new life and strength. His voice was deep-toned and merciless: Powerful, O Satan, is the adversary that confronts thee! And the malign spirit evidently understood, for it writhed and poured forth blasphemies. Two mighty champions, exulting in strength drawn from sources directly opposed, were now locked in a savage duel. All in the room had fallen on their knees and were wholeheartedly joining in the great battle.

"*Adjuro te*," thundered the priest. "*Adjuro te, omnis immundissime spiritus, omne phantasma, omnis incursio Satanæ, in nomine Jesu Christi Nazareni, qui post lavacrum Joannis in desertum ductus est, et te in tuis sedibus vicit. . . .*" The priest had begun on his knees, but here his zeal carried him away and he rose to his feet, standing alone in a silence that was now natural and earthly, of no significance except as a background to this conflict. And now the external world materialized, the world of earth-bound creatures who live in innocence, who are born in obscurity, who suffer, rejoice, and die in obscurity, according to the eternal scheme of things. And the hour of sunset could not be far off; a flood of warm light was streaming into the room, a golden dancing light which the curtains could no longer subdue; and in the distance the high mountain ranges stood darkly outlined against a pearly gray sky, the friendly evening sky, streaked with red, purple, and gold. And the very silence was part of the world of men, filled with the stir and throb of life, unspoken but human thoughts, and the muffled voices of all things that live and breathe. Beside the door of the room, bearing witness to the return of hope, stood a group of men and women. They were the household staff—the footmen, the cook, the steward; living men and women with their hopes and plans, for whom the future was still bright with promise. And meanwhile the struggle went on, and as the priest spoke Silvano translated: "Come forth, unholy spirit; come forth, thou monster, come forth in all thy horror; *for God willed that man should be His temple.*"

Then, in impassioned tones, the priest continued:

"But why shouldst thou dwell here any longer? Honor God the Father Almighty, before whose face all things bow down. Give way to Jesus Christ, who poured out his precious blood for man. . . ."

And at last, in a resounding, majestic voice, he proclaimed:

"Thy seat is the desert. Thy habitation is the serpent. Bow down and fall upon thy face. There is no time to lose. *For the Lord of Lords draweth nigh.*"

At that moment there was a sound of approaching footsteps; the household servants drew aside and Emanuele entered.

"You asked for me," he said. "Here I am."

Then the girl uttered a terrible, despairing shriek that rose and echoed in the stillness, and then died away. Something leaped from her mouth. Don Marcello bent down swiftly.

"Satan has left her," he announced.

His voice was hardly more than a whisper. He was hiding something in his clothes, and he looked all round him. Then he sank to his knees.

(27)

Behold the Little Valley of God

I AM showing you the Little Valley of God, I am showing you our Country. What is our Country, if not a land inhabited by men? The Little Valley of God is a land inhabited by men: it stands for our Country, it's a part that can be taken as a symbol of the whole.

I am showing you the Little Valley of God. But take a good look at it. When you arrive by the post-bus, and the sky is aflame with the sunset, and the mountains are darkening above your heads; or when you walk the burning, dusty roads, and the shrilling of the grasshopper sings in your heart, and you feel you are suffocating with the heat (oh, how sweet it is to die in such warmth!); or when you make your way to the church of St. Sebastiano, when the pealing of the bells is guiding your steps toward it and bands of girls in their Sunday dresses are talking and laughing on the road, quite close to you; or when your car breaks down at just the wrong moment and the peasants say to you: Go along to old Gallino, the man who writes magic formulas on scraps of paper—and you go, and you put the note under the bonnet of your car and it starts up and takes the road again; or when the peasants would like to kill the landowners over the question of leaseholds and the landowners would like to kill the peasants for the same reason, each side calling God to its aid; and in all other matters of life and death, day and night, black and white, dawn and high noon and evening, good and evil, sun and moon—take a good look at it, I say, take a good look at the Little Valley of God, our Country! At all times, latent in every aspect of its life and character, in things and men and events, there is a mysterious hidden meaning, the very soul of our land—and the object of my desperate unwearying search. The presence of this hidden meaning was made clear to me at the very moment when I first saw the light, in this plot of earth where my mother and father, too, were born, and my mother's mother and my father's father, and all my ancestors back to time immemorial, all from this plot of earth, a vast branching tree whose sap runs now in my veins, coming to me out of the dim past. The light went to my head like a strong wine and I was instinctively aware that in everything there was this hidden meaning; and I asked what it was, and there was none that could answer; and I asked again, and again, and there was none that could answer. And in the end I held my peace, with this terrible unsatisfied desire for knowledge in my heart; and since then other children have been born, and time has rolled on, and many old men who were alive then are lying now in our little grave-yard, beside others older than they; and still I am haunted by this desire to know, this unsleeping desire to know the true significance of our land; still it weighs upon my heart.

Perhaps, I say to myself, the explanation is to be found in Don Marcello's papers, in the notebooks and old tomes of the priest who loved his church more than his neighbor but who one day entertained an important guest and felt the presence of Love; perhaps in the sorceries of old Marion, who raises demoniacal powers with words of Holy Writ; perhaps in the tales Silvano writes, in his loves and aspirations; in the pleasure-seeking eyes of Signor Aquilante, at the table of Don Defendente Conelli, that learned man who would like to talk but cannot because his wife will not let him open his mouth. At the bottom of all these things, perhaps, lies the key to the mystery, the hidden soul of our Country. Or perhaps it is to be found in Simonetta Grei's holy relic, in the Marchesa Marianna's cigar, in the piano the Chevalier Catone played to himself in the deserted town, in Maddalena Amato's bed, in the flute and sightless eyes of blind Gio, who will nevermore leave the grave with which his whole life is now bound up, and his hopes that one day he will again see the light of the sun. Latent in all these things there is a mysterious significance, and for me that meaning, that mystery *is* the Little Valley of God, our Country, *the Temple of the Lord.* Shall I discover the hidden meaning one day, before death comes to me, or must I die with this restless yearning in my soul, this despair at the utter impossibility of voicing what is in my heart? I shall die—dust to dust, ashes to ashes—and still I shall have no knowledge of the hidden meaning of this corner of the earth, our motherland.

Once when I was on my way to the Little Valley of God I met an emigrant returning to his native country. He had been put next to me in the bus, a man who looked sixty or so; he climbed in, sat down beside me, and began to talk. I come from America, he said—just like that, in a perfectly natural tone of voice, exactly as he might have said: I come from the Town, or from Australia, or from the moon, or from Dolciacqua. He carried a haversack, and he was wearing an old American sweater and American shoes, a little down at the heel. Everything about him was foreign, except his speech. He asked: How's Untel? —naming a man who lived in the Valley; then he began to talk about him, about his childhood; and he recalled how they had gone to school together and what a lad Untel had been. A real little devil—he used to go and bathe in the river, and play tricks on the girls: how is he at the moment, can anyone tell me? All this was said in the old dialect of the Little Valley of God, with the same intonation, the same short or long vowels, the same stresses, the same light in the eyes, the same feeling. The others asked him: Is it a long time since you left the Valley? And he answered: Forty years, forty years have passed since I went away. But tell me, how's Truc? I remember that when he was a boy he couldn't pronounce his *r*'s. And he laughed. Quite well, said someone in the bus, he's fine. Forty years, did you say? Yes, he agreed, forty years. And during this conversation I was thinking what forty years represent in a man's life—the number of days and nights, the number of times he eats and drinks, smokes a cigarette, goes to bed with a woman, shaves, says his prayers.

(193)

Forty years. Then someone asked the old man: Why did you come back? Well, you know how it is, he answered. I'd put a little money on one side, my children were settled, I'd come to the age when a man thinks about retiring. That's the way things happen, life's like that. I said to my wife: Why don't we go back to the Valley? Let's go back—I want to go back to my own country. But you know what women are: Why? she asked—just as you did. And I replied: Where is our world; where do we belong? You said that? That's what I said—that's exactly what I did say. And your wife? My wife said: I'm a woman, my country is where my children are, they're flesh of my flesh, you know. I can't leave my children, they're part of me; so you go by yourself. And what did you say? I said: They're flesh of your flesh, I'll go alone. And here I am, I've come by myself. I can always come and see you, I told my wife, and she replied: That's all right, you can always come and see me. You do understand, don't you, that I can't leave my children? They're part of me. They're flesh of my flesh. Of course I understood; they're flesh of her flesh. But tell me, how's Machin?

While the old man was talking I thought I was on the point of discovering a secret, the secret of our native land; but he immediately changed the subject.

Another example: my friend Angiolino. He belongs to a patrician family in the Little Valley of God; he has a wealthy father, he owns lands and forests, and he has dozens and dozens of tenant farmers working for him and the future heir to his estates. Angiolino is an only son; uncles and aunts, cousins and grandparents, all keep him under their thumbs; they spend their days with him, looking after him, speaking of him. Oh Angiolino, Angiolino, all our hopes depend on you! And when he was twenty they began thinking of his marriage, of the woman who would become his wife, of the children who would be born to him. Oh Angiolino, our future depends on you! And my friend was silent; in the bosom of the greatest family in the Little Valley of God he was silent; and no one could give a reason for his dumbness. He was a highly cultivated youth, rather haughty and distant, morose, and with a hint of pain in his eyes, the suffering look of a man who must do something which he knows to be impossible. One day I asked him what was the matter with him; he did not reply immediately. The sky was dove-gray, a sky that threatened a storm; in the great stillness we could hear the creaking of the trees as they let fall the snow that had piled up on the branches. Listen! I said to him, there's always something in the countryside that sounds mournful. In summer, the grasshoppers and the crickets; in winter, the snow sliding from the tops of the trees. What's the matter with you, Angiolino? And then, suddenly, he began to talk; his voice was high-pitched and colorless, as though someone else were doing the talking for him. He said: My father wants me to marry, my family wants me to marry, everyone wants me to marry. But how can I get married? I am a homosexual.

"Homosexual" sounded like a word borrowed from a strange barbaric language that could not be the language of everyday. Listen, he said to me, I've been fighting this for nearly ten years. I first became aware of it at thirteen, when I fell in love with a boy in my class at school. How I cried in those days! I loved him so much. Even now I sometimes dream that I am clasping him in my arms and kissing his hair. Ivo, Ivo, I say to him; and I almost swoon with the feeling of protective tenderness he stirs in me. Until I was twenty I wept and suffered. After the tears came self-abuse. At the age when the mating urge is strongest I turned into a hermit, a man who can't bear even to be touched; and yet I was on fire with love, burning with love. At twenty I went to the brothel. No use. I went a second time and the girl made fun of me. She sat on the bed, utterly exhausted. But what's wrong with you, she said to me, what's wrong with you that you can't manage it? Oh, go to the devil! Since then I've been paying weekly visits; the girls send me away, they insult me, they jeer at me; but what can I do? I must marry; my family want me to marry; they all need a child of mine; and I must go on trying. And meanwhile I fall in love with every youth I happen to meet, peasants' sons, houseboys; I see them with their bare knees and short trousers; I look at their shining eyes and their ears and their hair; and O God, how much love there is in me, how much love! But what am I to do? I must go on trying. I must produce children for my family.

Once again, as I was walking in the quiet of the evening with the snowy whiteness of the earth underfoot and the gray pallor of the sky overhead, I seemed all of a sudden to grasp the significance of my native land. But Angiolino said: Give me a cigarette, will you? He lit it and added: Why is it that people don't understand certain things?

A third example: Felice the baker. Nowadays he's an old man who hobbles about painfully with a stick, but at the time when he learned that his son Bonifazio had a mistress he was still strong and active. Bonifazio has a timid, harassed look; on public holidays he sports colored waistcoats on which he hangs gold gewgaws. At the time of the story I'm going to relate he might have been about forty. One day Felice learned that every Saturday night his son went off to sleep with a peasant's widow, a very attractive woman. How did you manage this? he asked his son. Bonifazio reddened. How? Yes, how did you get her to sleep with you? Bonifazio looked at the ground. She loves me, he said. The old man hooted with laughter. But have you seen yourself? Look at yourself, Bonifazio, look at yourself, you fathead! Then he flew into a great rage. Fool, what do you do on these occasions? I give her money, Bonifazio admitted.

The whore, said the old man. The whore! He said it two or three times, then he said it again. He could not be five minutes in anyone's company without talking about Bonifazio and his mistress and saying: The whore! One day he chanced to be in the Shop at the same time as a farmer called Barnaba. The farmer heard him and felt like taking a rise out of him. If I hear you say a word like that once more, he declared, I'll inform the police. What word? said the old man. You know very well what word I mean. You can't say that word. Who do you think you are? It's slander. The old man looked at him with an air of stupefaction. But he gives her money, there's no doubt about it. . . . Doesn't matter, said Barnaba. That word is an insult, and you've no right to insult anyone. Well then, what ought I to say? demanded Felice. The farmer shrugged his shoulders. Why ask me? All I can tell you is that the word's an insult. Go to a lawyer. I know nothing about these things.

All right, said Felice, I'll go to a lawyer. He was a determined fellow who wouldn't be beaten; he harnessed his horse to his cart and off he went to the Town. Hat in hand, he introduced himself to the man of law and explained his case. You see what's happened; they sleep together and he pays her; and yet it seems I'm not entitled to call her a whore. The lawyer looked at him closely. What do you want me to do? he said at last. I want to know what I should say, the old man explained. I want to know if I can use that word. No, said the lawyer, better not; they might sue you. Ah, the swine! the old man exclaimed. They might sue me, eh? Well, tell me how I should put it so as not to get myself into trouble. Tell me what I can say to that cow.

Why don't you say "concubine"? suggested the lawyer. He went on looking at his client with obvious interest. Concubine, said Felice. Concubine. Does that mean the same thing? It does. The same thing as whore? Exactly. Good, what was it you said? Concubine. Concubine; good, write it down for me on a bit of paper; it's all Greek to me, you know. The lawyer did as he was asked and then pocketed his fee. That's money well spent, Felice said to himself as he went away.

From that day the old man got into the habit of looking at his bit of paper every time he referred to his son's mistress. He even went so far as to say concubine's son to a carter whom he hated like poison.

No doubt you will tell me that this is absurd. There's no sense in it; I'm just being frivolous. What connection has that with the secret soul of the Little Valley of God?

I tell you that there is a connection. Even in that anecdote may lie the explanation that I have been searching for all through my life. Our strength. Our violence. The fact that we are.

But who are we?

We are so strong that we can shake the mountains with our arms; and so weak that we crumple at the touch of a blade of grass. We are so generous that we can toss a morsel of our heart to a famished dog; and so mean that we can steal a crust of stale bread from an orphan's table. We are so lofty that we can touch the stars in the sky with our heads; and so lowly

(197)

that we can hide without shame in an animal's dung. We are so old that we can read the writings of the most distant past; and so new that we do not know the tongue of living men. We are so brave that we can die singing for a rag of cloth tied to a stick; and so cowardly that we cannot look into the depths of our own hearts. We are so virile that we would like to ravish all women; so effeminate that we are glad to yield to the first youth who comes our way. We are so violent that we can topple a whole world with nothing but the weight of our fury; and so docile that we can let ourselves be beaten for centuries without a murmur. We are so impatient that we cannot conceive of an instant's delay; and so patient that we can wait millenniums for our hour to strike. We are so soft that we can cover our fingers with jewels, our hair with perfumes, our limbs with sweet-smelling oils; and so hardy that we can live without a roof over our heads, without rest, without a place to sleep in, without bread. We are so just that we can define the idea of justice with absolute precision; and so deaf to the voice of justice that we raise pillars and monuments to a man who has killed and cheated. We are so thin-skinned that the blood of a lamb makes us retch in pity; and so insensitive that we can shed the blood of others with laughter on our lips as if we were at a carnival. We are so much the children of Christ that we cannot live without feeling Him constantly at our side; and so much the children of Satan that we kill Christ thousands of times in an hour. And we can love and hate, suffer and rejoice, be born and die, walk and keep still, slay and be slain, we can be the means and the end. We can be white and black and all the colors of the earth; and nothing is impossible for us; we are the salt of the earth.

But who are we really? What is our significance? What is the significance of our Country and ourselves? We know that we are everything and nothing; but who are we really?

This tale of the Little Valley of God has not been written without design. I tell stories and go on telling them, for I know that such is my destiny. But there is a purpose in every destiny. My purpose is to discover the secret significance of ourselves, our Country, and the world. The reality of our lives, which is Love.

(28)

A March to Glory Begins

IN these days Silvano's thoughts turned to the moment in the not far distant future when Barbara would at last be his. Gone were those hours of exaltation and ecstasy that had followed the fulfillment of the magic rite; he felt now that Sin, in its journeyings about the world, had chosen him among men, had rested its eyes upon him, and picked him out in the midst of the crowd. He felt the monster draw near; in the darkness he heard the padding of its feet and the sound of its rapid breathing. He knew that it was the whelp of Satan, inexorable as its father. He knew that all this spelled Death.

But it did not worry him and he even felt his body tingling with a sensation of unholy joy. Exultantly he waited for the great day.

He was equally indifferent to the transformation of the natural world that was taking place under his eyes. For him the dawns were now joyless and the skies bereft of light. The birds had fallen silent and earth's bosom no longer gave off its heady pungent scents. The universe was buried under an awesome silence that weighed upon him like lead. Over all brooded an air of expectancy and mystery. Silvano knew that he must cleave his way through it to reach the threshold on which someone was waiting, but he was not afraid. He lived as a man lives in a dream from which he knows he will awake.

It was the very core of the universe, the secret life-force in all created things, to which his senses were now dead. Once he had been aware of the throb and flutter of life in the rocks of the mountains, in the white pebbles of the brooks; for him they were now merely inert, lifeless objects. In his rambles about the countryside he now shamelessly insulted everything that he had respected and loved in his former existence; indifferently he tore branches from the vines, trampled the grass of the meadows underfoot, despoiled the flowers of the field, pillaged the hedge-rows along the streams as he went by; for the soundless agony of these creations of God no longer came to his ears. He was no better able to communicate with the tender hearts of animals; the dog that followed him faithfully till now had at last come to desert him, in sorrow and sadness. But Silvano hardly troubled himself about this defection; what was Aliofante to him if not some mongrel or other that he had found one night on a lonely road?

What was happening to Silvano happens to all men when life ceases to have meaning, when Satan steals or is about to steal upon their souls; Satan, the embodiment of what we call Sin or Death—for these are but different names for the one evil force, the great destroyer and denier of life.

In these days Silvano often went to Barbara's house at the summit of the pass. She would come to meet him and then shut herself up with him in one of the inner rooms of the old manor, where they would be safe from interruption. They rarely spoke; they sat holding each other's hands and gazing into each other's eyes. Sometimes Barbara would begin to cry and after a while Silvano would join her.

But their tears, produced by the tense silence, the hush of expectancy, like everything that befell them in their present existence, were painless and meaningless. They were useless tears.

One morning Silvano got up more quickly than usual, dressed hurriedly, and went out. The sun had not yet risen and the air was cool. The previous evening he had worked far into the night and written three different letters to three different people.

The letters were now spread out prominently on his desk, with the addresses carefully written in block capitals. At dead of night, having finished his correspondence, Silvano had taken a shiny black revolver from the drawer and looked it over. And now, as he strode along in the freshness of the early morning, he felt it weighing down his trouser pocket. The sensation was vaguely irksome. I won't be any good anyway, he said to himself, and as he walked he kept step to the rhythm of the words.

He marched with bowed head in the direction of Barbara's house. The stones on the precipitous path were wet and shining. The leaves of the trees and the gorse bushes that grew among the pebbles were still bathed in the dew that had fallen gently on the parched earth during the night.

Presently Silvano heard someone calling his name. He turned round and saw Emanuele sitting on the trunk of a fallen tree, with his white hands resting on his knees—watching him. The scene of this encounter was the exact spot where the path to Ca' d'Orso joins the gorge through which runs the mountain stream.

"Good morning, Professor," said Emanuele.

Silvano looked at him with a sort of resentment. He forgot at that moment how desperately he had wanted to meet the mysterious young man and how passionately he had exclaimed: Oh, if I could only talk to him for a moment! He merely told himself that at this moment Emanuele was standing in the way of his plans and delaying their fulfillment. So he did not stop; he merely slackened his pace and returned the greeting.

"Good morning."

Emanuele got up and walked a little way with him.

"You are in a hurry?" he said. "I'd like a few words with you." And he laid a hand on the other's arm.

Silvano swung round. "I must go," he said coldly. "Forgive me, I'm very late."

"I'm sorry," the young man murmured. He was smiling and his eyes had the same calm expression.

From deep within him, drifting up from a buried layer of memories, something rose for a moment into Silvano's brain; his irritation faded away and he said in a pleasanter tone, "Forgive me, I'm sorry too. I really am very sorry. But can't we arrange to meet at some other time? Tomorrow, for instance."

The young man's smile vanished.

"That won't be possible." He shook his head with a gentle obstinacy.

"Why not?" Silvano asked sharply. His former exasperation was returning; it annoyed him that the young man could speak with such assurance and self-possession. After all, he was only some laborer or other; what right had he to put on the airs of a superman and behave with this lofty detachment? Here he was, standing in the way as if to bar the path; what business was it of his? The sight of him and the realization that he was blocking the way stirred Silvano's resentment, transformed it into anger. "Why not?" he said again, more loudly. "When I tell you I haven't time to stop now, I mean it. Just be patient, we'll see each other again. I'd be glad if you'd get out of my way. And no more of this talk about not being able to fix up another meeting." He pushed past him. "See you again soon. Good-bye."

Emanuele gazed after him; he seemed disturbed and anxious. "I'm afraid you may have forgotten the oil for your lamp," he said.

Silvano was already some distance off, but he heard him. What oil? he wondered. What oil is that man talking about? Really, what a conversation. Aloud he exclaimed, "This country is full of madmen!"

In a few minutes he arrived at Barbara's house, where he was expected.

See, he has arrived at the old house; mark how solid and ancient it looks in the morning light. The sky is clear, the grass of the fields is still wet with dew, the sun, eternally spinning on its course, has now risen to illumine the earth. The gateway of Ca' d'Orso is black with age: the stone architrave is a little lighter in color; the old rough-cast walls have been covered for centuries with layers of blackened whitewash. Where is the door-knocker? See, he raps and raps and raps. O Silvano, can it be thy heart that is knocking thus? And now there is the sound of footsteps on the staircase.

(202)

What can I do for this child of mine? I have begotten him; until I created him he was as nonexistent as the ideas no one has ever conceived, the notes no musician has ever struck, the colors no painter has ever put upon canvas. I created him out of nothing. O Silvano, it was the fusion of my heart and mind and imagination that brought thee into the world. Silvano, thou art my child. And I have created for thee a world, a girl, a house, a heaven, and I have brought hither a Presence—for thy salvation.

But what can I do for him now? Nothing; he is slipping away from me. I cannot tell whether his future actions will mean death or life, joy or grief; all that is veiled from my sight. He is my child, and I can do nothing for him. I am not the arbiter of his destiny, and I have no knowledge of what is in store for him. I can say to my heart: Be still. That is all; I can do nothing for thee, Silvano, my child.

See, he raps at the door. Can you not hear the sound of his knocking as it echoes in the morning air? O Silvano, my child, that sound is the knocking of thy heart.

Silvano climbed the staircase. Pale as death, the girl stood halfway down the steps, waiting for him. They were alone; he took her hand and pressed his lips to it. As always when he did this, he was trembling. He said to her, "Barbara, how cold your hand is."

"I love you," the girl said, and she held up her face to him. She was pale and her eyes shone. She led the way across the vast floors of the house until they came to the drawing room. "Everyone is still asleep, but I knew you would come, Silvano."

"Is that true?"

"Yes, it's true."

"What's torturing us?" Silvano asked after a pause.

She shook her head. "I don't know. We're certainly in torment. D'you know that I didn't sleep a wink last night? I was thinking of you, I kept telling myself that you'd be sure to come."

"Is that true?"

"Yes, it's true," she repeated.

"I couldn't sleep either," said Silvano.

(203)

"Just like me."

"In fact neither of us could sleep. Isn't it strange? But d'you know why?"

"I think so," said Barbara.

"I'm sure you do," Silvano declared. He was sitting stiffly on his chair but as he spoke he leaned toward her. "The time has come, Barbara."

"That's just what I've been telling myself," she murmured. "Strange, how the idea entered my mind. What about you? What put it into your head?"

"Many things. It began to dawn on me last night after I'd left you."

"That's just when I began to understand."

"D'you know what will happen, once it's all over?" Silvano's voice sounded far away and he seemed to be talking like a man in a dream.

"I think I do," said Barbara.

"Tell me then."

"Why d'you want me to tell you?"

"I want to know, that's all."

"But it's so hard."

"Never mind, tell me. You must tell me, Barbara."

"I can't. It's more than I can bear."

Silvano laughed, a little bitterly. "All right, I'll tell you. We shan't love each other any more. When it's all over, we shan't love each other any more."

The girl avoided his eyes. "Exactly," she said. "I think that's how it will be."

"That's how it will be," said Silvano. "I've always known it, I've known it from the very beginning."

They were silent for a moment, and they were careful not to look at each other's eyes.

"But what's bewitching us?"

"I don't know," said Silvano. "I don't know, Barbara. I feel terribly unhappy. Do you?"

"I think so, I don't know. Are we really so unhappy?"

"Yes, we're unhappy."

(204)

"Why? What's this spell that's been cast on us?"

They were silent. Then Barbara said, "Well, what are we to do?"

"There's only one remedy left to us," Silvano said.

The girl grew paler than ever. "What's that?"

"Bring time to a stop," he replied in a loud voice. "Make that moment ours. Prevent it from escaping. Halt it forever."

She bent her head, remained thus for several minutes, and heaved a sigh.

"Yes," she said.

"There's nothing else we can do, my darling. Really, there's no other way out."

"Yes," she agreed, "it's the only thing we can do."

"How I love you, Barbara, my darling."

Love, love; that torturing word is everywhere and ever present—on every page of this book, at every hour of the day, at every moment of our lives. Everyone is either in love or would like to be, and love brings suffering to all, whether it comes their way or not. Everyone wants to live for it and everyone is ready to die for it. That is the true meaning of life; none escapes, we are all slaves of love. How I love you, Barbara, said Silvano.

After a while he said, "Barbara, we've got to do it, so why don't we do it now, this instant? Barbara, let's do it now. I can't go on any longer, my darling, I can't go on any longer."

She put a hand on his arm.

"Calm yourself. What's the matter with you?"

He started and drew away from her. "How should I know? I'm shivering, I don't feel myself, I think this is the end. Barbara, I'm trembling. Let's leave this house, Barbara, let's go a long way off. Now, this instant. . . . Barbara, I don't know what's the matter, but do listen to me and let's go!"

She looked into his eyes; she could do that now.

"Why of course," she said. Her voice was gentle and maternal. She put a hand on his brow. "Whatever you wish, Silvano."

"Let's go," he said, "let's go away."

(205)

"We will," said Barbara. "That's settled. Oh Silvano, how I love you!"

See, they are leaving the room, they are going down the stairs. What will happen to them? Life or death, good or ill, beauty or ugliness—what will happen to them? A mighty dream has them in thrall. Hearken, good people; now begins a march to glory.

(29)

"She hath washed my feet with her tears and wiped them away with her hair"

FOR several days Maddalena Amato had been seriously ill. And from the diary which she never failed to keep religiously, whatever the circumstances, we can see that it would have been beyond the power of any doctor in the world to cure the malady from which she was suffering.

Evening, September 6th

I don't know what's the matter with me. I cried all last night. Salvatore Gasparri came to see me just after noon, but I had to ask him to go away. He agreed willingly enough; no doubt he was shaken when he saw how white I looked. Yesterday evening, when Gentilino Lelli came, I had to treat him in the same fashion. He went away too, but rather scornfully.

All the time I want to cry.

Night, September 7th

Someone must have cast a spell on me. Once again I've passed a sleepless night. Finding sleep impossible, I got up, knelt down, and tried to pray. I must admit that my prayers didn't help me much; in fact they only made me feel more upset. I can't understand what's wrong with me. I opened my window, leaned on the balustrade, and waited for the dawn. A tomcat was howling not far from my window.

Yesterday evening I had to send Otello away. As he took his leave he inquired with an affectionate smile: What's the matter with you? Are you in love? I ask myself what this love is; haven't I had only too much of it in my life? The idea of going to bed with a man fills me now with a strange repulsion.

If that's what love is, there's no denying that love causes a lot of suffering.

Evening, September 9th

The terrible and indefinable sickness that torments me day and night shows no sign of abating. And I can't find any consolation in good works.

I told Sauro Diamente to go away. He was annoyed and nearly made a scene. After he had gone I cried and cried.

I'd far rather be beaten than have relations with a man. I don't hate anyone, no; but the very thought of my past life fills me with horror. Holy Virgin Mary, on this day when we celebrate thy birth, have pity upon me!

I pray and pray and I can find no comfort. Emanuele . . .

Evening, September 8th

I have hardly strength enough to write; my face is streaming with tears. I should never have thought one could weep so much and still go on living. I am very weak, I can eat nothing; I am reduced to a shadow of what I was. As I was in the garden feeding the chickens, Don Marcello happened to pass along the road. He gazed at me and then he smiled with such kindness in his smile that I felt myself blushing from head to foot, and I ran into the house.

I'm ashamed of myself, of what I have done, of my whole life. I hate men, I hate all men, I hate the whole world. I wish all men were dead, and myself too!

Later

Lord, forgive me for what I have just written! But I wish I had never been born, or rather I wish I were something blotted from human memory, utterly forgotten.

Afternoon, September 10*th*

I know that the men of the Valley are very angry with me. If they would put me out of my misery I should bless them for it!

At the Shop the men had at last been driven to admit that Maddalena might be ill. For three days everyone believed it or pretended to believe it. On the fourth Sauro Diamente struck the table a great blow with his fist and exclaimed, "If that little bitch isn't just putting it on, you can cut my head off!" Actually he said nothing about his head but alluded to quite another part of his anatomy. Suddenly there was a great silence in the Shop.

Young Fiorello, who had been leaning his elbows on the table, got up and went over to the man who had just spoken. His eyes were blazing with anger and the lower part of his jaw was trembling. He stepped up to Sauro Diamente and said to him in a hard voice, "Just say that again, will you?"

"Boys . . ." began the woman who kept the Shop. But Sauro Diamente did not hear her. He got up, looked round arrogantly, stuck out his chest, and exclaimed, "What I said was, if that little bitch isn't joking, you can cut my——off!"

Fiorello struck him full in the face; they heard his jaw crack and he fell against the wall. A great uproar followed. In the end Fiorello, surrounded by his friends, had to admit, "Bah! Maybe Sauro Diamente is right."

And so, at the Shop, there was no longer anyone to champion Maddalena Amato.

Two days later a procession consisting of about a score of men left the Shop and set off toward Maddalena Amato's house. For the most part they were young and sturdy, with rough hands accustomed to manual labor, to working the harsh earth of the Little Valley of God. Sauro Diamente was in the van; and on the short journey they made plenty of noise. When they arrived in front of Maddalena's door they stopped and began to whistle.

This happened toward ten in the morning, on a beautiful day, full of warmth and sunshine. Gentle Maddalena, who had once been the very incarnation of the lusty health and vigor of the

(209)

young folk of the Valley, was now lying pale and still, like a corpse, on her unmade bed. When the noise of the mob came to her ears she got up, trembling all over. She who had never known the meaning of fear was suddenly seized by a crazy terror.

She went to the kitchen and opened the shutters. When she appeared at the window the catcalling broke out again, louder than ever. Sauro Diamente took three paces forward and said coldly, "You bitch."

It was the tone in which the words were uttered, rather than the words themselves, that restored something of Maddalena's old self-possession. Her awareness of danger gave her back her courage, and it was with a bold front that she asked, "What do you want with me?"

Sauro Diamente went forward under the window, his hair glistening in the sunshine, his lips clearly defined in his great swarthy face, and exclaimed, "What we have always wanted, baby. Your body." And he broke into a harsh laugh.

As she heard that laugh Maddalena felt the blood freeze in her veins. The fluttering panic of a moment before now took complete hold of her. With a note of entreaty in her voice she protested, "But you know very well that I'm ill. Leave me alone."

The men said nothing; Sauro Diamente seemed quite un-affected. He was immediately below the window, and looking up he sneered, "So you're ill, are you? I just don't believe it, baby, nobody believes it. Ill or not, we want you just the same, it makes no difference to us." On this sunny morning he was dominated to his shame by those twin furies, Violence and Lust. He went on, "What's all this fuss about? Shall I tell you something, baby? Even if you had the most shameful disease in the world I'd still go to bed with you!" And pushing open the door he made his way into the house.

The other men did not move. Maddalena remained at the window for a moment as if out of her wits; then she heard the man's foot on the staircase. And she began to shriek in a frenzy of despair.

Having finished the celebration of mass, Don Marcello retired to the vestry and divested himself of his robes; then he knelt down in the choir of the church and began to pray. Rapt in his devotions, he paid no attention at first to the savage yelling of the mob outside Maddalena's house, but her screams brought him up with a start. Almost without knowing what he was doing, he got hurriedly to his feet, passed in front of the altar, bowed, and rushed out of the church.

He was scarcely outside when the sunlight smote him a violent blow. The sky was deep blue, the mists had rolled away, and it seemed to stretch beyond the edge of the world. The countryside lay smiling in the sunlight, crowned by soaring blue mountains, a little darker than the sky. The shrieks rent the stillness, and Don Marcello asked himself: Whatever is the matter? Then his eye fell on the group of men, silently waiting.

His eye fell on the group of men, and the first thing that struck him was the contrast between the shrieking of the woman, who was hidden from view, and the men's stubborn silence. The contrast was sharp and startling; it seemed symbolic of a great injustice. For a few seconds Don Marcello stood thus without moving or uttering a word, quite unable to grasp the true significance of what was happening; then he pulled himself together and looked up at the window. He saw a man fling himself on a woman and try to bend her to his will, regardless of her shrieks and struggles. The woman was Maddalena Amato. Maddalena, thought Don Marcello, and at that moment something stirred in him—a blazing anger, such as he had never known before in all his life, suddenly shook him to the depths of his being. He had a sensation of physical pain, as though someone were raining blows on him, and he gasped for breath; he looked round for something that would give outlet to his raging resentment. Beside the church door he noticed a massive cudgel which a stranger had apparently left there and forgotten. He pounced on it, snatched it up and, brandishing it like a club, mounted Maddalena's narrow staircase at a run. All the while, without even realizing what he was doing, he kept shouting, "You devil, you devil!" His voice resounded in the well of the narrow stair like a clap of thunder.

Sauro Diamente had managed to wrench off the clothes that were covering Maddalena's breasts; frenziedly, he clasped her in his arms, tried to imprison her legs between his, and pressed his mouth to her skin. He was thirsting for her flesh; avidly he sought her lips, her throat, and the white breasts that jutted, amazingly pointed and provocative, from her torn gown. At the same time he was struggling hard to pin down the woman's legs with his own, crush them between his knees, and eventually possess her. Intent on pushing aside the last of her defenses, he slipped his hand toward the hem of her gown; to tear it from her, to have his way with her, would then have been the work of a moment, no trouble at all. Inflamed by this fierce struggle, lost in the blind fury of his passion, Sauro Diamente did not even notice the presence of Don Marcello, did not hear the curses leveled at him, did not see the priest stop on the threshold, with a stick tightly gripped in his hands.

Don Marcello advanced into the room and struck him savagely over the head with the full weight of his club. And uttering a low groan Sauro Diamente sank to the floor.

Still holding his stick with both hands, Don Marcello began to examine the body stretched out at his feet. The heat was less overpowering, or so it seemed. A feeling of complete emptiness gripped the pit of his stomach and made his head swim. For a few seconds longer he kept gazing down at Sauro Diamente; then he raised his eyes, as if looking for some other object to engage his attention; but very soon he was forced to lower them again. He could not drag them away from the man lying senseless at his feet, from the contorted body, the swarthy face, the gleaming oily locks. He went on staring until he became conscious of someone moaning and gasping for breath close beside him; then the spell broke and he was able to turn his thoughts to the young woman, who sat huddled under the window.

"Please put on your clothes." And very slowly, moving one step at a time and still grasping his stick, he crossed over to the window. Maddalena shrank away. "It's unfortunate, very unfortunate," the priest stuttered, and he heaved a gentle sigh.

When he had reached the window, Don Marcello let go his stick and leaned out. He saw the men whose silence had made such a deep impression on him as he came out of the church; they were still silent. But their silence had quite another meaning now. Don Marcello sensed it and understood that now they were waiting for something very different from what they had been waiting for then; something equally mysterious and important, but different: *mysterious yes, but different*. There they are waiting, the priest said to himself. Then, raising his voice, he asked them, "What do you want, my children?" and in the quiet of the sunlit countryside his question echoed like a bugle blast. Yes, the priest repeated to himself, they're waiting. And he said again, "What do you want?"

The men made no reply. Don Marcello looked at them for a moment and then said, "Go home, my children." And he saw that this was exactly what the men had been waiting for him to say; what they expected of him.

But they expected something more; other words. Everything was so clear now. Don Marcello fully understood that he had to talk to them. He had to talk to them, that followed inevitably. Everything was so straightforward.

"My children," he said then, "I don't know what brought you here—or rather I do know, only too well; it was one of those abominable impulses that often rise up in our hearts; but it seems to me there's no point in describing your feelings. Let's be clear about what happened. I was praying in the church when I heard shrieks. I ran to this house and I saw a man trying to ravish a woman; and the woman was half-naked and pleading for mercy. I had a stick in my hands; I can't remember now where I got it from, but it's a fact that at that particular moment I found myself with a stick in my hands. Goodness knows where I could have picked it up. Right; I had a stick in my hands; I flung myself on the man and I struck him on the head, and now here he is stretched out on the floor. He isn't showing any sign of movement and he may be either dead or alive—who can tell? My children, do you know who reduced him to this state? It was I—I, an old priest; at the very moment when I have a feeling that my days are numbered, at the very moment when I've just discovered the true meaning of this thing that I thought I understood and in fact knew nothing whatsoever about—this thing that we human beings call love. Love, love! the word is on our lips at every hour of the day; but how very few of us know what it means! Yes, my children, it was at such a moment that I did what I have just done. And I'm quite sure that if I told you what my feelings are as I stand here you would be extremely surprised, for I should have to say to you: My children, I am happy! I am glad to have struck this man, proud to have done such a deed; and if it had to be done again I would do it again. Yes, I couldn't stop myself from beginning all over again now that I know how one feels when doing such a deed! And all this is the result of having discovered the meaning of that word love; and everything appears to me now in a truer light; as it is written in the Gospel: the soul of man is as the temple of God, woe unto him who violates its sanctity! Yes, it is written in the Gospel. And that is why I tell you—I, an old priest, I who have baptized not only you but your fathers and mothers, I who am on the brink of the grave: Go home, my children, and never forget what has just happened. Never forget it; tell it to all so that the memory of it shall endure forever; let the whole of the Little Valley of God learn of it from your lips. Say: that was what Don Marcello did, that was what he told you. And say he added as his last word that he was very happy about what he had done, that he was almost sure it was one of the finest actions of his miserable life!" Here the old man paused for a second, drew a handkerchief from his pocket, and mopped his brow; then, heaving a sigh, he added, "And now, go away. But first, will two of you lads volunteer to come up and carry this man back to his home? He must be heavy."

The priest left the window, turned to Maddalena, and said, "It's all over, Signorina." His voice was kindly and tired.

Two young men appeared on the threshold.

"Father," they said, "give us Sauro Diamente's body."

"Over there," said the priest, and he added, "Poor fellow, so it's Sauro Diamente, is it? The son of Gustavino Il Moro? Never mind, he won't be any the worse, you'll see."

Without a word the two youths carried the unconscious man away. Don Marcello was left alone with the woman, much to his embarrassment. He began to examine the room with a great show of interest. Maddalena had put her clothes on again as best as she could, but it seemed that she did not dare leave the corner of the window, and her wide-open eyes were still filled with terror and stupefaction. The priest walked a few paces across the room, toying absently with the wretched trinkets on the furniture. He touched a majolica statuette of St. Rita with the tips of his fingers and murmured, "Pretty."

At that moment a voice from the road below broke into the silence. It was the high-pitched, plaintive voice of a woman who had apparently been running hard and was out of breath.

"Don Marcello, Don Marcello, come down quickly, Don Marcello-o!"

The priest listened attentively, muttering something to himself. Then he flung up his arms.

"Today is a day of miracles. Good-bye, Signorina." And making for the door with a briskness surprising in a man of his years, he bounded from the room.

For a few seconds Maddalena Amato stood motionless; then Emanuele came in.

He was in his usual working clothes, threadbare in places and carefully darned. He had come up the staircase so quietly that Maddalena's first reaction was one of astonishment; then she looked at his feet and saw that they were bare. As if in a dream the thought passed through her mind: That's why I didn't hear him come up—and suddenly her cheeks flamed and she felt herself blushing all over.

Emanuele stood smiling on the threshold. "Good day," he said.

Maddalena could not reply.

"May I sit down?" he asked. "I was passing, I saw the door open, and I couldn't resist the temptation to come and pay you a little visit."

Maddalena was still trembling. She was incapable of making any movement, but she managed to get out one word, "Yes."

Emanuele sat down and began to look round the room. At last his gaze rested on Maddalena and remained there for a moment.

"How nice it is here!" he exclaimed gaily.

The young woman continued to stare at him with her great wide-open eyes, and at last she replied, "It's a poor room. I'm poor."

"Of course I wasn't talking so much about the room," the visitor explained. "I was merely remarking that it's nice to be here with you."

Again Maddalena made no movement.

"Me?" she said.

"Yes. You, Maddalena."

Then, slowly and with dignity, Maddalena began to undress. She took off the great shawl that she had wrapped round her chest; and her white breasts appeared through the torn gown. Swiftly she took off her gown, revealing her white arms, her white legs, her white body.

She said, "If that's what you want, I can still do it for you." Her voice was gentle but not happy, resigned rather than joyful. She glanced in the direction of the big bed.

Emanuele went on smiling at her, distantly, oh so distantly.

"No, Maddalena," he said, "that isn't what I want. But thank you all the same."

She stopped beside the bed, almost naked.

"No?" she murmured. "You don't want to?" And suddenly she blushed furiously.

"You mustn't sacrifice yourself for me," Emanuele said gently.

Maddalena's voice hardened.

"I'm not sacrificing myself!" she cried. "I've done it for so many others in my life! I've always done it, I can always do it, don't you understand?" She bent her head. "I can still do it for you. It would give me pleasure to do it for you."

"Why?" the young man asked, with his distant smile.

Maddalena did not look up. "There's nothing I wouldn't do for you," she murmured.

"Why?" Emanuele asked for the second time.

Then the woman suddenly came to life, as though waking from a deep sleep. She raised her head.

"Why?" she cried in a shrill voice. "Because there's something I must tell you. I, Maddalena Amato, I who have given myself freely and gladly to all comers, I, the harlot of the Little Valley of God, I'm in love with you, I'm in love with you! I'm in love with you!" she shouted, and then her voice failed her. "I love you, I've loved you since the moment I saw you, and there's

(216)

nothing I can do myself, Emanuele, I just can't stop loving you! And though my love for you has made me hate every man in the world, though the life I've led up to now fills me with shame and disgust, though I'm ashamed of my body and look upon it with loathing—yet, in spite of all, you'd only have to say the word, Emanuele, and I'd give myself to you, I'd give myself to you day and night, for ever and ever! Oh Emanuele!" Then she knelt on the floor and began to kiss his feet, to touch them with her hands. She was weeping and crying, and she spoke wildly, without thinking what she was saying. "Your feet, Emanuele! Oh, Emanuele! I've always loved you, have pity on me! Oh, who will have pity on me? No one, no one, no one. Oh, I've always loved you, I've waited so long for you! Oh, have pity on me, Emanuele!" She went on weeping and crying, her arms clasped round his feet. "Oh Emanuele, Emanuele!" And suddenly she felt the marks of two healed wounds, one on either foot, like two deep furrows, and she put her lips against them, filled with tenderness and love and a longing to lose herself in him. "Oh Emanuele, your poor feet! Oh Emanuele, I've loved you so much, have pity on me, I've loved you so much!"

Emanuele let her do as she wished; and the distant smile was still on his face.

(30)

The March to Glory Goes On

THE sun was already shedding its beams over the world and the
earth was full of light. But Silvano and Barbara saw only the
light that burned in their eyes. Darkness covered their souls,
their bodies, the whole world; the luminous globe which
the human race inhabits seemed to them on this morning to
have reduced itself to the radiance shining from their eyes, beyond which nothing existed. The sun in the heavens, the leaves
on the trees, the reawakening of life with the coming of daylight, the sap flowing under every clod of earth, the pristine
essence of all dumb creation—stones, trees, animals—nothing of
this existed any more. Nothing. They were alone in a desert.

Silvano was explaining to Barbara in a strangled voice, "We're
alone, Barbara." He gave a ghost of a laugh and then asked with
a kind of strained enjoyment, "Can you imagine a time when
there were other people in the world besides ourselves?"

Barbara kept her eyes on the ground; perhaps because the fire
that smoldered under Silvano's eyelids was more than she could
bear.

"Sweetheart," she said, "what are you talking about? What
people?"

Silvano laughed out loud. "Those who go about the world,
those who once existed."

"No," said Barbara, "you're wrong. Before us, no one ever
existed."

"You think not?"

"I'm sure of it. No one."

Silvano was content with this reply. Nevertheless he asked, "What about your grandmother?"

"What grandmother?"

"Yours. Donna Elena."

"She has never existed," Barbara said firmly.

He kept on questioning her. "What about Donna Teresa—the woman who wanted me to marry her daughter?"

"She has never existed," Barbara said again.

"And the lady who took me into her house—Carmela Cavalli?"

"She has never existed," the girl said for the third time. "We have always been alone in the world, Silvano. Just you and I."

"Adam and Eve," Silvano said. And he seized hold of her hand. How it burned against his. . . .

They resumed their walk. The sun was now high in the heavens, but they were unaware of it. Suddenly Silvano asked:

"What about Maddalena? And Gustavino?"

"I've never heard of them," Barbara said. And she was speaking the truth, for on this warm September morning Love had made her a new woman.

"This is very beautiful," Silvano said with emotion. And then he asked, "Tell me, what are we going to do?"

What are they going to do? The storyteller cannot answer; once again he must move away, once again he must say to himself: O heart, be still! And yet he would so much like to break in and alter the course of events. Everything impels him to intervene—his feelings, the story of his life, all the things he has longed for and never had, all the things that have come to him unsought. How marvelous it would be to turn the world upside down, to hurl the stars to the bottom of the abyss, to banish forever the travail that men have been enduring through all the ages, and make way for the triumph of Love, whose glory is the glory of this earth! But all this is only a dream. The storyteller cannot escape from the fixed objectivity that is required of him; and his words can never do more than bear witness to the secret stirrings of his heart.

He is chained by his obligation to be impartial, and he bears the full grievous weight of his shackles. He can neither laugh nor weep, he can neither sway nor foresee events, he can neither pray nor determine a course of action; forced into indifference by fatal necessity, he can only tell his tale, for such is his appointed lot. All of us carry in our hearts the story of Silvano and Barbara, we know that the fate of the world is linked with their fate; those words "What are we going to do" can be heard breaking over the shores of the earth like the flaring of the trumpets that shall sound on the Day of Judgment. For what they are going to do does not concern them alone, but the rest of us too, we people of the Little Valley of God whose name signifieth world, universe, earth—the Earth; and each of us is bound by the others, Don Defendente to blind Gio, Simonetta Grei to young Piero the Vagabond, Don Marcello to Gastone Ferro; and all other men to other men; I who write at this table am bound to thee, reader whom I know not and shall never know; the man who is not bound to other men does not exist; and the death of one is in some sort the death of all, the pain of one is the pain of all, the life of one is the life of all, and a plot of earth is the whole Earth. That is why the question Silvano has asked Barbara is our question too: the love of one is the love of all.

The love of all. But give ear, good people. The march to glory goes on.

Neither of them answered the question. After a few moments Silvano stopped and asked, "What's holding us?"

"Who," Barbara corrected him.

"Who's holding us, Barbara? Don't you feel as if there's some kind of presence within us?"

"It's Love that has entered into us," she said. "Can't you hear him?"

Silvano listened intently and then remarked, "That doesn't sound like Love."

"Who is it then?" Barbara asked.

Silvano would not say it, but he had realized that the intruder was Death.

(220)

"Listen," he said after a moment. The sun had risen high, very high in the heavens.

"Sweetheart?"

"I met Emanuele. You know, the young man everyone talks about. Would you believe it, he didn't want me to come and see you." Silvano gave a short laugh; and then he noticed that she was silent. Brutally, he questioned her, "Tell me, why don't you laugh?"

"I don't know," Barbara answered dreamily.

Silvano flew into a rage.

"Laugh!" he shouted. "Why don't you laugh? What's Emanuele to us? So far as we're concerned," he stormed, getting more and more worked up, "Emanuele doesn't matter in the least, he doesn't exist!" Then, noticing that the girl was not laughing even now, he caught her by the shoulders and shook her with unconscious brutality.

"Laugh!" he shouted. "For God's sake, laugh!"

"Don't pronounce that name, Silvano," Barbara murmured. And she began to cry.

Silvano stopped. The sight of the tears running down her cheeks caused him acute anguish. He took her in his arms.

"Darling," he said tenderly. "My sweet. Don't cry, Barbara, darling." And he kissed the tears from her cheeks. "Darling, don't cry. Barbara, why are you crying?" The sun was blazing fiercely in the heavens.

"I don't know," she said; and then she asked, "When will the time come?"

Silvano saw that she was trembling.

"Soon," he said. "Soon, my sweet. Oh, my darling."

They sat down on the grass of a meadow, in the shade of a great oak. But, beyond the radiance of their eyes, they saw nothing.

(31)

The Visions, Death, and Glory of a Poor Servant of God

IN his desperate hurry Don Marcello had forgotten that he was clutching the letter which was, in fact, what had sent him dashing off under the blazing sun. His shiny black robe was accentuating the whiteness of the sheet of notepaper, making it stand out with cruel prominence, and the flooding sunlight heightened the sharpness of the contrast. Light, light . . . the whole earth was dissolved in light; it drenched every clod of earth and every tree; the very droning of the insects was suffused with it. The letter shone in the priest's hand like a mirror; or like a piece of glass caught in the shine of a lamp.

Don Marcello was hastening along the main road, and the hem of his cassock was very soon ringed with a broad circle of white dust. It was Signorina Carmela who had come shrieking under the window and brought him the letter. Now she was toiling behind him; she wanted to catch him up and by a super-human effort she was dragging herself along on her poor swollen legs. Holy Mary, the old man's going much too fast for me. Dear God, how does he manage to run like that? And oh, that boy, that boy! It was a long time (how long? ah, many, many years) since she had allowed herself to call the Professor a boy. That was what she called him now. And in her anguish she added: Perhaps he's already dead, we'll never know.

But Don Marcello had turned round.

"Don't try to follow me!" he cried to the poor woman. "It's much better for me to go on alone; you women are often more of a hindrance than a help. Holy Mary, if you want to make yourself useful go and see Barbara's grandmother. Go and keep her company!"

And seeing that Signorina Carmela, in spite of what he had said, was redoubling her efforts to limp after him, he flapped his hands at her as if he were chasing away hens. "Off you go, be off with you. Shoo, shoo!"

What an extraordinary morning this was!

Now the priest left the main road and plunged along a stony path. I'll get there quicker this way; the wood, then Martino's vineyard, then the wood again, that never-ending wood, and at last the meadows. Holy Mary, the meadows. . . . The path was strewn with sharp pebbles; from time to time the priest trod on a stone more pointed than the rest and then he felt a fierce pain running up his leg as far as the knee; higher still, as far as the groin. The heat was overpowering and his face was streaming with sweat; what an astonishing morning! Presently the old man said to himself: Would you believe it, I've forgotten my handkerchief! Angrily he scolded himself: You stupid old priest, you old donkey. . . .

Lord, if only I can get there in time. The cicadas shrilled around him, the eternal cicadas of the Little Valley of God. How late was it? What with sun time and clock time you got completely muddled. How blue and cloudless the sky was! The dog days had come back; what weather for September! The path kept on rising and the priest reached the edge of the wood. Ah, he said to himself, if I go on walking like this I shall be there in thirty minutes. One, two, three, four, five, twenty. . . . Half an hour isn't really very long. But can I go on walking like this? He felt his heart thudding in his chest like a drum. Thud, thud, thud. How much longer can I go on like this? You old donkey, he said to himself, is this all you can do? Why, you're no good for anything. Come along, you old donkey, get a move on, get a move on. . . .

All of a sudden he realized that he was holding a sheet of paper in his hand. What's this? he wondered. It seemed to him that he had never set eyes on it before. What's this? Then something awoke in the inner recesses of his memory. It's the letter, he explained to himself. Professor Silvano's letter. And what a mess I've made of it! He felt almost like laughing. I've been using it as a handkerchief without realizing what I was doing. Gracious heaven, the letter! What a stupid old fellow I am, I might be in my second childhood. . . . The notepaper was moist, sticky, and shapeless; nevertheless the old priest kept on clutching it in his hand. Professor Silvano's letter. The heat was suffocating and Don Marcello began to undo the buttons of his cassock. After all, he said to reassure himself, there's no one to see me. But something answered him: The Lord sees you. Yes, for Thou art everywhere, O Lord, the heavens and the earth are full of Thy glory. Ah, never mind, the Lord will forgive me. Heavenly Father, Thou wilt forgive me.

Then he began to think about this business. The shade of the wood was now protecting him a little from the heat—but very little, alas, too little. The world has gone mad, Don Marcello said to himself, and immediately the reason was clear to him; the Lord has forsaken it. This generation is out of its senses; in my time it was different. He tried to imagine this sort of thing happening in the days of his youth—when, for instance, he was a student at the great seminary on the banks of the river. The letter said in effect: Dear Signorina Carmela, I'm going to kill myself with Barbara, my fiancée, because—but why? why? let's see, ah yes—because I'm sure our love will come to an end and I want it to last for ever and ever. We shall walk into the fields that were mined and we shall be blown sky-high; I want our love to last for ever and ever. Isn't that what the letter says, more or less? I want our love to be eternal. Lord, what a word. Eternal, eternal. But what is eternity? It was said of old: Before Thy face, O Lord, the seasons. . . . Very well. And if the Father Superior, now, had received a letter like that, how would he have taken it, Holy Virgin?

The Father Superior. And the thought of his old master

stirred a gentle emotion in Don Marcello as he toiled breath-lessly along the path. I was young then, he thought with a tight-ness in his throat. The great seminary on the banks of the river! Once again he saw the recreation ground, the tall green and white poplars, the willows, the shady oaks. That bench he was so fond of—wasn't it under one of those oaks? I picked it out from among all the others on the very day I entered the seminary. What a funny little chap I was then with my cropped hair and frightened eyes! And Mama came with me on that day, carrying a haversack stuffed with cakes and a roll of sausage and pairs of socks. She was anxious and excited. Eat the sausage, she whis-pered in my ear; they'll hardly give you enough to eat in this place and my little boy must keep his strength up. Eat the sau-sage, my precious. My dear little priest must keep his strength up. That was all you thought about, Mama—the roll of sausage and your ambitions for your son. Your son a priest; what a bless-ing to have a priest in the family! You were only a poor work-ing woman and all your hopes were centered on that. You kept on talking about the sausage, but wasn't it to hide your tears; tell me, Mama, wasn't it to hide the tears that came secretly into your eyes on that autumn morning? Ah yes, I'm pretty sure it was. And afterwards there was the stone bench, my old friend, my favorite place for reverie. Often on a Sunday I would ask to be excused from going for a walk with the others, and I would sit down there and read and think all by myself, in peace and soli-tude, until the sun vanished behind the horizon. I used to read the lives of the saints: St. Catherine, St. Teresa, St. Rita, St. Margaret, St. Anne. The saints I loved long ago. I loved the saints in those days.

And now this old man hastening through the wood, bent by the weight of his years, the effort of walking so fast, and the burden of his acute anxiety—this old man was summoning up the thoughts and emotions that had filled him in those days now gone forever. The saints—the chaste affection he had for them used to quiet the fierce clamor of his senses, just as one can feel a deep spiritual love for a woman and forget that all the time desire lies in ambush ever on the alert. Don Marcello's eyes grew moist, and this could hardly have been because sweat was pouring in great rivers from his exhausted old body; no, there was another reason for it. The saints—how dear they were to me! And then that phase of his existence had ended and other loves had come into his life; love for a quiet parish, for regular daily meals, for the white sheets of his bed, for old churches, witness to the history of bygone centuries; and for books, fresh linen, for distinguished company, for the rich of this earth; self-love, for that was what it all came to in the end. So many different kinds of love! And never the love that is real, the only love that matters. O, Love, where wert thou? I knew thee not, I knew thee not!

And now Don Marcello had crossed the wood and was in Martino's vineyard. Suddenly he was jerked back to the reality of the present moment. Perhaps there's still time, he said to himself; and he turned beseechingly to the saints. My dears, he said, let me get there in time! He appealed to them all without making any distinction between them, all those he had loved so much in the days of his youth. Teresa, Margaret, Anne, Catherine, Rita, Rita. Listen to me, you can at least listen to me—meanwhile he wiped away the sweat that was dripping from his forehead and making his eyes smart—you can at least listen to me, that doesn't commit you to anything. Do listen to me, my dears. Let me end my life to some purpose, let me get there in time. Grant me this favor—you can so easily answer my prayer, without any trouble at all.

(If this were a matter that concerned me alone I wouldn't have asked; I should have said: Let your will be done, let your will be done. Teresa, Margaret, Catherine, Anne, Rita, let your loving will be done. But I'm not asking this for myself; I'm asking it for others. It's on their behalf that I'm beseeching your aid. I'm invoking a love greater than mine when I refuse to say: Blessed saints, let your will be done.)

Then once again Don Marcello's thoughts dwelt on those two young people who were hastening toward their deaths. The world has gone mad! he told himself at this point; but he remembered that he had already said it and he thought it was an idle reflection which he ought to be ashamed of and he wished he had never uttered it. God could not have forsaken the world because the world was His Kingdom. It was stupid to say that the world had gone mad; naïve and stupid. Wouldn't it have been better to seek the reason for these happenings? There was a reason for everything, there must be; but where was it to be found? O God, where was it to be found? Don Marcello thought and thought and was deeply distressed because no answer came to him. There must be a reason. Good; now what were the facts? Two young people, the Professor and Signorina Barbara, had fallen in love with each other. Weren't they at the age when men and women fall in love? Of course, there was no doubt about that; and the love young people felt for each other was natural and normal, a noble and generous emotion which had the blessing of God. They were in love with each other; then why on earth did they want to kill themselves? Suicide: a grand, high-sounding word. Suicide, suicide, suicide. There was a fine ring about it. But why shouldn't they get married, why shouldn't they let the Church consecrate their union? Suicide . . . Who could have opposed their marriage? No one, for sure. Well then? O Lord, inscrutable is the mystery of Thy designs.

Martino's vineyard was behind him; the priest was again penetrating into the wood, where there was a little shade. But the sun was blazing under his skin, boiling in his veins; what relief was there from its scalding heat? For a moment the priest's thoughts turned to Martino Lamorte, brother of that Simone Lamorte who had come to such a pitiful end. What a place it was, this Little Valley of God! And yet it had a name that seemed to promise so much; such a holy name. If I were the Lord, the priest said to himself, it would give me great pleasure to tread this plot of earth, I should be glad to come down from heaven and walk about in this land. Disguised in the cast-off garb of a beggar, a wandering minstrel, a laborer, a soldier, or even—why not?—an archæologist. To the eternal mind of God every calling in this world is good and worthy of respect. But all this is but daydreaming—if only I get there in time! Blessed saints, listen to me, and take no notice of my babblings, it's old age that makes me drivel away like this. Grant me what I ask—

you can grant it so easily, without any trouble at all. O God, I'm finished. It's old age that makes me talk this drivel. Oh, how blue the sky is. It's like a brazier, it's coming down through the trees, it's sinking into the earth. O God, the fire in my veins! Lord, protect Thy servant. Heaven and earth are filled with Thy glory. . . .

Disguised as an archæologist, a historian. Why not? Why shouldn't the Lord deign to come down upon earth wearing the outward aspect of a scholar? Hosannah to Him in whom is all knowledge and understanding. O Lord, Thou knowest all things: the name and date of every object, the beginning and the end of every epoch, the glories and the crimes of every civilization, the least little episode in the history of the world. O Lord, Thou knowest all. Hosannah to Him who reigneth through all eternity, who knoweth all things. Just like young Emanuele, that mysterious laborer fellow. (But what brought his name to my mind? Lord, how did that come about?)

The heat was crushing him like a dead weight and the furnace fire of the sun, blazing through the trees, was pulsating in his body; his veins throbbed and his heart and every particle of his flesh; and there was a sledgehammer in his chest, a heavy pounding in his chest and his veins and his heart. O God, to fling myself on the ground, to lie on the earth, to lay my face against the earth, to fling myself on the ground in the shade of this wood, in the shade of this wood, O God!

Then Don Marcello said distinctly in a loud voice, "At the end of this wood I'll come to the place where the forsaken meadows begin. O Lord, let me reach them."

The priest had come to the edge of the minefields; he stopped, looked about him in a dazed way, and then began to shout. He felt his voice burst from his throat and heard the sound of his shout rise to a great height through the quiet of the morning, and then die away in the distance. He called six or seven times and each time he was astonished by the strength of his voice. "Professor, Barbara! Professor, Barbara! Profess-or!" He went on calling—seven, eight, nine times; and his voice came back at him, echoed and re-echoed, lost itself in the depths of the vast deep blue sky. Then he stopped and listened with his head on one side, hoping to hear a call. But under the glorious sky only the mocking echo of his voice answered him.

"I must find them," he said loudly and clearly. "Glory be to God. . . ."

He made the sign of the cross and deliberately advanced across the meadows which the enemy had sown with his murderous mines at the time of the fighting and which had since been carelessly abandoned.

It must be close on noon; the sun was nearing its zenith, the sky was a deep clear blue, and the grasshoppers shrilled without a moment's pause. The soil was burnt up—how long was it since any rain had fallen?—and in places there were great white boulders, cruelly reflecting the glare of the sun. From the earth rose a strong scent of mint. Birds were tracing patterns in the heavens, with light twittering cries; and then plummeting down into the depths of the great valleys.

The priest walked on in the blinding, unreal light; from time to time he shouted two names across the lonely wilderness: "Professor, Barbara!" and his monotonous call merged into the sounds and scents of the countryside, merged into the shrilling of the grasshoppers, the sharp smell of mint, the light wind that skimmed the surface of the earth. Glory be to God. Everything was radiantly beautiful, like the perfect image of an ideal world long sought and desired; so beautiful that once again the priest felt a constriction in his throat. In all my life, he asked himself sadly, how often have I come up here? Twice or thrice at most; and that was long ago. Without stopping, the old man surveyed the deep valleys spread out under the radiant sky. Glory be to God. . . .

And, in a flash of intuition, he understood that the life animating them was more symbolic than real, more of heaven than of earth. Here were houses and roads, haystacks that gleamed like gold, distant vineyards, woods and waters—the material symbols of life. *Life,* Don Marcello said to himself, almost in tears, the life created by the Lord. Glory be to God! No one has the right to stop it, no one. And as he gave one more shout he felt his voice quiver.

At that moment a prolonged convulsion shot up from the earth and engulfed him. Then everything was quiet, and the priest found himself on the ground, bathed in his own blood. Above his head stretched the blue depths of the sky, so blue, so deep, a great peacefulness that went on forever.

I feel a little sleepy—it's the sort of drowsiness that steals over you at dawn, when you're waiting for the daylight—and I feel weak. I feel as if I were choking, I feel that I am going to die, but it's a gentle sensation, soft and gentle—now I know what's happened, Don Marcello said to himself. A mine has exploded. I trod on a mine, it exploded, and it's blown my legs off. A mine exploded, I've been killed by a mine. I'm a dead man; or rather, I'm going to die. Die, die, die. That might be the thudding of a sledgehammer, mightn't it? I'm bleeding to death, my life is over—Emanuele.

Why does that name come to my mind? he asked himself. It's hot and the sun is glittering overhead. What a lovely sky for the end of summer! Look, there isn't a cloud in it. And I'm going to die. Yes, I'm going to die, the priest repeated three or four times as if to convince himself that it was as he said; I'm going to die, I'm lying here on the ground, waiting for death. And the name Emanuele keeps running through my head. Oh, Emanuele!

How hot it is! The sky is blue and there isn't a cloud to be seen—nothing but sunlight. Oh, this heat! I'm wet all over. I might be in a bath. It must be perspiration, it's so hot today. I'm an old man and nearly eighty. And the priest smiled up at the sky. It must be sweat, but it's warm and sticky, whatever is it? Blood? Yes, it's blood. I'm going to die. Die, die, die. That sledgehammer again—just listen to it. It's Death knocking on my door, Death has come for me. Well, so be it, I'm ready, I'm an old man. Have pity on me, Lord, have pity on Thy servant, have pity on me. Life only have I loved; I used to preach sermons about death, and I thought only about life. Have pity on me, Lord, now that Death draweth nigh. Oh, that hammering! I thought only of the church of St. Sebastiano and the church of St. Donato and the church of St. Rocco, especially of the church of St. Rocco, and who founded it I never could discover, but soon I shall know. Out of the depths have I cried unto thee, O Lord. . . . Soon I shall know—will that hammering never stop? I'm covered with blood—for the dead know everything. Have pity on me, Lord, I have never understood the meaning of death. Out of the depths O Lord . . . I have never understood what it means, and now I'm dying, O God, I'm going to die. I'm going to die, and I don't understand the meaning of death and blood. Out of the depths O Lord. Even now I can't understand. . . .

(He gazes at the sky, lying there in a pool of blood. And the earth drinks his blood greedily, like a vintage wine, for the earth is a selfish mother and cares not whom she slays, when her children have to be nourished. She cares not whom she slays. And now her children, the grasses and the insects she carries half-hidden in her bosom, are all athirst; they are all parched by the burning summer and they are all athirst. See, here is a rich red blood that will refresh my children, the fruit of my womb, the life I bring forth eternally, from century unto century, the life that must come to birth, the life that is in my children. O life, life, life, life! The sky is blue, the grasshoppers are shrilling on the distant plain; where is that thunderous roar of a moment ago? The white boulders glitter beneath the sun; a sharp smell of mint rises into the air, a sharp smell of blood; where is that thunderous roar of a moment ago? Gone into the air; circling the world. The old priest weeps because that thunderous roar of a moment ago is something he cannot understand; he cannot understand it because—O God!—he cannot understand the meaning of death.)

Out of the depths have I cried unto thee, O Lord—that I be not confounded for all eternity.

I have never understood Death; this is my punishment. Death draws nigh, I hear him overhead, but I don't know who or what he is. Good or ill, sweet or bitter, joy or pain, black or white— O Death, I know not who thou art. I have prayed with the black stole about me, I have swung the censer three times around the catafalque, I have seen thee in the eyes of men and women, on their sunken chests and bloodless lips, I have often met thee in my path—for fourscore is a great age, and thou art seldom far away. I have besought my God to keep thee from me, and now my time has come. O Death, *who art thou?* Good or ill, sweet or bitter, joy or pain, black or white, I don't know. And now I'm about to die. Out of the depths have I cried unto Thee, O Lord. . . . Death, who art thou, who art thou . . . ?

(While he is weeping and wailing something comes into his head; like a fanfare in the stillness of a city that has been dead for many centuries, like a sudden unexpected light flashing up from the pitch-darkness of midnight: the name Emanuele and two other names, Silvano, Barbara. Ah, I mustn't die, I mustn't die, he cries in anguish. Death, let me alone, I mustn't die. My life doesn't matter, but there are two other lives I must save, that's why I came up here, because I know now what love is—life itself! Silvano, Barbara! Hi there, Silvano! Are you there, Silvano! I must shout—leave me here a little longer. I must vanquish thee, O mine enemy, because I understand now that love means life and perhaps death too. I must shout, I must call to them. Silvano-o-o, Silvano-o-o! My children, you've got to live! O Death, I must vanquish thee. You've got to live, my children, life, life, life. . . .)

For a long time he wept and shouted in this fashion, remembering nothing except that he must keep calling their names; trying to drag himself upright on his torn stumps so that his voice would carry farther; arching his back like a cat; bathed in blood and remembering nothing except that he must keep on calling, wholly bent on saving these two beings, Silvano and Barbara, Silvano and Barbara. And now, God alone knew why, another name mingled with those two names, growing larger and larger: Emanuele, Emanuele, *Emanuele!* And it burned itself into the brain of the dying man, fraught with mystery, terrible in its intimation of eternity, fierce in the thunder of its sound, burned itself so deeply into his brain that suddenly he understood its significance: all-consuming love, GOD WITH US.

(232)

("*Now all this came to pass, that it might be fulfilled which was spoken of the Lord by the Prophet, saying; 'Behold, a Virgin shall be with child, and shall bring forth a son: and they shall call his name Emmanuel, which being interpreted is, God with us.'*")

At that moment the priest heard a step quite close to him; and beyond that he heard nothing at all. He turned round and recognized young Emanuele.

He stood beside him, but the priest—perhaps because of the tears in his eyes—saw him bathed in light, and his feet, it seemed, were not touching the earth but raised lightly above the ground; and his whole body was radiant and transparent, shining against the horizon.

The priest looked at him for a moment and ceased moaning; through the signal grace that had come upon him from on high he suddenly understood the nature of this Man. It isn't the tears in my eyes! he thought proudly, and he murmured as though to an old friend, "Lord." He had no fear; on the contrary, he felt happy and confident. "Lord Jesus!" he murmured again. There was a sound of singing, a sweet perfume rose into the air; it seemed to him that he had been lifted above the earth and was flying through the blue of heaven. "Lord Jesus, my Master," he said for the third time; and he understood then there is no death, that life alone exists, the miracle that is in men, animals, insects, grasses, fish, flowers, stars, passions, colors, clouds, sounds, houses, virtues, angels, in all creation: life alone exists. Life! and *I have seen Thee, O Lord!* And so Don Marcello closed his eyes forever, carrying with him in his heart a certainty born of the meaning of those words he had understood in his last hours: Life, Love, and *I have seen Thee, O Lord.* Glory be to God.

Emanuele bent over the priest's bloodstained body and gently drew down his eyelids. Then he said, "So died a poor servant of God." And he went on his way—for the story of the Little Valley of God makes it necessary—toward the place where Silvano and Barbara were blindly looking for death.

(233)

(32)

The March to Glory Ends

THE radiance of their eyes dazzled them like a lamp shining in the darkness. The air was black, the bare earth they trod on was black, and the sun was a black flame.

They walked hand in hand, preoccupied, lost to the world; they talked, but their conversation was not a duologue for there was a dark haze over their minds and they were each busy with their own thoughts. It would have been frightful indeed if they had stopped talking, for the whole world hung by a thread, their lives hung by a thread, and that thread was the sound of their voices.

"When I was six," Barbara said, "I used to play ninepins in my room. I remember they had been given to me as a present by my father, who's dead now. They were red and they were very tall; when the ball hit them they swayed for a moment and then they toppled over with a crash. And when they were all on the floor I wept."

"I know," Silvano said. He was walking by her side, but he did not look at her. "I remember. You were sorry for them."

"You were there too, were you? Do you know what I used to sob? They're dead, they're dead, and I've killed them! I was terribly upset and I cried."

"You were terribly upset," said Silvano. "In those days you wore braids and your mother used to tie a ribbon in your hair."

"My mother is dead. How can anyone tell what I was like in

those days? My mother . . . I never knew her and I've never been able to picture her. I cried. I killed them, I used to say."

Silvano lowered his eyes to shield them from the black glare of the sun. "What about Gustavino?" he asked suddenly.

"Who?" said Barbara.

"Gustavino."

"He doesn't exist."

"She was rather like you," Silvano resumed. "A little paler, a little taller. Your mother, I mean."

"But you never knew her."

"She had the same eyes, the same hair, the same mouth, the same hands. She talked like you and she had your walk."

"But you . . ." said Barbara. She changed the subject. "What about Maddalena?"

"What are you saying?" Silvano murmured. "And when she looked at anyone she had your look."

"But," said Barbara, "you never knew her."

"I've known everything you've known," Silvano declared. "I've seen everything you've seen. We've breathed the same air."

"Yes, I believe you," said Barbara.

"No one ever has existed," Silvano went on gently. "Gustavino, Maddalena, your grandmother, Don Marcello—all just like ninepins. Click! they sway and then over they go."

"And I used to burst into tears."

"Yes, but from now on you aren't going to cry any more."

"That's true. I think . . ."

"You aren't going to cry any more," Silvano persisted. "No more tears, ever again. Do you know why?"

"I know," said Barbara.

"Good."

"I hear a voice," the girl exclaimed. "Someone calling in the distance."

"When I was small I believed that at night, while everyone was asleep, the animals started talking to each other, just like human beings. If you listened very quietly you could hear them. That's what I believed, once upon a time."

"And now?"

"Darling," said Silvano. "Darling. My sweet."

(235)

"You remember Clotilde?" Barbara said. "She told us the mayor's motorcycle was a horse without legs. It's sad. What good is a horse without its legs? But I hear someone calling."

"A motorcycle. After all, motorcycles are alive too. And they can talk. I know a motorcycle . . ."

"I hear someone calling."

"Clotilde. But who is Clotilde? Does she exist?"

"No."

"Clotilde is a ninepin. Click, and there she is on the floor."

"Silvano."

"Of course I was there too, why do you ask me such a question? I have always been wherever you were. I've breathed the air you've breathed."

"Who's caught hold of us?"

"Who? I tell you . . ."

"I've a feeling that we're prisoners."

". . . I tell you that wherever you have been, I've always been with you. There has never been a moment . . ."

"We're prisoners, but whose? Who's caught hold of us?"

Silvano did not look at her. "Love," he said. "We're Love's prisoners."

"Love," echoed Barbara.

"Love. What a word! I have always been with you, you know. Even when you wore your hair down your back and your mother . . ."

"And you had short trousers? I know . . ."

". . . used to tie a ribbon in it. Did you say you heard a voice? I don't hear anything . . ."

". . . you were there too. I don't feel the least bit tired, I feel light as thistledown, I feel I could float."

". . . so it was probably a voice in the air. Do you think notes and words and cries just vanish? Of course they don't, they live forever. Listen to me, Barbara. Say Hi! after me. Really loud."

"Hi!"

"You hear it? Hi, hi, hi! Do you hear it going round the world?"

"I hear it."

"It's leaving the Valley, it's away beyond the Town, it's reaching the sea. Can you smell the salt water?"

(236)

"The little boats have colored sails—all the colors of the rain-bow—with a sun painted on top."

"It's the sea and the waves are sparkling in the sunlight. Your Hi! is over the water now, it goes on and on, it's reaching Amer-ica. It's in New York, in San Francisco, in Connecticut, in Texas. Listen, it's in Mexico, and now up it goes, up and up until it reaches the stars. There is Orion."

"The Twins," said Barbara. "The Great Bear, Sagittarius."

"Capricorn. Can you hear it?"

"Do you know," said Barbara, "I thought I heard a call."

"You had your hair down your back. . . . What are you say-ing? It flies through the blue of heaven and it climbs up and up . . ."

"A voice . . ."

". . . like a song."

". . . calling, calling."

"There are so many voices in the air. Besides, who could it be? We are alone in the world, you and I."

"Yes, we're alone."

"Alone, alone. Just you and me."

"But tell me, what have you done?"

"They're all dead. Click, and they're flat on the ground. They sway, and over they go. Click, and over they go. What have I done, did you say? I don't know what you mean. Ninepins, flat on the ground."

"But what have you done? Have you put your arm in the fire?"

He laughed. "And we're alone. Maddalena, Gustavino, your grandmother, Donna Teresa Conelli, Signorina Carmela, old Marion, Piero Zei the Vagabond, the dog Fiorella—all gone, all tumbled over like ninepins. There's nobody left. We're alone, you and I, alone . . ."

"But look, you've burned your sleeve!"

". . . alone in the world. Now when I was six years old I used to talk to dogs made of cardboard. We didn't have a dog and I so much wanted one. Do you know what I did? I drew them on a piece of cardboard, then I cut them out and I said: Your name is Bonzolino, and you, you're called Mirondella—you're a girl-dog. And you there, you're a mongrel—your name is Tarabaralla.

Oh, that mongrel Tarabaralla! And I used to talk to them for hours on end."

"I know," said Barbara.

"For hours on end. Oh, what talks we had, Tarabaralla and I! I tell you . . ."

"I know, I know!"

". . . these dogs were . . . But what was that you said? Fire? Did I hear you mention the word fire? Oh, that mongrel Tarabaralla!"

"I was talking about those burns on your sleeve. They look just like the marks of fingers. One two three four five—five scorch marks. As if someone had laid a hand of flame on your arm, Silvano."

"Darling, tell me. . . . Flame, did you say?" And Silvano's voice was uneasy.

"It's nothing. What did you want to ask me? We're alone, Silvano. I . . ."

But he was no longer listening to her. "It's that man who touched me," he said in a hoarse voice. "That man they call Emanuele." Something was dispelling the haze that had been clouding his mind, something like a chill of fear. . . . "Let's walk on, let's walk on," he said, and he trembled all over.

Barbara herself seemed thoughtful. "It's odd," she murmured.

Holding each other by the hand, they walked a few steps farther. Then Barbara said slowly, "I would like to know one thing, Silvano."

He was calmer now. "What is it, Barbara?"

"It's this." She hesitated a little. "How can we make our love eternal?"

"You know," said Silvano. "You've known since the beginning, Barbara. By dying."

She bowed her head.

"I know that."

"Then what is it you want to know?"

Expressionless and far away, Barbara's voice rose in answer. "I want to know how we shall die—how we shall kill ourselves."

(238)

Then Silvano said, "Very soon now we shall reach the edge of the minefields—the meadows that were mined by the enemy when the fighting came this way. We'll walk into them with our arms round each other, my love, you and I. And sooner or later we shall hear a terrific explosion, and all will be over." He added fiercely, "It will be wonderful, Barbara!"

"And we'll fall down like ninepins," she said. "Yes, it will be very wonderful, Silvano."

They went a few steps farther and then Silvano stopped, turned toward the girl, and kissed her passionately on the lips. They felt their souls mingle and unite, and a new radiance blazed forth, shining through the darkness of eternity.

Silvano released her and said, "This is where the minefields begin."

"Love," murmured Barbara. "Love. . . ."

Hand in hand, they walked toward the meadows.

A prolonged tremor shook the ground, followed by a heavy and sinister rumbling. Startled birds flew up into the sky. A blast of icy wind swept over the deserted meadows, bending the grasses double and withering the flowers. The sun clouded over, and a gray curtain descended upon the dumb earth.

Silvano and Barbara stopped, with their arms clasped tightly around each other's waists.

"Something has happened," murmured Silvano. Then he added—and what joy there was in his voice!—"But we're alive, we're alive!"

They waited tensely, without moving. Then Barbara lifted up her voice and said, "Here is the young man they call Emanuele."

He came forward smiling. He said, "They who believe in Him who sent me have passed from death to life."

Silvano trembled. He put his arms round Barbara and said, *"Si, Signore."*

And so they made their exit from this story of the Little Valley of God.

(33)

Significant Conversation between Two Tramps on the Subject of the Little Valley of God
(by way of an epilogue)

WHEN you come to the bend in the highroad the whole sweep of the Valley is suddenly revealed. One of the two men who were moving along the road turned to the other and said, "There is the Little Valley of God." And his voice betrayed the naïve complacency of one who knows he is well informed. He was a tall thin man, covered with dust from head to foot, and carrying a travel-stained pack on his shoulders.

The other did not reply immediately. After a moment's silence he asked pensively, "Why do they give it that name?" He was shorter than his companion and his face shone with an expression that was uncommonly appealing. He too was white with dust.

The First Tramp did not know what to answer. What a funny sort of question to ask! His self-esteem was wounded and he shrugged his shoulders.

"Who can tell why a thing is called this or that?" he replied. "Can you tell me why bread is called bread? Or why cows are called cows? There's no reason, my friend."

"Just so," the Second Tramp solemnly agreed. "I asked a stupid question. There are many things in the world that one can't altogether account for. I beg your pardon, brother."

"Not at all," said the First Tramp, somewhat mollified. It was the hour of sunset, and in this exceptionally fine Indian summer the air caressing their faces was soft and mild. From the height on which they now found themselves they saw the houses and hayricks over all the Valley. The Second Tramp said in a voice full of hidden meaning, "O Lord, how beautiful it is!" Then he heaved a sigh.

The companionship of this man was giving the First Tramp a curious urge to talk. He was glad to have found a comrade, even though the fellow had just annoyed him slightly. Tonight he wouldn't have to stretch out alone in the hayloft, he'd be able to have a little chat before going to sleep, and how pleasant that would be! He asked, "Why are you sighing, my friend?"

The other contemplated the landscape in silence.

"At sundown," he said, "my heart fills with longings and I feel sad."

"Will you tell me what they are?"

"Well, to give you an instance, I long for a house, a home of my own. I'd like to live always in the same place, get to know it well, associate with the men and women who inhabit it—in short, I'd like to have a little kingdom of my own. Do you know what I've been saying to myself? I've been saying that this region might be just the sort of world that would give me my heart's desire. What do you say its name is?"

The First Tramp shook his head and smiled. "Careful, my friend," he said, "don't let's walk into the trap!"

"What trap?" asked the Second Tramp.

The other shrugged his shoulders. "Can't you see that some-one's playing a game with us?"

"I don't understand."

"Listen. The two of us are walking along the road and there's a vast panorama unrolled beneath us. Houses, roads, haystacks, dogs barking at the sunset, men and women. Isn't that so?"

"That's so."

"Now follow me carefully. What's my first move? To give this valley a name. People say that it's called the Little Valley of God."

(241)

"And then?"

"It's quite simple; follow me and don't let anything I say surprise you. The next step is to make us talk."

"Us?"

"Us."

"But who does this?"

"Someone who can do it. Don't you see that we're only puppets?"

"I don't understand."

"I'll explain. We're made to talk. And do you know why? Because there's someone who can't talk himself, who must stand in the wings. Someone who wants to talk, who wants to talk."

"And he can't?"

"No."

"Why not?"

"He can't, that's all there is to it. He can't talk himself; so he makes us talk instead. You'll see that we'll have to say this, that, and the other. Hoopla! the trap's laid. Let's look where we're going, friend; don't let's walk into it!"

The Second Tramp did not reply immediately. After walking for a moment in silence he asked with a curious smile, "You think that's how it is?"

"Oh, I'm sure of it."

"Then listen, brother." And the Second Tramp's smile became still more remote and mysterious. "Would it surprise you if I asked you a favor?"

"A favor? What is it?"

"Let's play our parts in this. Let's play our parts, brother. Just once. Are you willing?"

The First Tramp stared at him for a long time, unsmiling. "All right. Why not?"

His companion heaved another sigh. "Thanks," he said. "Thanks, brother."

The First Tramp understood quite well what his companion was saying, though it surprised him a little. He replied, "The Little Valley of God."

"Well, this Little Valley of God could be a world in miniature for someone like me. You see these lovely houses? I'm willing to bet that at this moment the women are in the act of laying the table for dinner. Then the lamps will be lit and the whole family will sit down to table, and afterwards they'll all be together until it's time to go to bed; the old women will spin wool for the winter, the boys will make love to the girls, the men will play cards or discuss the grape-gathering. They are happy people, they have a little world all to themselves. Now do you understand why I give a sigh! We don't have a world of our own, we have only *the* world. It's too much. It's far too much."

"All the same," said the First Tramp, "I don't think these people are completely happy."

"The people of the Little Valley of God? But of course they aren't, brother; there you've uttered a profound truth. They're not happy because they don't know how to be. And who has a right to reproach them? Alas, it's nearly always like that. Every one of us has his vexations: worries, taxes that must be paid, rheumatism, differences with a landlord, a cow that has calved badly, unrequited love; in short, misfortunes. Men let such things get on top of them, and they nearly always forget that life is a great blessing. I'm going to tell you something: the people of the Valley, like all others, would have to know death in order to learn the proper value of life. They would have to die before they could be born again."

"That's very true," agreed the First Tramp, filled with admiration for his companion. "But what's to be done about it? When people are dead, they're dead for good. There's no hope of return. No one can restore life, no one!"

"That," observed the Second Tramp, "is not quite correct. There is someone who can restore life to corpses, brother. I'm speaking of God. He has resurrected the dead, and He did it because He wanted to show us that life is a great blessing."

"That's true," the First Tramp was forced to admit. "But these things happened a long time ago; nowadays God is so far away from our earth."

"Because men have kept Him at a distance!" the Second Tramp exclaimed indignantly. "The fault is entirely ours, not God's. Don't you know that He created men to dwell in them? And if people would allow Him to dwell in them, then they'd

(243)

be happy! If they called to Him once, only once in their lives, that would be sufficient; He would instantly come down into their hearts. *For man is His temple:* and when it's God who dwells in the temple the world is filled with joy and love is enthroned as the king of life!"

The sun had now gone down behind the ring of mountains but it had left in the sky great channels of red and purple that were lighting up the whole Valley. The Second Tramp's voice carried growing conviction.

"Do you know," he went on, "I'd even say that if I were God —don't laugh—I should so much like to come down upon earth and live among men. And I should see to it that they all—good or bad—got to know me and loved me. And I should teach men to live." Smilingly he ended: "And I'm pretty sure that if, being God, I had decided to come down again upon earth, even though men hadn't summoned me, out of the whole wide world this is the spot I would choose—perhaps because of its name, brother. And I should bring to it a very important thing: Love."

He fell silent.

Whereupon the First Tramp said, "Will you stop here with me, friend? I'm going to stay nearly a week in this neighborhood. I've been asked to play the accordion at a grand wedding. Why don't you come with me? I'll say that you're my partner. You would hear me play; and let me tell you in all modesty that it's difficult to find a musician who plays the accordion as I do."

In the gathering dusk the eyes of the Second Tramp shone with joy.

"May I?" he said. "May I, really? Is it your accordion that you're carrying in that case?"

The other felt that he could afford to be magnanimous.

"You certainly can! So long as you're with me, no one will dare say a word to you. Besides, everyone will be on holiday, you'll see; a young writer is marrying a beautiful girl. They've asked me to play the accordion at their wedding. Stay with me, friend, we'll have a jolly time. Man can't live by himself!"

The Second Tramp seemed profoundly happy.

"Certainly I'll stay, brother," he promised. "Oh yes, I'll stay in the Little Valley of God!"

(244)

About the Author

CARLO COCCIOLI *ranks with Alberto Moravia as one of the leading novelists in the present postwar renaissance of Italian letters. He has written many novels, one of which,* Heaven and Earth, *has already appeared in the United States.*

Signor Coccioli was born in Livorno in 1920, studied in Africa and Naples, and took part in the resistance movement during the war. He has lived in Florence and Paris and is now living in Mexico. He writes both in Italian and in French.

DATE DUE
